THE TRICK OF THE TREASURE

SILVER AND GREY
BOOK 4

MARY LANCASTER

ARE YOU SIGNED UP FOR DRAGONBLADE'S BLOG?

You'll get the latest news and information on exclusive giveaways, exclusive excerpts, coming releases, sales, free books, cover reveals and more.

Check out our complete list of authors, too!

No spam, no junk. That's a promise!

Sign Up Here

www.dragonbladepublishing.com

Dearest Reader;

Thank you for your support of a small press. At Dragonblade Publishing, we strive to bring you the highest quality Historical Romance from some of the best authors in the business. Without your support, there is no 'us', so we sincerely hope you adore these stories and find some new favorite authors along the way.

Happy Reading!

CEO, Dragonblade Publishing

ADDITIONAL DRAGONBLADE BOOKS BY AUTHOR MARY LANCASTER

Silver and Grey Series
Murder in Moonlight (Book 1)
Evidence of Evil (Book 2)
Ghost in the Garden (Book 3)
The Trick of the Treasure (Book 4)
Word of the Wicked (Book 5)

One Night in Blackhaven Series
The Captain's Old Love (Book 1)
The Earl's Promised Bride (Book 2)
The Soldier's Impossible Love (Book 3)
The Gambler's Last Chance (Book 4)
The Poet's Stern Critic (Book 5)
The Rake's Mistake (Book 6)
The Spinster's Last Dance (Book 7)

The Duel Series
Entangled (Book 1)
Captured (Book 2)
Deserted (Book 3)
Beloved (Book 4)
Haunted (Novella)

Last Flame of Alba Series
Rebellion's Fire (Book 1)
A Constant Blaze (Book 2)
Burning Embers (Book 3)

Gentlemen of Pleasure Series
The Devil and the Viscount (Book 1)
Temptation and the Artist (Book 2)

Sin and the Soldier (Book 3)
Debauchery and the Earl (Book 4)
Blue Skies (Novella)

Pleasure Garden Series
Unmasking the Hero (Book 1)
Unmasking Deception (Book 2)
Unmasking Sin (Book 3)
Unmasking the Duke (Book 4)
Unmasking the Thief (Book 5)

Crime & Passion Series
Mysterious Lover (Book 1)
Letters to a Lover (Book 2)
Dangerous Lover (Book 3)
Lost Lover (Book 4)
Merry Lover (Novella)
Ghostly Lover (Novella)

The Husband Dilemma Series
How to Fool a Duke (Book 1)

Season of Scandal Series
Pursued by the Rake (Book 1)
Abandoned to the Prodigal (Book 2)
Married to the Rogue (Book 3)
Unmasked by her Lover (Book 4)
Her Star from the East (Novella)

Imperial Season Series
Vienna Waltz (Book 1)
Vienna Woods (Book 2)
Vienna Dawn (Book 3)

Blackhaven Brides Series
The Wicked Baron (Book 1)
The Wicked Lady (Book 2)
The Wicked Rebel (Book 3)
The Wicked Husband (Book 4)

The Wicked Marquis (Book 5)
The Wicked Governess (Book 6)
The Wicked Spy (Book 7)
The Wicked Gypsy (Book 8)
The Wicked Wife (Book 9)
Wicked Christmas (Book 10)
The Wicked Waif (Book 11)
The Wicked Heir (Book 12)
The Wicked Captain (Book 13)
The Wicked Sister (Book 14)

Unmarriageable Series
The Deserted Heart (Book 1)
The Sinister Heart (Book 2)
The Vulgar Heart (Book 3)
The Broken Heart (Book 4)
The Weary Heart (Book 5)
The Secret Heart (Book 6)
Christmas Heart (Novella)

The Lyon's Den Series
Fed to the Lyon

De Wolfe Pack: The Series
The Wicked Wolfe
Vienna Wolfe

Also from Mary Lancaster
Madeleine (Novella)
The Others of Ochil (Novella)

CHAPTER ONE

CONSTANCE SILVER APPROACHED the black-painted door, her stomach in knots. The shining brass plate beside the door, which proclaimed *Silver & Grey*, took on a massive new significance in her mind.

Several of the people who had crossed this threshold since the sign went up must have felt similar nervous attacks—wondering if their problems would be believed or accepted, cringing at the personal and family secrets they would have to reveal in order for their inquiries to be carried out. Constance had no such excuse. She was one of the firm's two partners and did half of the inquiring.

Since the last thing she wanted was to be seen hovering coyly by the door, she fished out her keys from her businesslike bag and let herself in. It was foolish, of course, but she no longer had any idea how to greet her partner and friend Solomon Grey. Because last night, he had asked her to marry him.

Or at least to contemplate the possibility. At any rate, they had agreed to consider themselves engaged.

It was utter madness on his part, of course. He was a wealthy, respected businessman while she was not respectable at all. Her personal wealth was founded on immoral earnings, her most notorious and successful venture being the discreet and hideously expensive house of ill repute nestling among the mansions of Mayfair.

She was acquainted with dukes and government ministers

and bishops, but none of them acknowledged her in front of their wives.

And yet the trivial problem exercising her mind was how to greet her betrothed. Should she kiss his cheek in public or in private? Or merely say good morning?

The low murmur of a male voice came from the first office on her left—Solomon's. Their expected client must have been early. Relieved to have her decision put off by the closed door, she began to take off her hat as she walked on toward her own office.

"Good morning, ma'am," Janey said, bustling up from her cubbyhole where she kept the appointment book and managed the post.

Constance raised one eyebrow, for she could tell from the girl's unusual politeness of manner that they were not alone. Janey jerked her head in the direction of the waiting room and grinned.

This really was excellent—a client with Solomon and another waiting in line.

Janey followed her into the office. "Got some water heating for fresh tea. And a fine gent in the waiting room—name of Mr. Lloyd. His card's on your desk."

Having hung up her hat and coat, Constance glanced at the good-quality card. *Barnabas J. Lloyd, Esquire,* with a good address on the edges of Mayfair.

"He didn't have an appointment, just dropped in. Thought you wouldn't be long, so I asked him to wait. Very civil, he is, with a twinkle in his eye."

Janey noticed such things. Even when Constance had first taken her in, an excessively foul-mouthed prostitute, she had been observant. Her ambition then had been to give up the old life that was killing her and become a lady's maid. She had begun by practicing on Constance, but since Silver and Grey had begun, she had found this position suited her much better.

Which left Constance without a maid, though Janey still

appeared to bring her coffee in the morning and to unhook her at night.

"I'll bring him in here," Constance decided, "and you can bring us both tea. Tell Mr. Grey when he is free."

"Right you are," Janey said cheerfully.

Constance followed her from the room and crossed the hall to the waiting room, where a gentleman sat in one of the two armchairs, calmly reading a newspaper.

He was a healthy-looking man perhaps in his early forties, with chiseled features, sun-bronzed skin, and a very silky-looking moustache. He glanced up as Constance entered and rose at once to his feet.

He did indeed have a twinkle in his eye.

Well, Constance was used to dealing with those.

"Mr. Lloyd, good morning," she said cheerfully, walking toward him with her hand held out. "I am Mrs. Silver. Would you care to come through to the office?"

He took her hand and bowed over it, undisguised admiration on his face. "How do you do? Thank you." He released her hand, folded the newspaper, and laid it on the table before following her across the hall.

Leaving the door ajar—a concession to respectability that amused her—Constance chose to bypass the comfortable armchairs grouped by the fireplace and go straight to her desk. "Please, sit down and tell me how we can help you."

He looked startled as she sat behind the desk, though at least he did lower himself into the visitor's chair. "Is Mr. Silver about to join us?"

It was not the first time she had encountered this mistake. "There is no Mr. Silver, sir. I am the Silver half of the partnership."

His eyes widened, though with more amusement than outrage. "Really? How very intriguing! I apologize for my misunderstanding. In the circumstances, I believe I shall wait until Mr. Grey is free."

Janey entered with the tea tray, giving Constance time to smooth her hackles.

"Is Mr. Grey free?" Constance asked.

"No, ma'am," Janey said, obedient to the unspoken instruction.

Constance smiled. "Be assured, sir, we consult and investigate each case together. It does not greatly matter which of us you speak to initially."

She could tell from his fixed expression that it mattered a great deal to Mr. Lloyd. At least he did not get up and walk out, but as he graciously accepted a cup of tea from her, she suspected the gleam of admiration in his eyes had little to do with her abilities and all to do with the way she looked. Appearance was a double-edged weapon.

She drew her notebook toward her. Though she remembered every conversation in detail, it generally impressed clients if notes were taken. And, in truth, they sometimes helped her to see connections and patterns.

"How might we help you?" she asked.

He met her gaze consideringly, but did not answer at once. In the silence, she heard footsteps in the hall, the opening and closing of the front door.

Mr. Lloyd sipped his tea. "Mrs. Silver—"

She never discovered if he meant to reject her or not, for a brief knock on the door heralded the appearance of her partner.

Solomon Grey was a tall man, slender and elegantly dressed, and the sight of him affected Constance with more than usual disturbance. Under any circumstances, he had the kind of charismatic presence that drew the attention. As his newly affianced bride, Constance was tongue-tied.

Fortunately, he was not. "Ah. Good morning. My apologies for interrupting."

"Not at all," Constance managed calmly. "This is Mr. Lloyd, who was about to explain his business with us. Mr. Lloyd, my partner, Mr. Grey."

Lloyd rose to shake hands, his glance friendly and yet definitely assessing.

What did he see? A gentleman of his own class? A servant yet to prove himself? Solomon could pass for a European or an African—unsurprising, since he had both in his parentage. To most of Constance's acquaintance this made no difference, sparking mere, occasional curiosity. As a successful and wealthy shipping magnate, Solomon Grey had most of the world's respect. But she had also come across a few people who were shocked, or even outraged, that a person of his descent should regard himself as a white man's equal.

She was glad to see that Lloyd shook hands with perfect civility. Although he appeared to be the quintessential Englishman, his skin was not dissimilar in shade to Solomon's.

Solomon brought up another chair and sat at the corner of the desk.

Mr. Lloyd lifted his cup from its saucer once more. "Someone has stolen my treasure," he said. "And I have no idea how to find it."

Carefully, Constance and Solomon did not look at each other.

"What kind of treasure?" she asked pleasantly.

"Oh, the usual kind. Gold, Spanish coins, jewels, antiquities. Some silver. I returned with it aboard my own ship, removed it to the strong room of my own home, and in the morning, it was gone."

"Then presumably very few people had access to it? Who had keys to your strong room?"

"Only myself. I keep it with my other keys, locked inside the drawer at my bedside—which can of course be unlocked easily enough, but not without waking me. I am, of necessity, a light sleeper."

Constance pounced. "What necessity?"

"Preserving my life, of course. I have slept in some very hair-raising places." He smiled faintly from Constance to Solomon. "I should perhaps explain that I am something of an adventurer. To call myself an explorer is, perhaps, somewhat grandiose, though I have done my own modest share of that, too."

"Your treasure is a result of this—er…adventuring?" Solomon asked.

"Indeed."

"Over many years?" Constance asked.

"No, it was all one collection in its own chest, which I dug up on a small island off the east coast of Africa. No one lives there and it has never been named on the maps. I believe pirates buried it there some forty years ago." He smiled. "I know. It sounds like a children's story, but I assure you it is true."

"Have you alerted the authorities to this theft?" Solomon asked delicately.

Lloyd appeared to understand at once. "Indeed. It was inspected by customs officials before I took it off the ship. And I reported the theft to the police yesterday. I gave them the same detailed description I will give you, should you decide to assist me, but they seemed to hold out little hope for the treasure's discovery."

"One never knows where things will turn up unexpectedly," Constance said, thinking of a recent case. "So there is always hope. When did you last see this treasure with your own eyes?"

"When we placed the chest in the strong room, the evening before last. When I opened the lid yesterday morning, everything had gone save one Spanish doubloon."

Solomon stirred. "Tell me about your strong room. Does it have windows?"

"No," Lloyd replied. "All its walls are internal. There is no damage to the room at all, and nothing else in there was taken. Nor had the door lock been forced."

"A mystery indeed," Constance murmured, intrigued in spite of her original doubts. "Is there any way someone in your household could have made a copy of your key? Even years ago? What happens to it, for example, when you go off adventuring?"

"It stays locked in the drawer by my bedside," he admitted.

"But I cannot imagine any of my servants would do such a thing."

"Sadly," Solomon said, "if your house was not broken into, the members of your household are the likeliest suspects. Perhaps we could speak to them?"

Lloyd's eyes flickered uneasily. "My wife will not like the servants to be further upset. The police have already interrogated them."

"Were you present for those interviews?" Constance asked.

"My wife, my son, or myself were always present."

"Then you and they could probably tell us most of what was said, leaving our own questions to a minimum."

Lloyd still looked doubtful, but Solomon distracted him by asking casually, "Was this treasure insured?"

"No," Lloyd said bleakly. "Not yet. Neither my shipping nor home insurance would cover this loss."

"What did you plan to do with the treasure?" Constance asked.

Lloyd shrugged. "Various things. I meant to keep a few pieces for my own collection, donate some to the British Museum, perhaps, and sell the rest at auction."

Which would seem to discount any insurance fraud as the motive. Besides, involving private investigators as well as the police was not the act of a man who did not want his treasure found. Her gaze met Solomon's briefly.

In response to the answer she read there, she opened her desk drawer and took from it a sheet of printed paper on which Silver and Grey's charges were listed.

"If you still wish to go ahead," she said, "we require part payment to secure our services and the rest upon completion as agreed by both parties."

As HE SHOWED Mr. Lloyd to the door, Solomon was not entirely surprised when his new client said confidentially, "Man to man, old fellow, the lady is calling herself your partner. Some people won't like that, for any number of reasons."

"But the lady *is* my partner," Solomon said gently. "In the firm and in personal matters, since we are engaged to be married. One has to be strictly honest and transparent in business, I'm sure you will agree."

Lloyd blinked, accepting his hat from Solomon in a slightly flustered kind of way. "I daresay you know your own business best. Until this afternoon, Mr. Grey."

"Mr. Lloyd." Solomon bowed and closed the door behind him.

He hesitated minutely before he turned and walked back to Constance's office. He had looked forward to greeting her this morning with a kiss that he hoped would remove any lingering doubts about marrying him. But their early client had been even earlier than expected, and she had been five minutes or so later than normal. Nor had she joined him in the consultation, preferring to see the unexpected Mr. Lloyd.

Was she embarrassed? Or had she changed her mind?

She had moved to the comfortable chairs with her notebook, where she was scribbling something down and did not glance up.

"What was Mr. Mostyn's problem?" she asked.

"Marital. He wanted us to spy on his wife, whom he suspects of infidelity."

She stopped writing and looked up, frowning. "Oh dear. I don't want such a case."

"Neither do I. He began by saying it was for his wife's protection, because she had been receiving unwanted and threatening attentions, but the truth soon came out. I said we could not help him and suggested he actually talk to his wife. Which, it transpires, he does very little. He departed somewhat miffed and offended."

"Good," said Constance roundly. "What do you think of Mr. Lloyd?"

"A basically conventional man," Solomon said, sitting down beside her, "doing unconventional things."

"Adventuring and treasure hunting?"

"While his wife stays at home keeping his house and looking after his children."

"Maybe she's not the adventuring kind," Constance suggested.

"It's possible. I look forward to meeting her. You didn't tell Janey."

"About what?"

"About our engagement," he said dryly.

A faint flush stained the delicate skin of her cheeks. "Oh. Neither did you."

"I didn't want to assume you hadn't changed your mind. Have you?"

She held his gaze. "No. Have you?"

"No." He smiled at her, but her response was uncharacteristically distracted and she quickly began talking about the case.

"On the face of it, the thief must be someone who lives in the house. Which limits it to his wife, Christine, his unmarried sister Audrey, his son Sydney, and his two daughters, Jemimah and Rachel. Or one of his servants."

"Your theory being," he said, "that one of them copied the strong room key while he was away adventuring, waited until something really valuable was stored there, and then quietly extracted the treasure the very night he brought it back? How did they get it out of the house without being seen?"

"We don't know that they did. It could still be there. Though I don't see Mr. Lloyd giving us permission to search the house, including the bedchambers of his family."

"He might let us search the servants' quarters," Solomon said, "but I doubt there's much point. I can't see a servant hanging around with his loot. Wouldn't he or she bolt?"

"They would only be brought back by the police. Most domestic servants are so respectable that they'd have no idea how to lose themselves in London, let alone find someone to fence such a collection. Although," she added, sitting straighter, "if they had planned it well enough, they could already be on a ship to America or anywhere…"

"*Could* they plan it so well?" Solomon argued. "They can't have known exactly when Lloyd's ship would dock, or when his treasure would enter the house, so booking passage on a ship would be risky."

"And expensive on a servant's wages. My money is on the household. I wonder what his wife is like?"

"I wonder what his strong room is like."

CHAPTER TWO

As a precaution, since neither Constance nor Solomon knew anything about the Lloyd family—none of the gentlemen frequented Constance's establishment nor shared business interests or charity board membership with Solomon—they first called upon Lady Grizelda Tizsa.

Griz was a duke's daughter who had disgraced herself by marrying a poor doctor who also happened to be a revolutionary refugee. As a couple, they were highly curious by nature and inveterate solvers of puzzles. It was amid one such puzzle involving an old acquaintance of Constance's that she had first met them and been introduced rather dramatically to Solomon. But that was not the only reason she liked them. They treated everyone the same way, with courtesy, friendliness, and sincerity. They were also funny, eccentric, and charming, hanging on to the fringes of many societies.

Griz was delighted to receive them. They found her sitting on the floor of her drawing room, which looked more like a study, playing with her gurgling, kicking baby. An untidy young woman with golden-fair hair and spectacles, she seemed either unaware or uncaring of her own subtle beauty. She jumped up as soon as the maid announced them, and, smiling in welcome, swiped the child up with her.

"Come in and sit down! I'm so pleased to see you again. How are you both?"

"Well," Solomon replied, "Constance has just agreed to marry me."

"Goodness," Griz said with awe but very little surprise in her smile, while she continued to bounce the happy baby up and down on her knees. "You will make a positively dazzling couple."

"Like you and Mr. Tizsa?" Constance said, unreasonably irritated.

"Lord, no," Griz said vaguely. "Congratulations. I know you'll both be very happy together."

"In among the challenges," Constance said.

"But it's the challenges that make it fun." Griz might have sensed Constance's discomfort, for she changed the subject. "Did you come about something in particular?"

To many, the engagement would have been something very particular. Solomon's lips twitched with amusement, but he said, "We were wondering if you had ever come across a family called Lloyd? Here's his card."

Griz took it and adjusted her spectacles. "Lloyd… I don't think so, not at that kind of address. But then, I never moved in Society a great deal. Azalea and Eric might know."

They were her sister and her brother-in-law Lord Trench. Constance had once discreetly attended a charity ball at their home, but she balked at making an open morning call upon on Lady Azalea. Solomon, of course, had business dealings with Lord Trench.

"Come to think of it," Griz added, "so might my brother Horrace, who should call this afternoon. Let's have tea while we wait."

Their conversation became more general while the maid brought tea and scones. The baby fell asleep in Grizelda's arms and she took it upstairs to its cot.

"Would you like to have children?" Solomon asked idly.

Oh, dear God… "It's not always up to us," Constance managed, annoyed with herself for blushing. Had she ever blushed before she met Solomon Grey? What child would not be ashamed of a courtesan for a mother? Thankfully, she knew more than most about preventing conception, but nothing was ever certain. "Do you?"

"Yes, one day…"

Fortunately, Griz re-entered the room with the guilty glee of many a parent on enjoying their hour of freedom, and before their tea was finished, the maid announced, "Lord Horrace, my lady."

On the face of it, Lord Horrace Niven was nothing like his sister. He was tall and distinguished and very precise in his dress and in his manners. Griz introduced them quite casually, and his lordship bowed and shook hands with great affability. His eyes, however, were cool, hard, and unreadable, as he accepted a cup of tea from Griz.

"Dragan is at the clinic," Griz told him. "But he said just to leave the parcel here."

"Then I will," Lord Horrace replied.

"Also," said Griz, dropping Lloyd's card into his saucer, "are you acquainted with this fellow?"

"Barnabas Lloyd?" Lord Horrace said in surprise. "Yes, a little. Adventurous sort, always exploring unlikely places or finding treasure…"

"He found some on an island off the East African coast," Solomon said. "It was stolen from his London home and he has asked our help to recover it. We are concerned that his family or close friends may be involved, so an unbiased view would be useful."

Lord Horrace's gaze was direct and perceptive. "I see."

Griz said, "They are private inquiry agents, Horrace. A more professional version of Dragan and me. I can vouch for them."

How much weight that endorsement carried with Lord Horrace was debatable, but he said, "I know nothing against any of them. Except all that adventuring has played ducks and drakes with the family fortune. He bought his own ship and finances his own expeditions. Not sure his findings ever justify it."

"Interesting," Constance said. "So the treasure he's just

brought back is rather vital to him."

"Then I hope it was insured," Lord Horrace said.

BARNABAS LLOYD AND his family lived in a large townhouse with a gracious, porticoed front door. It appeared to be well maintained both outside and in. Solomon and Constance were admitted by a smart, unsmiling footman, who showed them to a small reception room near the front door where, only moments later, they were joined by the master of the house.

"Let me take you to the strong room," Lloyd said as soon as polite greetings were over.

Obediently, they followed him to the staircase and along the passage to a door on the right. It looked like every other door in the house—white-painted, paneled wood—but clearly appearances were deceptive.

Reluctantly, it seemed, Lloyd took a ring of keys from his pocket. There were four of them, the largest of them very complicated in shape.

A maid bustled past with a shawl in her hands, pausing only to curtsey, her eyes down, before vanishing through the double doors on the left of the passage. Probably the drawing room, Solomon guessed.

"This is odd," Lloyd said ruefully. "I have kept the secrets of this room for years. It seems wrong now to be showing it to so many people—the police inspector yesterday, you today."

"Our discretion is total," Constance said mildly.

Solomon watched very carefully as Lloyd inserted the large key into the lock and turned it clockwise. A heavy metallic clunk was the only clue that this was anything other than an ordinary door.

"There is steel behind the wood of the door," Solomon guessed.

"And lining the walls." Lloyd turned the key again then removed it. To the right of the door handle, he lifted a panel that had been previously invisible, and revealed another, smaller keyhole. Into this Lloyd inserted another key, which he turned anticlockwise. He then put the large key back into the first hole—and this time it seemed to slide further in—and turned it clockwise.

Lloyd removed it and dropped the key ring into his pocket before depressing the handle, which clearly offered more resistance than an ordinary one, and pushed the heavy door open.

It was more of a cupboard than a room. A few deed boxes sat on a shelf on one side. But it was the wooden chest on the floor that drew the eye. About three feet in length with a curved lid, it almost filled the space. Although it had clearly been cleaned up to some degree, the wood was old and thick and dark from ingrained dirt. Its lock hung open, an iron flap hanging down from one loose hinge.

Lloyd stepped inside the strong room, bent, and lifted the lid to show the chest was empty save for one shining gold coin. Just as he had said. Beside it was a heap of what look like old gardening tools, a broom head, a rusting shovel, a hammer, a few rocks, and odds and ends of wood and metal.

"What is that junk?" Constance asked.

"What I found in the chest yesterday morning with the single doubloon. Whoever stole my treasure clearly thought it was funny."

"So, when exactly was the chest locked up in here?" Solomon asked, while Constance squeezed past him and crouched down to look at the chest, lifting the flap at the broken hinge, inspecting the old gold coin within. "Did the chest travel from the ship directly to this house with you?"

"Yes, it did, and I supervised its removal from under the carriage seat and up to the drawing room. I think it must have been about five o'clock in the afternoon when we reached the house."

"Were you showing the treasure to your family in the drawing room?" Constance asked.

"Yes, I was rather proud of it," Lloyd said, sighing.

"Did they know about it before your arrival?"

"Not until my wife and my sister came on board to greet us."

"Us?" Solomon repeated.

"My son, Sydney, accompanied me on the voyage. Did I not say so previously?"

"No."

"Well, he did. I thought it was time he saw the world."

"So, you had not written to your wife to expect you?" Constance asked, straightening.

It brought her pleasantly close to Solomon, her scent arousing his senses, her wide skirts catching around his leg. He had to restrain the urge to put his arm around her.

"She knew of the ship's approach," Lloyd said, "and I sent a messenger as soon as we docked. Of course, we had to wait for customs inspections and so on."

"Did your wife and sister see the treasure when they came on board?"

"No, the chest was already tied up on deck and ready to go."

Solomon nodded. "How long did it spend in the drawing room with you?"

"Oh, an hour or so." A smile flickered on Lloyd's lips. "After the long voyage, it was good to be home, surrounded by my family, teasing them…"

"Who was in the drawing with you?" Constance asked. "All your family?"

"Yes."

"And servants?" she asked.

"Only Garrick, the butler, who brought in champagne and announced dinner."

"Did you leave the treasure unattended in the drawing room while you dined?"

"No. Sydney and Harry the footman carried the chest to the strong room. Then Sydney ran upstairs to fetch the keys for me. I found myself somewhat prophetically reluctant to leave the treasure for a moment."

"Did the footman wait with you?" Solomon asked.

"No, I sent him back to his dinner duties. I never open the strong room door when anyone is watching."

"Did you wrestle the chest in here by yourself, then?" Constance asked.

Lloyd smiled slightly. "I didn't need to. Sydney and I moved it together."

"Then your son saw you open and close the strong room door?"

"Yes, but he already knew how. I showed him on his eighteenth birthday. I live an adventurous life, which is not without its dangers. It seemed only sensible that someone else should know, in case of my death."

Carefully, Solomon did not glance at Constance. There seemed to be several things Lloyd had not thought to mention at their initial interview. "Who else knows how to open it?"

"Only the locksmith. And there is a sealed note with my solicitor with instructions."

"Perhaps you would give us the directions of both these gentlemen?"

"If you wish, but I can assure you, they were not in the house last night. I employ a night porter and the doors are locked every night. In any case, even if they were not the most respected men in their professions, how would they have known the treasure was there that particular night?"

"What else do you keep there?" Constance asked. "Money? Jewels?"

"From time to time. But it would hardly be fair to deprive my wife of her jewelry for months at a time while I am out of the country."

"When was all this security installed?" Solomon asked.

"About ten years ago, when I brought the first treasure home."

"Then this was not your first?" Constance moved past the men and out into the passage.

"No, we found a wreck on a sand bank, close in to the Jamaican coast."

Solomon looked up quickly. Everything to do with the island of his birth drew his attention. "When were you in Jamaica?"

"Oh, must have been ten years ago? 1842."

Too late. His brother David had vanished from Jamaican shores ten years before that.

"The wreck had gone down during the earthquake of 1692," Lloyd continued, "and was never found until I did so, with the aid of some other sea divers. At low tide, we could reach it and bring things up. Not quite as fabulous as my African treasure—mainly gold and silver plate—but it gave me a taste for treasure seeking."

"Then you had the strong room installed while you were away?" Solomon asked.

Lloyd looked slightly sheepish. "No, I commissioned it when I came home. I'm afraid I kept the valuables under the bed until I sold what we did not wish to keep. So you see, my house, and my household, is secure. But the strong room was common sense. It even has a special coating to help protect it from fire. And the other valuable artifacts I obtained after it was built—from Egypt and Greece and the Middle East—have been stored quite safely in the room from time to time. Have you seen enough?"

"For now, yes, thank you," Solomon said, backing into the passage and watching Lloyd close and relock the door, going through the same motions as for unlocking, only in reverse.

Constance asked, "Did the same people as now live in the house ten years ago, when you installed the strong room?"

Lloyd blinked at her. "Of course."

"Even the servants?"

He led them into a bright, pleasant room, scattered with antique vases and exquisite ornaments carved from wood and marble that he had no doubt brought home from his travels.

"Yes, mostly," he said, closing the door and gesturing for

them to be seated. "Garrick, of course—the butler—has been here since my father's time. So have the cook and the night porter. I can't really remember when the younger staff joined us, but most of them came from our country estate in Berkshire. Loyal people."

"What do *you* think happened here, Mr. Lloyd?" Constance asked.

"If I knew, I would not have consulted you," he said sharply.

"There is a difference," Solomon pointed out, "between suspicion and knowledge based on evidence. Do you have suspicions or even vague thoughts?"

"No," Lloyd said, almost between his teeth. "Frankly, I'm flummoxed. And I'm guessing from your questions that so are you."

Constance bestowed one of her full smiles upon him. He was not immune, judging by the glint rising in his eyes. A man used to following his desires and not to being thwarted. Solomon smoothed his own hackles. Gentlemanly instincts would probably keep Lloyd from pursuing her for now—providing he never learned her more notorious profession.

"On the face of it, the theft appears impossible," she said. "But clearly it isn't, for your treasure is gone. We shall not give up just yet. Do you know how the police are approaching the investigation?"

"I believe they are looking for the items themselves and mean to trace them back to the thief."

Solomon caught his gaze. "You may not like what we find. Or what we stir up while we are looking."

"I want my treasure back," Lloyd said steadily.

"Very well. Then I'm afraid we need to speak to your family, to your servants, and to anyone who visited the house on the evening you came home."

"I told my wife to expect guests for tea. But, to my knowledge, no one visited the house the evening we returned."

"Then your family is aware you have employed us?" Constance said.

"I shall not keep it secret." Lloyd took out his pocket watch and glanced at it before rising. "Shall we go in to tea?"

There were three ladies in the drawing room when they entered. The room itself was a little too opulent and busy for Solomon's taste, having too many frills to curtains and cushions, and the surfaces so packed with pretty things that he was reminded of Constance's mother's shop.

One of the three ladies rose immediately from the chair by the fire and walked gracefully toward them. A mature woman with beautiful skin, fashionably gowned, she smiled at her husband's guests.

"My dear," Lloyd said fondly, "allow me to introduce Mrs. Silver and her betrothed, Mr. Grey."

Constance's gaze flickered with clear surprise, quickly covered by a smile as she took her hostess's proffered hand. "Mrs. Lloyd, how kind of you to receive us."

"I am always pleased to meet Barnabas's friends." Mrs. Lloyd turned to Solomon. "How do you do, Mr. Grey?"

"Delighted to meet you, ma'am."

"You must let me introduce you to my sister-in-law, Miss Lloyd." She indicated a very different lady in appearance—older, wispy, fluttery, and untidy—who dropped her knitting into her lap and then tipped it onto the floor as she rose to greet them with vague, gentle amiability. "How do you do? So pleasant to meet new young people…"

"And my elder daughter," Mrs. Lloyd proceeded inexorably, "Jemimah."

The third lady could not have been more than sixteen years old, a remarkably pretty girl with gleaming chestnut hair and vitality leaping from her bright blue eyes. Admiration for Constance's beauty stood out in her face as she curtseyed to them. She still looked dazed as she turned to Solomon and smiled brilliantly.

"Come and sit by me, Mr. Grey," said Mrs. Lloyd, taking his

arm to give him no choice in the matter. As they sat down on the sofa, a footman wheeled in a large tea trolley, and he and a maid began laying out plates of sandwiches, elegant savories, scones, and cakes. The teapot and matching cups and saucers were laid before Mrs. Lloyd.

"So," she said brightly, "how do you know my husband? Did you meet him on his travels?"

"Why, no, ma'am—we met here in London when he asked us to look into the theft from your strong room," Solomon replied.

Her amiable mask slipped for an instant, from perfect hostess to stunned, slightly irritated wife. Solomon glanced quickly at Lloyd and found a very curious expression on the man's face—amused, avid, and somehow not pleasant.

A silence followed Solomon's words as everyone stared at him with dismay.

A young man, impetuously entering the drawing room, glared at his father. "Seriously, Papa? You brought a *policeman* to tea?"

Constance saved the day. "Oh, no, we are not the police," she said. "We merely help people with their problems."

"Is there much call for finding lost treasure in London?" the young man asked, a shade insolently.

"A great deal," Constance said. "Although I suppose it all depends on what one regards as treasure."

"My son," Lloyd interjected at last. "Sydney, Mrs. Silver and Mr. Grey."

The youth bowed, his gaze lingering on Constance. He walked toward her as though drawn by an invisible thread. Solomon knew the feeling.

He turned back to Mrs. Lloyd. "We will do our very best to help get your treasure back. Finding it gone, as it were, must have been a great shock to you."

"I was never more shocked in my life," Mrs. Lloyd said. "Indeed, I could not think it was true—I thought Barnabas was playing some trick on us."

Solomon raised one eyebrow. "Why should you think that?"

She blinked a little too rapidly. "Well, it was in the *strong* room. We have never been robbed before, and frankly, I do not see how it can possibly have happened."

"It is quite a mystery, is it not? I understand the treasure spent some time in here before your husband and son took it to the strong room. Were you in the drawing room all of that time?"

"Yes, I was."

He gestured discreetly to include the whole room. "And all your family were present then too?"

"Yes."

"Was anyone else?" he asked. "Any visitors? Servants?"

"No visitors. No one would call without invitation on the evening of my husband's return. I think only Garrick—our butler—entered the room with wine and left again. Oh, and he announced dinner, which was when Barnabas decided to lock the chest away. Harry—the footman—helped Sydney carry it up."

The story was just the same as Lloyd's, and yet to Solomon something was not quite right.

"Where are the keys to the strong room kept?" he asked, mainly to see if she would tell him.

"Locked in my husband's bedside cabinet—when he is away. When he's at home, he keeps them about his person."

"Are you a light sleeper, Mrs. Lloyd?"

Her eyes widened. "I beg your pardon?"

"I mean, if someone was moving about the house during the night, would it normally waken you?"

Obviously, she saw the point of the question, because she answered easily enough, "It depends whether or not I take my drops to help me sleep."

"Did you take them the night before last?"

"No," she said, color staining the pale, perfect skin of her face. "My husband had come home after an absence of many months."

Intrigued by her blush, Solomon wanted to ask if they had

separate bedchambers, and if so, in which of them they had spent their reunion night. If in hers, then however lightly she slept, she needn't have heard the keys being taken from their usual place. Though why would Lloyd not have told him? Because he imagined it was none of his business? Solomon had come across other rakes who were extremely prudish about their wives.

"Then you did not hear anything unusual during that night," he said smoothly, making it more of a statement than a question.

"Nothing. Oh dear."

The last was uttered involuntarily as another young man walked into the room.

CHAPTER THREE

ONSTANCE SAW AT once that the newcomer had caused a subtle stir. Beside her, Sydney Lloyd tensed. His mother, seated beside Solomon, looked positively dismayed for the tiniest instant before she smiled in welcome and went to greet him. Only the elder daughter Jemimah looked uncomplicatedly delighted as she bounced up and reached the visitor before her mother.

"Ben, how wonderful! You may greet Papa at last. Papa, you remember Sydney's friend, Mr. Devine?"

Mr. Devine was a pleasant-looking young man with a shy smile but sharp eyes. He bowed to the room in general, and to Mrs. Lloyd in particular, before allowing himself to be hauled before his host, who smiled somewhat glacially and invited him to sit.

Jemimah brought him a cup of tea and offered plates of sandwiches and cakes to everyone.

"*Your* friend?" Constance murmured to Sydney with a hint of teasing.

"Well, he was," Sydney replied wryly. "Though he's likely to end up as no one's if my father takes him in dislike."

"Why should he do that?"

Sydney regarded her. "When we left England in the spring, Jemimah was fifteen years old, still in short skirts with pigtails and puppy fat. Now look at her. And poor old Ben in attendance. Not easy for a father to watch his daughter growing up."

"But he didn't, did he?" Constance said. "It was you he was watching grow up when he took you on his treasure hunt. Did you enjoy it?"

"I did," Sydney replied, his eyes gleaming rather like his father's. "I can see why my father is so addicted to his adventuring."

"Then you intend to follow in his footsteps?"

"Oh, it's too early to say," Sydney murmured.

Constance took a dainty little cake from the plate offered by a distracted Jemimah and smiled her thanks at the girl. Sydney snatched a couple of sandwiches.

"Tell me about the treasure," Constance urged before taking a bite of cake and placing the rest back on her plate.

"You mean how it was pinched? Dashed if I know." A smile came into his eyes. He would break hearts in a year or too, Constance thought, if he wasn't doing so already. "Are you really going to find it for him? One would think he might find it humiliating—the great treasure seeker used to braving hostile lands needing a young woman to track his property down in his own country."

"Well, the criminal world of London requires a different kind of knowledge."

"And *you* have such knowledge?" he asked. "How does that come about?"

"Secret of the trade, Mr. Lloyd," she said vaguely. "Were you upset by the loss?"

"Shocked," he answered. "It makes one think."

"What does it make you think?"

"Well, either some stranger has access to our house and wanders about at will in the middle of the night, knowing everything of my father's habits, or someone already in the house has betrayed us by stealing."

"And which do you believe?" She sipped her tea.

"Neither seems credible, to be honest. And yet it's gone."

Constance picked the last piece of cake on her plate. "You fetched the strong room keys from your father's bedchamber, the evening you came home."

"I did."

"Did anyone see you do so? Was anyone else in the passage when your father unlocked the strong room?"

"No, the servants were all downstairs getting ready to serve dinner."

"What about the footman who helped you carry the chest upstairs?"

"Harry? He went back down as soon as we dropped the chest outside the strong room. Papa and I lifted it inside."

"And then what?"

"We left it there and joined the others in the dining room, where Mama was worrying about the soup going cold."

"Did your father not lock the strong room door?"

Sydney blinked at her. "Of course he did."

"You mean you saw him do it? Or you merely assume he did?"

Sydney smiled with something very like delight. "You think he just forgot to lock the door? And someone just happened to try it and nabbed the treasure?"

"Is it a possibility?"

"Sadly not," Sydney replied. "I watched him lock the door and pocket the keys, and then we went downstairs together."

Constance changed tack. "What did you do for the rest of the evening? After dinner?"

"Came in here so we could regale everyone with more of our adventures over the last eight months."

"Who is 'everyone'?" she asked.

Sydney looked amused again. "My mother and sisters and my aunt."

"Did you have any visitors that evening?"

"No, it was a strictly family evening."

"When did the family party break up?"

Sydney smiled at her. "Goodness, you are more thorough than the policeman in your questions! It must have been just before eleven. And yes, I went straight to bed. If you want the truth, I was exhausted and had, besides, drunk too much champagne and port. We didn't have such luxuries on board the ship—which is a mistake, in my view."

"Well, that is an argument for another day." She finished her tea and set down the cup. "Did you sleep all night? Did any unusual sound disturb you?"

"Such as the clank of keys or the squeaking of the hinges on the strong room door? Sadly not."

"How did you learn that the treasure had been stolen?"

Sydney grimaced. "My father creating a one-man bawling match. He was up with the lark as usual and went straight to gloat over his treasure—or to let Rachel poke around it, maybe."

"Who is Rachel?"

"Rachel is my younger sister. She's twelve years old, so fortunately you won't see much of her. Would you excuse me? I should shake hands with poor old Ben."

"Of course," Constance replied.

As he rose, her sweeping glance caught the figure of his aunt, Miss Audrey Lloyd, knitting contentedly, quite alone by the fire. There was something oddly touching and yet unbearably lonely in the vignette—the maiden aunt living in another woman's house, always there and yet, it seemed, used to being barely noticed.

Constance stood and walked across the room to her. "Miss Lloyd?"

The lady looked up in surprise, peering over her spectacles. "Indeed. How do you do, Mrs. Silver? What a lovely name to have."

Constance drew forward the nearest chair and sat beside her. "Do you think so?"

"I do. Did I hear aright that you and Mr. Grey are helping Barnabas find his lost treasure?"

"We shall certainly do our best. It is quite a bizarre happening."

Audrey shook her head. "Most peculiar. I can't imagine what… Or who, which is even worse, don't you think?"

"Yes, it might well be. Where does Mr. Lloyd keep the keys to the strong room?"

Constance asked mainly to see if his sister knew, but she answered immediately.

"On his person. Or in the drawer by his bed. Everyone knows that."

"Everyone in the house?" Constance asked. "Or is there a wider community of family and friends who are aware of his habits?"

"Oh, I don't think so," Audrey said vaguely. "But then, I don't pay a great deal of attention. I have my own interests."

"May I know what those are?"

"Oh, just a few little charities."

Constance glanced at her work. "What are you knitting?"

"A scarf. For the poor."

"That is kind."

"Not very," Audrey said distractedly. "A mere drop in the ocean, really. One does what one can, when one has so much while others have nothing. Imagine not being able to keep your children warm in winter, or even fed. It is a great gift, to be born into a wealthy family, don't you think?"

Those weak eyes blinked up at Constance, who, on impulse, spoke honestly.

"I'm afraid I wouldn't know. I made my own way in the world."

Audrey smiled at her. "Did you, dear? I admire that. When will you marry Mr. Grey?"

The question flustered Constance. "We have not yet set a date."

"You should. If you love him."

Oh, I love him. That was never the issue…

"I suppose he is different," Audrey said. "Does your family not approve?"

"My mother would marry him herself if she could."

Audrey laughed, an unexpectedly merry sound. It lightened her tired face and the weak eyes behind the spectacles. Constance thought that she was probably still on the right side of forty, although she looked older most of the time.

"So what do you think happened to Barnabas's treasure?" Audrey asked.

"I don't honestly have a clue," Constance admitted. "Yet."

All the same, she had noticed Jemimah casting both anxious and imploring glances at Mr. Devine, who was now in laughing conversation with Sydney. Jemimah alone had been unsurprised by the young man's visit. No servant had shown him in, which meant that the security of the Lloyds' abode was less than perfect. Or that the servants were so used to his being received that they let him find his own way—the privilege, surely, of only the most frequent and favored of callers. Interesting.

Excusing herself to Audrey, Constance walked over to join Jemimah at the table, where she was replacing the plates she had just been offering to the guests.

"What a beautiful gown," Constance said, guessing what would most please the girl at this moment.

"Oh, do you think so? Thank you! It's new."

"I can see that," Constance said gravely. "Quite the height of fashion, too."

"So is yours," Jemimah replied with just a hint of wistfulness. "I wish I were as beautiful as you are."

"I'm not really, you know. If you behave as if you are, people tend to believe it."

Jemimah's eyes widened. "Really?"

"I have found so."

She frowned. "How does one behave as if one is beautiful?"

Constance leaned closer. "Well, for one thing, one does not keep trying to catch the eye of the gentleman whose admiration she wishes to attract. She ignores him, in the knowledge that he will come to her."

Jemimah blushed, looking guilty. "What if he doesn't?"

"That rather depends on the gentleman in question. Are we talking about Mr. Devine?"

"Does it show?" Jemimah asked ruefully.

"What it shows to me—and probably to your father—is that Mr. Devine is a more frequent visitor to the house than your father might like."

Jemimah blanched. "Oh, please hush! I have done nothing wrong!"

"My dear, I am hardly here to judge you," Constance said. "My only concern is with who was in the house on the evening of your father's return."

"Oh, no, he wasn't in the house," Jemimah assured her with relief.

"You met him in the garden?"

"Well, yes, just for five minutes."

"I suppose he calls on you often," Constance said neutrally.

"Well, he has been quite attentive in the last few months, but we have known him forever. He and Sydney went to school together, and he frequently stayed with us."

"What does he do now?"

Jemimah shrugged. "His father wants him to join the family firm—they are involved with cotton mills in the north—but Ben wants to be a great writer."

"A worthy ambition."

Jemimah beamed at her. "I think so."

BARNABAS LLOYD WAS glad to see the back of all his guests. Admittedly, Grey and Mrs. Silver had only gone as far as the kitchen to interview his servants, but at least Ben Devine was out of the house. Jumped-up puppy.

He waited until the children and Audrey had gone off about

their own business and the tea things had been taken away. His wife sat by the fire, opposite him, busying herself with embroidery work. He folded his newspaper.

"How long, Christine, have you permitted young Devine to run tame about this house?"

"Run tame?" she said a little nervously. "I would not call it that, my dear!"

"Would you not? He appeared to wander in here off the street."

"Not without Garrick's knowledge. There's no need for such a fuss, Barnabas. He has stayed here in the past, and his parents are friends of ours."

"Acquaintances," he corrected her. "I hope you have not encouraged him to sniff around Jemimah."

"They are children, Barnabas."

"You were barely a year older when I married you. I expected you to have more sense than to allow this."

"Allow what?" she asked with irritating defiance, her needle poised.

"Utter impropriety. She will be ruined at the age of sixteen! She's a child, and yet you let her put up her hair and let down her hems. What were you thinking of?"

"That she is a young lady and must learn to behave as one," Christine said tartly.

Barnabas rose and walked the few paces toward her, watching the courage fade from her eyes and the nervousness turn to alarm. He halted and bent over her deliberately.

"You are at fault, my love. Grievously so. Were she three years older, I would not give my daughter to Ben Devine. You are responsible for chaperoning her at all times."

"He is not her only admirer," Christine said defensively. Her breathing had quickened, as it always did when she was frightened. "As you will see when you escort us to the opera tomorrow evening."

"I'm not sure either of you are fit to be allowed out."

Her eyes fell. "If I have made a mistake, then I am sorry for it. I only did what I thought was best for a restive girl. I took her to tea with me a few times when I knew other young ladies and gentlemen would be present. That is all."

"Am I likely to come upon her swains prowling about the house?"

"Of course not."

He straightened and heard her sigh of relief. "Then we shall say no more about it for now. I'll speak to Garrick and put a stop to young Devine treating the house like his own."

THE LLOYDS' STAFF seemed to be everything good domestic servants should be, loyal and close-mouthed to strangers, even under instructions from their master to co-operate.

Constance and Solomon spoke first to Garrick, the haughty butler, whom they found in the kitchen conferring with the cook, a grim-faced woman of middle years who looked more likely to curdle the milk than produce food to make the senses sing.

Garrick's nostrils flared at sight of them in his domain. The cook turned away, banging the rolling pin in her hand down on the table with unnecessary force.

"Forgive the intrusion," Constance said amiably. "We shall not disturb you for long. I believe Mr. Lloyd has already informed you we are looking into the mystery of his missing treasure."

"Indeed," Garrick uttered.

Constance persevered in the face of his obvious discouragement, bestowing an understanding smile upon him. "It would help us enormously to know what you observed on the evening and during the night of Mr. Lloyd's return."

Garrick said nothing.

"When did you first see the treasure chest?" Solomon asked.

"When it was brought into the house. Sir." There was just

enough of a pause before the *sir* to be insolent.

Solomon ignored it. "Who brought it in?"

"Harry and John. Footmen."

"Where did they take it?"

"Upstairs, to the drawing room."

"Directly? Or did it lie in the hall for a while."

"Directly."

"How was it closed?"

"It was bound with rope."

"What happened once the chest was in the drawing room?"

"You must ask the master. I was not there."

"Then the family was already in the drawing room?"

"Indeed."

"When you brought wine to the drawing room, was the chest open or closed?"

"Closed."

"Bound still with the rope?"

For the first time, Garrick hesitated. "I couldn't say."

"And when you announced dinner?"

"I didn't notice. Mr. Lloyd asked for Harry to help carry it up to the strong room."

"May we speak to Harry?"

"According to the master. Harry." There was no change in his tone as he summoned the footman—the same brawny young man who had admitted them into the house.

Constance left Solomon with his thankless task and sidled up to the cook, who was snapping at the kitchen maid chopping vegetables beside her. The girl looked frightened enough to cut her fingers by mistake.

"I'm Mrs. Silver," Constance said pleasantly. And when the cook did not trouble to reply, merely continued rolling her pastry with brisk brutality, she asked, "What is your name?"

"Mrs. Smith," the cook said without looking up.

Constance turned to the maid. "And you?"

The girl dropped her knife. "I'm Rosie, ma'am. Kitchen

maid." She bobbed a quick curtsey and picked up the knife again.

"I was wondering if anyone not of the household visited the kitchen the evening before last."

The cook cast her a glance of contempt. "We got no time for visitors."

"I'm sure that doesn't stop them dropping in at inconvenient moments."

"Not here, they don't." Mrs. Smith threw down her rolling pin and lifted the pastry with surprisingly delicate hands, to place it in the waiting pie dish.

"Then a simple yes or no will suffice," Constance snapped, tired of the attitude. "Did anyone visit the kitchen that night?"

"No," the cook answered, snatching up a knife with which to trim the pastry.

"What time did you retire?"

"Half past ten, when the family did."

Constance glanced at Rosie the maid, who said hastily, "Ten o'clock, ma'am, on account I have to get up early to see to the fire."

"Where do you sleep?" Constance asked.

"Attic, ma'am."

Constance sighed and looked at the cook. "And you?"

"Attic. We all sleep in the attics."

"Were you disturbed at all by any unusual noises in the house? Or outside the house?"

"No," said Mrs. Smith.

Rosie shook her head.

Constance was not really surprised. Most hardworking servants were so tired that they slept soundly until wakened by someone else or by their own trained body clock.

"What time did you rise in the morning?" she asked the maid.

"Five o'clock, ma'am."

"And did you see or hear anything unusual then? Was the back door locked?"

The maid's eyes widened. "I never checked, ma'am. It was

closed. So was the area door at the front."

"And no one else was moving about?"

"Not until about six, when everyone else came down."

In this case, "everyone" appeared to mean the other servants. "Then none of the family was up and about at that time?"

"Course not," said Rosie. "Even the master don't rise *that* early."

"And you used the back stairs to come down to the kitchen?"

"Of course," Rosie said again, clearly shocked at any other possibility.

Constance smiled. "Even so early when no one would see you? I would be tempted."

"You," said Mrs. Smith, "ain't her. She uses the back stairs, and she'd be dismissed for anything else."

Constance let it go.

CHAPTER FOUR

"**I** THINK WE should call on my mother," Constance said, by way of explanation as to why she had instructed her coachman to take them to Covent Garden.

"To see who is likely to fence the treasure?" Solomon said.

"Or if she has heard any rumors. I learned long ago never to discount my mother's wealth of low knowledge."

"Will you tell her about our engagement?" he asked.

They were seated side by side, so she had to turn her head to look at him. "I suppose it would kill two birds with one stone."

"Are you afraid she will make a fuss?" he asked wryly. "Or forbid the banns?"

"I'm afraid she'll laugh."

"Am I so laughable?"

"Engaging yourself to me? Of course you are! But it's *me* she will be laughing at." Constance shifted restlessly. "And no wonder. I don't know what a wife *does*, Solomon. Except turn a blind eye when a husband visits a woman like me."

"Constance." He took her hand, his fingers warm and firm around hers. "There are no other women like you."

For a second, she clung to his hand, longing for his fidelity. She hated being on that side of the fence. All she knew about marriage was from the unfaithful, and she doubted she could be like these tolerant, ladylike wives. She was more likely to revert to her upbringing and break bottles over his head.

With a breath of laughter, she thrust such personal thoughts aside, withdrew her hand, and said, "Have we learned anything useful?"

Solomon shrugged. "That the servants are well trained and loyal."

"And tense," Constance added. "They didn't strike me as a happy group. They're much too defensive. Though I suppose they can't be blamed for that, since servants are always under suspicion whenever anything goes missing."

"They were unusually obstructive," Solomon agreed. "And they told us nothing new about the theft. Only Garrick the butler knows where the keys to the strong room are kept at night and when Lloyd is away."

"And we do know Mrs. Lloyd has entertained several times during her husband's absence," Constance added. She had learned that not from the cook but from John the footman. "There have been sizeable dinner parties with old friends and new and frequent morning callers, all Mrs. Lloyd's acquaintances but some of them Jemimah's friends and admirers. Like Benjamin Devine."

She must have been frowning over that, for Solomon said, "You are suspicious of young Devine?"

"No more so than of any of the other visitors to the house, although he does seem to have had carte blanche to wander about the place in search of Jemimah. No, what worries me about Devine is that no one seems to have told Lloyd about his friendship with Jemimah. Apart from her, the whole family was dismayed to some degree by his arrival."

"Mrs. Lloyd certainly was," Solomon agreed.

"Like many fathers, I daresay he doesn't like his daughters growing up. Sydney implied as much. And the transformation apparently happened while they were away."

"What did you think of Sydney?" Solomon asked.

"Actually, I'm not sure what to make of him. He is very young, of course, and in his father's shadow, but he does seem rather…offhand—about the treasure and everything else. The selfishness of youth, I suppose."

"Lloyd didn't tell his family about employing us," Solomon said thoughtfully. "He sprang us on them without warning."

"You think he suspects one of them and was trying to make them betray themselves through surprise?"

"Maybe. He plays his cards close to his chest. I wonder what he has not told *us*?"

Constance thought about that, too, then turned to the matter of their suspects. "On the face of it, the family is likeliest," she said. "Any of them could have taken the keys while he was away, copied them, and opened the strong room during the night."

"Except Sydney, although he could have copied them earlier. We need to talk to the locksmith. Would you like to go to the opera tomorrow evening?"

Constance, who had been gazing out of the window as the carriage rumbled its way through Covent Garden, turned to him in surprise. "It's very public."

"Do you mean to hide?" he asked.

She took a deep breath. "I may not affect your business, Solomon, but I will affect your social standing."

"I have never sought social standing, and I very much doubt I have any."

"More than you know," she said seriously.

"Are you saying no to the opera?"

"No. I'm saying…" Actually, she didn't know what she was saying, except that attending the opera with him in the full glare of, she was sure, many of the gentlemen who attended her establishment on a regular basis was both damaging for him and terrifying for her.

"Don't lose your courage because of me," he said. "It is one of the things I first loved in you."

The carriage had halted without her noticing. He opened the carriage door and alighted before holding out his hand to her.

She stared at him. *He loves me. Solomon Grey loves me.*

The miracle of that would always take her by surprise.

Closing her mouth, she swallowed and took his hand to step

down in front of her mother's new shop. "Of course I will go to the opera with you."

HER MOTHER'S SHOP consisted of an eclectic display of antiquities and curios, the valuable and the valueless, the beautiful and the frankly ugly. Spread out around the shelves and cabinets, in the bright light gleaming through the large window and glass door, they presented a fascinating array to browsers and collectors. Two sets of customers were already wandering around. A third was having something wrapped by the proprietress.

Juliet Silver had found her element. Dressed in a unique, exotic style of flowing gowns and shawls, she looked like some Byzantine princess of ages past. Constance felt her lips twitch, just as her mother glanced up and saw them.

She beamed, for she and Constance had recently reached a sort of rapprochement. It might not have been total understanding, but it was an acknowledgment of affection, a bond that could not be broken.

"Good afternoon!" she said. "I shall be with you shortly."

It had become habit between them to pretend no relationship, mostly so that neither could be used against the other by the nastier of the criminals who had inhabited both their worlds until recently.

Constance wandered over to a small but eye-catching porcelain tea set. The shapes were exquisite, the painted design of interlocking flowers beautiful and somehow happy. She had a sudden vision of serving tea in them to Solomon and the Tizsas and other shadowy friends.

Where will we live? she thought in sudden fright.

Not in her establishment—that would never work. She felt more than a flicker of regret for that. She wondered about his little house behind the Strand. Or would they choose somewhere new?

"Gerry," her mother called through the door into the back of the shop, and the familiar figure of the lad who had been her gatekeeper in her old—rather less salubrious—quarters emerged. He looked somewhat self-conscious and stiff in his smart new suit, but he had scrubbed up remarkably well.

Constance smiled, glad to see him still with her mother.

He grinned back. "Afternoon, Miss Connie."

"Watch the shop, there's a love," Juliet said, holding the inner door for Constance and Solomon. "To what do I owe the honor?"

"We're picking your brains, Ma," Constance said, sitting down at the comfortable table and producing from her bag Lloyd's inventory of his treasure. "Have you heard a whisper of stolen treasure coming on the market? Unusual items? Anything about the items on this list?"

"I don't hear what I used to, being respectable now," her mother said virtuously, eyeing Solomon, who was her landlord. "But no, I haven't heard anything in particular." She took the list from Constance, and her darkened eyebrows flew up as she read. "Where does all this come from? A museum?"

"It was stolen from a private home," Solomon said.

"Very well, I'll keep my eyes and ears open for a word, but this lot would need to be sold to a private collector. Whoever pinched it would get a tiny fraction of its worth. I presume the police are already looking for it?"

"Yes, but it's possible our thief is somewhat naïve in the ways of stolen goods," Constance said, "and has no idea how to earn usable money from his loot."

"I'll listen for that too. I daresay I'll have the peelers poking their long noses and clumsy mitts into my business again." Juliet looked up from the list. "Did you consider it might have been a private collector who stole it?"

Constance felt her eyes widen. "Actually, no, but that makes perfect sense." Presumably the Lloyds numbered several eager collectors among their friends. "We should look into that. Who would you suspect of such practices among the wealthier of your clientele?"

"You mean the *outwardly* respectable?" Juliet thought for a little, then pulled a piece of paper in front of her and took a pencil from a hidden pocket behind her shawls. She started to scribble a few names, some with addresses beneath.

When she paused in her writing, Constance said, "Solomon and I are engaged to be married."

A slow smile tugged at her mother's lips before she looked up. She wasn't laughing, though her eyes did gleam. "Congratulations, Solomon. Con, I knew you'd turn respectable one day, even if it took a man like our Mr. Grey."

"Women like me are never respectable," Constance snapped.

"Why not?" Juliet retorted, spreading her arms wide. "Look at me."

Constance was obliged to laugh. "You are right, of course. There are many shades of respectability. Your shop appears to be blooming."

"It's a novelty right now, so people are curious. Not everyone who comes in is here to buy. But trade is brisk and I can't ask for more. I had to get Gerry in to help mind the shop just so I can attend to the rest of the business. And yes," she added, scowling at Solomon, "he knows the rules and keeps his nose clean."

"I never thought otherwise," Solomon said mildly.

SINCE THEY WERE making use of Constance's town carriage, she had instructed her coachman to go first to Solomon's house behind the Strand.

"I'll collect Janey from the office," she said, as Solomon sat down beside her. "She won't close up until one of us tells her to."

"Will you tell her we are engaged?" he asked as the horses pulled them forward.

She shifted position, gazing out of the window. "I don't know."

He was silent for several heartbeats, though she could feel his gaze on her averted face. "If you don't want to do this, tell me."

Blindly, she reached out, seeking and finding his hand, though she would not turn her head. "I do," she whispered, gripping hard. "I just don't know where to start. I can't tell Janey because she will tell the girls, even by accident."

"Then why don't *you* tell your girls?"

"Tell them what?" she demanded. "That I am about to make them homeless, turn them out, sell the roof over their heads? Sacrifice their future to mine?"

"*This* is what's been bothering you?"

After a few moments' more silence, he touched her chin and she closed her eyes as, inexorably, he turned her face toward him.

"Constance. I would never ask you to sell your establishment. I understand what it means to you and the good you do there."

She forced her eyes open, furious that a tear—of pure frustration, of course—caused her to dash her free hand across the corner of her eye and glare. "Do you also understand that when I marry you, you will own everything of mine? *You*, Solomon Grey, will be the owner of a brothel!"

His lip twitched. Was that laughter glinting in his eyes, or just relief? It was hard to tell in the flickering lamplight.

"That is certainly not respectable," he said gravely. "But I doubt anyone but the reformers will hold it against me. It might cause a certain amount of ribald laughter in the clubs, but in gentlemen-only matters, few will care."

"They will when your wife is seen there," she retorted. "And I do need to be there, Solomon."

"To live?" he asked expressionlessly.

"No… But my frequent appearance is necessary, not just to keep the place running smoothly and safely, but to keep the girls and the clients happy. I haven't given those duties up for Silver and Grey, and I don't want to now. Only…" She sucked in a wobbly breath. "There is you. I don't want such a wife for you."

His thumb caressed her chin. He leaned forward, his hat obscuring the lamplight from the window, and softly kissed her lips. "There is a solution, Constance. There is always a solution to our puzzles, is there not?"

Her smile felt a little tremulous. "So far."

"It will require some thought. In the meantime, might you not just tell them you are engaged to be married but that the establishment will remain under your control?"

"I could tell them that," she said, doubtfully. Some would know he could sell the place without her consent or even her knowledge if he so chose, but the women trusted her, and Janey would speak up for Solomon. It was a short-term solution while they solved the real problem, and for the first time, she began to think they might. Together.

She squeezed his hand gratefully and he sat back, rather to her disappointment. She liked his kisses… "Do you suppose every couple faces so many complications?"

"Probably. But they needn't all be troublesome ones. Don't you think it will be fun finding a new home and making it our own?"

She peered at him. "You want a new home?"

"Mine is too small. Yours is too scandalous. Shall we devote some time to that too?"

"Yes," she said, straightening with a smile. "Why don't we?"

The carriage drew up outside his front door. In sudden panic, she realized he was leaving her again, and she didn't want that. She clung harder to his hand, as if he had been trying to withdraw it—which he hadn't.

"We should dine together," she said abruptly.

Either the invitation or her tone surprised him, for his brow twitched very slightly. "I would like that."

"Does your man cook?"

"We have an actual cook. Tomorrow is the opera. Shall we say the day after?"

"What's wrong with tonight?"

He smiled and raised her hand to his lips. "Tonight, you have to tell Janey and the rest of your staff." He kissed her gloved fingers, then drew back her glove and kissed the inside of her wrist. "And then you will be more comfortable. Goodnight, Constance."

She sighed. "Goodnight, Solomon."

TO CONSTANCE'S SURPRISE, there were no lights in the offices of Silver and Grey. She had just discovered that the front door was locked when Janey came flying around the corner from Chandos Street and skidded to a breathless halt.

"Ah, there you are, ma'am! I locked up, but I can get you some tea if you want to go back in?"

"No, we can take the carriage home now."

Janey grinned, for she loved a carriage ride, and opened the door for Constance with an exaggerated flourish.

"I got loads to tell you," she said as soon as she landed on the seat opposite Constance.

The horses eased forward while Constance regarded her former handmaiden. "New prospective clients? You and Lenny Knox have discovered something about the Lloyds?"

"What's Lenny Knox got to do with anything?" Janey demanded aggressively, although betraying color was seeping into her face.

Lenny had proved useful very useful in discovering the truth about their previous case—in which he had begun as a suspect—and since he needed the work, they had agreed to call on him whenever necessary. He, a recent and devastated widower, and she, a former prostitute, had become unlikely friends.

"Nothing, except you are good for him," Constance said. "And I would be glad someone other than my mother was keeping an eye on him."

Janey waved that aside. "It's not about Lenny or the Lloyds. It's about Bibby Barton."

Constance blinked. "Who's Bibby Barton?"

"Working girl, on the game over by Haymarket. Told you about her the other day 'cause I don't think she should be on the streets. Too young and too soft to last many winters."

Constance rubbed her forehead with consternation. "You did tell me. I'm sorry, I can't have taken in her name. I've had a lot on my mind. What about her? Is she ill?"

"Only in spirit. All she has in the world is the locket her ma gave her when she left her in the orphanage as a baby. It ain't worth anything, trashy thing really, but she loves that locket and she's gone and lost it. Devastated, she is. I was helping her look around for it, then I thought I'd better dash back here in case you or Mr. Grey showed up. I didn't leave the office until five," Janey added defensively.

"You are more than conscientious, Janey," Constance said.

Janey grinned. "I know I am. Thing is, I told Bibby I'd speak to you about the locket. About finding it."

Constance blinked. "How are we to do that? Did someone take it?"

"Might have done. Can't trust men. She had it when she went out but not when she came home. We searched her lodgings and the place she waits for business, but saw no sign."

"You didn't give her hope, did you?" Constance said uneasily. "We both know she'll never see it again. A child might have picked it up off the street, one of the women might have found it and kept it, or it might just have been lost in the rubbish…"

Janey's face fell.

"I'll go and see her," Constance said. "But the best I can do for her is take her back to the establishment—and I will if you're vouching for her."

"I am," Janey said, with a quick smile, but even in the gloom of the carriage, Constance could see she was still troubled.

Constance took a deep breath. "Look, I think it's a lost cause and a waste of time. But I could be wrong, so if you think there's a chance of finding this locket, you can spend half your day doing so. You know what to do—speak to the girls who were close by, speak to her customers, find out if anyone saw anything, and who passed by at the time. See if anyone wished her ill for any reason, who fought with her."

"No one fights with Bibby—she ain't that kind of girl. But I'll do all the rest. Thanks, Mrs. S."

"Ask Lenny to help, if you like," Constance offered recklessly. She was already lending out a paid employee of the firm for no return, and now she would have to pay Lenny too.

Janey looked horrified. "God no, I couldn't do that! He might find out—" She broke off, turning her head away.

"Your past?" Constance said calmly. "If he is ever to be a real friend, he will have to know. Besides, he's the sort of man who understands about desperation and poverty. He'll be proud of what you're doing now. Which reminds me, I have news, too."

Janey turned back to face her. "Really?" she asked eagerly. "What?"

"I'm going to be married." It didn't seem to get easier to say, and the reactions were never quite what Constance expected, either.

Janey stared at her, jaw dropping. "Who to?"

"Mr. Grey," Constance said frostily.

Janey's hunched shoulders relaxed. She even grinned. "Oh! Well, that's all right, then. I like him. He's a good man, if there is such a thing. In fact, wouldn't mind—" She broke off hastily. "No wonder your mind's wandering! Bloody good excuse for a party, though—I'd love to dance at *your* wedding!" She frowned. "Mind you, he won't want the likes of us there..." Her eyes suddenly widened. "Wait, though, what about Silver and Grey?"

"It will still be there," Constance said. "In fact, when I tell everyone at home, I'm relying on you to help reassure everyone that there will no changes to the establishment."

Janey's eyes widened. "Likes of him wouldn't come and live with us there!"

"No, of course not. But even if I am there less, I *will* be there and I will be in charge."

"And he doesn't mind that?"

He must do. He has always minded… "He knows what and who comes along with me." Constance noticed she had crossed her fingers and hastily uncrossed them.

BARNABAS LLOYD TOOK the newly delivered parcel into his study after dinner. It no longer seemed quite so exciting to unwrap the objects within. But it was the only way to admire his treasure, the only proof he had that he had ever found and possessed it.

Slowly, he unwrapped the parcel and spread the contents over his desk. Several glass plates and the photographs printed on paper from them. Some were taken on the island, amongst the reedy, swampy ground where they had dug the treasure up, some on the deck of the ship.

Quickly after that, he found his favorite. Barnabas himself, dressed in his light suit and sun hat, stood beside the chest, which was held open by two of his men grinning at the camera. Sydney and the others crouched around it looked awed and happy.

All the photographs were unexpectedly clear and sharp—Sydney, his chief informant about the latest process, was right about that—and this one managed to portray something of the sparkle of the treasures visible within the chest. Barnabas wished the picture could show the extraordinary colors, rather than the mere shades of light and dark. But even so, it was a fine photograph, and one he would have been proud to show in the exhibition of his treasure he had planned to hold around the auction.

His smile faded. Someone in his household had betrayed him.

He wanted to believe it was an outsider who had somehow broken in without leaving a trace, but that was even more unlikely than the alternative. Perhaps the strangely refined Silver and Grey could find out and relocate his treasure. Perhaps the police could.

Unlikely. It would be broken up and sold for a pittance.

He ran his finger over the photograph, almost caressing the flat, colorless treasure.

A brief knock sounded at the door.

"Enter," he called.

Sydney wandered in. "Garrick said you wanted me."

"Just to show you these, since you were so interested in the process."

"The photographs!" Sydney's step sped up until he peered over his father's shoulder. "These are excellent. I still wonder if there is a way to make a living in photography?"

"You are a gentleman," Barnabas snapped. "You do not *earn a living.*"

"Then I'm likely to starve," Sydney retorted. "Since your precious strong room couldn't hold the treasure that was to save the family fortunes. At least until the next expedition."

Barnabas curled his lip. "Then by all means go out into the world," he said, spreading his arm toward the window. "Make your own way. Don't let me hold you back. I'm sure there is a place somewhere for a talentless dilettante who is best at drinking, gambling, and whoring."

Sydney straightened. "Which reminds me," he drawled. "Best get on. Goodnight, Papa."

Barnabas felt like hurling the glass plates after his son as he sauntered insolently out of the room. Fortunately, he had not reached that level of self-destruction.

CHAPTER FIVE

"How did it go?" Solomon asked Constance when they met over coffee in the office the following morning.

Janey, who had opened up before he got there, had already greeted him with a beaming smile and a startling kiss on the cheek, so he knew the word was out and his doubts about Constance's commitment to their marriage began to evaporate. Still, he wanted to hear the news from her point of view.

She did not pretend to misunderstand his question. She never played such games. "They were somewhat surprised, and all wished us well. I *think* they are reassured. Janey helped."

He nodded and left the matter alone. "To the case, then. What should be our next step forward? Finding out if the Lloyds are acquainted with any of the collectors on your mother's list?"

She nodded. "I think so. Also, any other serious collectors who have ever been in the house. Perhaps look into the Devine boy, too, since Jemimah met him in the garden after the rest of the house retired."

"It strikes me we should also speak again to Jemimah herself. And to the rest of the family. Something is wrong there."

She nodded. "Perhaps you should go back there. I am not quite dressed for it."

For the first time, he realized she was in her dull clothes. In fact, he rarely noticed what she wore, for it never changed who she was or dimmed her beauty.

"I have a slightly different errand this morning," she said

ruefully. "Establishment business. But it should not take me long. I can find Benjamin Devine after that and meet you back here for luncheon?"

"Hopefully, we shall have some new clues to follow by then."

"Um…one more thing." She smoothed her hand over her skirts. "I have given Janey leave to pursue another case for a friend who cannot pay. I've also said she can employ Lenny Knox should the need arise. I know it's not Silver and Grey business, so I am happy to pay for Lenny and the inconvenience of not having Janey here all day."

By the time he had disabused her of that notion and heard the story of Bibby Barton, they had finished their coffee.

"It will do the firm no harm, if word of us spreads further," he said, rising to his feet. "Though I could wish the chances of success were higher."

"So could I," she said. "I thought you were a hardheaded man of business, Solomon."

"So did I."

She smiled and, to his surprise, reached up to kiss his cheek, a small gesture of affection that touched him far more deeply than it should. But he was smiling as he picked up his hat and left the office.

On arriving at the Lloyds' residence, he was informed by Garrick, with unnecessary relish, that Mr. Lloyd was not at home.

This rather suited Solomon, who had a notion to see the family without the overwhelming presence of the master of the house.

"Perhaps Mrs. Lloyd?" he suggested.

"Madam has not yet come down, sir."

Clearly, the butler thought he had stymied the intrusive upstart. Solomon gave him a gentle smile. "It seems I would be best employed below stairs until the family is available."

In fact—for the moment, at least—Solomon was not much interested in the servants, but he was well aware his questions had flustered and outraged the staff, who were already threatening to give notice and leave Garrick with a considerable problem.

"I'll see if Mr. Sydney is available," Garrick said grandly. "If you will please wait in here."

The butler showed Solomon into the small, cold reception room where the fire had not been lit recently. If ever. When Garrick had gone—without attempting to take his hat and coat—Solomon laid his hat on the small table and sat on the chair by the window.

From the hall came a casual, if musical, humming. A moment later, a girl of about twelve years old wandered in with a not very convincing air of surprise.

"Oh! Good morning. I'm Rachel Lloyd."

Solomon rose and bowed. "Solomon Grey."

"Papa is off to his clubs."

"So I heard."

"Ah, you are one of Jemimah's admirers."

"How could one not be?"

"Now you're being polite," Rachel said unexpectedly.

"So are you, greeting me on your family's behalf."

She grinned, unabashed. "Actually, I saw you from the schoolroom window and thought you looked interesting—different from our usual callers."

"How did you escape your governess?" he asked, thinking that it was just like Lloyd to leave such a person off his list of residents.

"Oh, I'm between governesses just now. Mama sets me copying work to do, but it's very dull."

"It sounds it," Solomon said sympathetically. "How did you scare off your last teacher?"

"I'm not very sure." The child looked genuinely regretful. "Actually, I rather liked her, but I suspect she didn't like me."

Or the Lloyds had run out of money to pay the woman. "I'm trying to help your father find his missing treasure."

"I hope you do, because it would make everyone so much happier again."

"Including you?"

"Oh yes. I never even saw it, you know!"

"You didn't?" Solomon sat back down. "I thought you were all in the drawing room together while your father showed you the treasure chest."

She grimaced. "He did show us the chest. He just didn't open it. Can you imagine how maddening that was? Is!"

"No," Solomon said slowly. "I'm not sure I can imagine anything like it. Did none of you ask to see it?"

"We all did! Except Sydney, of course, who'd seen it already, since he was present when they dug it out. *He* would have shown us, but Papa made him sit back down again."

This was sounding increasingly bizarre. No one else had mentioned this odd behavior. In fact, everyone had contributed to the notion that the treasure had been much admired before being taken to the strong room before dinner. Was the child lying? After all, why on earth would Lloyd not let them see the dazzling fruits of his months-long expedition?

Because he had already hidden it elsewhere to fool would-be thieves? Or was the whole treasure story made up to swindle the insurance? Which would mean, of course, that Lloyd had lied about not having insurance. Looking into that shot up Solomon's list of priorities.

"How will you set about finding the treasure?" Rachel asked.

"Oh, asking questions, mostly," he said vaguely.

"That doesn't sound *very* exciting."

"No. It can be interesting, though. Tell me, why would your father have taken the chest into the drawing room if he did not mean to show you the treasures within?"

"Teasing us," Rachel said. "He's always doing things like that. I daresay he would have shown us that evening, eventually, only dinner was announced at just the wrong moment. I was allowed to have dinner with them that night," she added proudly.

Was this teasing? Or evidence of Lloyd's exertion of petty control over his family? Like not telling them what he and

Constance were doing in the drawing room yesterday...

With a hint of anxiety, perhaps aware she had chattered too much, Rachel said, "Papa took me to the strong room first thing the next morning to show me the treasure."

"Just you?"

"No one else was up but he and I. I don't sleep much. That is," she corrected herself, "Aunt Aud was already up and out upon her good works. She's my father's sister, and we call her Aud because she is—odd, I mean. Sydney thought of it, and I suppose it's funny, but she isn't *really* odd, just disappointed in love. Are you going to marry the beautiful lady? Mrs. Silver?"

Solomon blinked, suspecting the child had won many a confidence in this apparently artless fashion. "Yes," he said, and endeavored to bring the conversation back under his own control. "Your father must have been completely stunned to find the treasure gone."

The faintest giggle escaped her lips and was immediately swallowed. "Amazed," she agreed, clearing her throat. "And absolutely furious. I've never seen him in such a rage."

"It does not appear to upset you," Solomon noted, taking in her innocent expression.

"Oh well, I'm sure he is very scary when he's enraged, only I have no... What is the word? Sensibility?"

She certainly did not look remotely frightened of her father. Who was? *Is your mother frightened of him? Is your brother?* He could not ask a child such a thing. Apart from anything else, he couldn't see how it might be relevant to the current mystery.

"Good grief," Rachel said with exaggerated surprise as a swift step sounded from the hallway. "Sydney is up! Morning, Syd," she added as her brother did indeed stride into the room.

"Morning, pip-squeak," he returned cheerfully. "Scarper! Mr. Grey, how pleasant to see you again." He held out a careless hand to Solomon, who gripped it briefly while Rachel edged very slowly toward the door. "Papa is out, you know."

"So I have been told," Solomon replied. "But I thought of

another few points you or the rest of the family might be able to help me with while I wait." Since one of the things preying on his mind was the truth of Rachel's story of never seeing the treasure, he gazed at her expectantly until Sydney noticed and advanced upon her purposefully.

"Oh, very well, I'm going," she said with a sigh, though she still dragged her feet, and Solomon was fairly sure she went no further than the other side of the door. Her brother closed it, probably in her face, before sitting in the chair next to Solomon's.

"Little sisters are a plague upon the world," Sydney remarked without rancor. "What can I help you with, Mr. Grey? You must know we are all under instruction to co-operate with you in full."

"I'm sure finding the missing treasure must mean as much to you as your father. After all, you helped to dig it up, did you not?"

"With these not-quite-so-fair hands." He spread them, inevitably sun and sea bronzed, for Solomon's appreciation.

"How did that come about?"

"Oh, Papa decided I should go with him, since I wasn't doing anything else except wasting his money." He shrugged. "I didn't mind. I thought it might be amusing."

"Was it?" Solomon asked.

"In places. Though I admit I was getting a bit fed up with hiking across the dullest of little islands under the blazing sun, when we finally found what we were looking for."

"How did you know where to look? Was it mere chance?"

"Lord, no. Papa had an actual map—though it helpfully omitted any names or compass bearings. He got it from some old sea dog—I think he'd sailed with Papa on earlier expeditions until he got too ill. Papa looked after him a bit, and in gratitude the old fellow gave him his treasure map. Anyone else would have said a polite thank you very much and burned it with the rubbish, but not my father. He believed him, and as it turned out, he was right."

"It must have been very exciting."

"It was certainly funny," Sydney said. "I had to eat my own

words of doubt, which had become increasingly loud over the preceding week, and for once I was more than glad to."

"I suppose you were owed a share of the treasure?"

"I was," Sydney said fervently, "and I don't mind telling you it would have been damned useful."

"May I ask what you meant to spend it on?"

"Wine, women, and song, of course. Preferably without the song. Either that or to set up in photography. I believe that will be a valuable business investment. Such a useful science, and artistic in its own right."

"Really?" Solomon said. The various processes he had come across were clever, but he had never thought the end results either artistic or useful. Stern portraits without character or spontaneity, landscapes without color. "Perhaps I should look further into the matter."

"Get my father to show you his photographs from the expedition. They were delivered last night."

"I will," Solomon said. "Do they show the treasure?"

"They do. Well, just the chest in most, but there are a couple with it open, where you get a pretty good view of the contents."

"Your little sister seemed very disappointed that she never saw the actual treasure."

Sydney smiled wryly. "Papa's little joke. Not that it makes any real difference who saw it."

So Rachel had told the truth. "I had the impression before today that you had all seen it."

Sydney's eyes slid away to the window. "Oh well, we none of us like to spread about Papa's less successful jokes. Some of them can seem almost cruel to strangers. Papa does not mean them that way, of course. He's just teasing and thinks everyone is as entertained as he is."

"Were you?"

"Not really. Mama and the girls would have loved to see it. I do hope you get it back for us."

"So do I. Do you or your father have any enemies, any ill

wishers who might have stooped to robbery?"

Sydney rubbed distractedly at the side of his nose. "Not unless his seamen decided they deserved more pay. Or there's Terrance, I suppose."

"Who is Terrance?"

Sydney grimaced. "Mark Terrance. Boring, ill-natured old duffer who fancies himself as a collector of valuable antiquities. He rants against my father's knowledge whenever anyone will listen—mostly because Papa refused to bid at auction for some vase or other than Terrance paid a fortune for. It turned out to be fake, and Terrance insisted my father knew and kept quiet deliberately."

Sydney stretched out his legs and yawned. "Which he might have, to be fair, but it's hardly Papa's fault Terrance was gammoned. Anyway, I don't see how either disgruntled seamen or Terrance could have got into the house, let alone opened the strong room."

"Was Mr. Terrance a frequent visitor to the house?"

"Lord, no, shouldn't think so. Not after the vase incident, anyway. A couple of years ago, that was. I do remember his popping up here occasionally before that. You should ask my mother."

"I will," Solomon assured him. "I believe Benjamin Devine is a friend of yours?"

A hint of amusement crept into Sydney's eyes, though he kept his face straight. "So far."

"Meaning your father might banish him for his interest in your sister?"

"Be fair, sir. Jemimah's only sixteen years old."

"It wasn't a criticism," Solomon said. It had, in fact, been a deliberate provocation to see if Sydney would defend his father. "I merely wondered if Mr. Devine is interested in antiquities too."

"He's interested in beauty," Sydney said. "So he might be, if his father didn't keep him on such a short leash. Wants him in the family mill, but Ben's more of a poetry man. You don't suspect him, do you?"

"We can't rule out anyone familiar with the house."

Sydney met his gaze, the amusement more pronounced now. "Especially those who live here and know where the keys are kept? Want to search my room, Mr. Grey?"

Solomon smiled back. "I have no such authority, Mr. Lloyd, nor, at the moment, any such interest."

"No point anyway," Sydney said. "My father's already roared through every room in the house."

Well, that explained why the servants were so uppity. A mixture of outrage and fear, and yet still loyal. Solomon hoped his client was worthy of that.

"I say, it's dashed cold in here, isn't it? Shall we go somewhere warmer? I daresay it will be more comfortable in the drawing room. Will the charming Mrs. Silver be joining us today?"

"Not this morning," Solomon said, rising and picking up his hat to follow.

Surprisingly, Sydney said, "Give me your hat and coat, sir. Garrick can't have thought you were staying."

"Wishful thinking, no doubt. Thefts often lead to difficult times for domestic servants."

"Very tolerant fellow, aren't you?" Sydney said, leading him upstairs. "I suppose you have to be... In your line of work, I mean," he added hastily.

On the landing, Sydney opened the double doors of the drawing room, which was indeed considerably warmer than the reception room below.

A fire blazed welcomingly in the grate. Solomon was glad to take the chair next to it when offered.

"Want some tea?" Sydney asked, hovering. "Something stronger?" He made a half movement toward the decanter on the cabinet near the fireplace.

"Not for me, thank you."

If Sydney was disappointed not to have the excuse of brandy

well before eleven o'clock in the morning, he didn't show it.

Instead, he sat in the chair opposite Solomon's and asked amiably, "How does one come to the career of a private agent of inquiry?"

"I imagine former policemen are very good at it."

Sydney's lip curled. "Yes, but *you* were never a policeman, were you?"

"No. I rather fell into it by degrees after some property was stolen from me. It became something of—er…a hobby before I had the notion of making it a business interest."

"Not many men marry their employees," Sydney drawled.

"You might be surprised there. But Mrs. Silver is not my employee. She is my partner." Solomon fished Juliet Silver's list of collectors from his pocket, unfolded it, and leaned forward to pass it to Sydney. "Might I ask you if you know any of the names written here?"

Looking faintly amused once more—whether at Solomon's partnership or the list before him was not clear—Sydney cast a quick glance at it. "Can't say I do. Who are they?"

"Collectors of antiquities."

"I see." He read the names again more thoroughly and began to look more thoughtful. "You know, this fellow sounds familiar for some reason. Arthur Fenwick… Fenwick…"

The drawing room doors opened again and Mrs. Lloyd swept in with her elder daughter, saying briskly, "I am not saying that, my dear, merely that Mr. Devine will be treated with the same respect as any other visitor to our house and not left to find— Oh." She broke off, actually halting in her tracks as Solomon rose and bowed. "Mr. Grey. Good morning. I was not told you were here."

"Garrick told me instead of disturbing you," Sydney said easily. "Come and look at these names, Mama. Don't we know an Arthur Fenwick?"

"I don't believe so. Who is he?"

"I believe he collects antiquities," Solomon said, giving his seat next to the fire to Mrs. Lloyd, who was now reading his list, with Jemimah peering over her shoulder.

She waved at him to be seated once more. "We know the Graftons, though."

"Are they frequent visitors? Old acquaintances?"

"Not so very old, only in the last few years or so. Mrs. Grafton and I are friends. She calls occasionally for tea. We dined with her family last month, and the month before they dined here."

Jemimah nodded. "He loves Egyptology. She always looks harassed by the thought of dust on the millions of objects displayed in their drawing room. They have a daughter a couple of years older than me who always looks down her long nose at me."

"If it's that long, she probably can't help it," Sydney said helpfully, ambling toward the door. "I'll bid you good day, Mr. Grey. I have an appointment to keep." With a casual wave of the hand to his mother, he departed.

"I don't believe we are acquainted with any of the others on your list," Mrs. Lloyd said, returning the paper. "But my husband may know them."

"I shall certainly ask when I next speak to him. I believe you are acquainted with another collector, a Mr. Terrance?"

"The vase man," Jemimah said with a wicked grin.

"I heard about the accusation he made against Mr. Lloyd," Solomon said. "What sort of a man is he?"

Mrs. Lloyd sighed. "Lamentably quick tempered, but there is no harm in him."

"Then he does not bear a grudge against your husband?"

"Oh no. He and his wife came to dinner in… When was it, Jemimah?"

"August, I think," Jemimah said, perching on the arm of her mother's chair. "It was a very warm evening, anyway. He was charming. If you ask me, Papa provokes him deliberately. He's quite different when Papa isn't around."

"Have you ever discussed with anyone in his family such

matters as security? The strong room, for example."

"Oh no!" Mrs. Lloyd looked shocked. "I doubt anyone knows we have one."

"When they came for dinner," Solomon pursued, "did either of them have any reason to go upstairs? To a retiring room, perhaps, or to make use of your boudoir?"

"Oh, no. You cannot suspect our friends, surely!"

"It must be someone who knows your household well," Solomon pointed out. "Someone who knew about the strong room and the keys and the precise night the treasure arrived there. There are surely a limited number of people who could possibly have committed this crime."

"Oh dear. Oh dear!" The poor woman sounded so distressed that Solomon began to feel guilty.

Her daughter, however, while patting her shoulder, did not seem unduly disturbed. In fact, the gleam of curiosity in her face resembled her little sister's.

CHAPTER SIX

J ANEY WAS RIGHT. Bibby Barton would never last on the streets. Clearly undernourished, she shivered constantly in her thin, ragged clothes and torn shoes that were too big for her. She looked and sounded as if she were just recovering from one illness, for her chest still wheezed, and was about to come down with another that might just carry her off. She was too thin and too sharp of feature to be either pretty or popular with potential customers. On top of all that, she looked utterly morose.

On the other hand, she had quite a sweet, shy smile and seemed overwhelmed that Constance had deigned to visit her dingy room.

"Janey's told me all about you, ma'am. She said she'd ask you about the locket—I'm so grateful for your help."

"Actually, it's Janey who will be looking," Constance said. "And I have to warn you, the chances of finding your locket are not high. But she will do her best. I've come about something else entirely…"

Half an hour later, they left the dingy room together with Bibby's pitifully few belongings in a bundle—a comb with several broken teeth, her shabby working dress, and a battered, shapeless hat for Sundays. They caught up with Constance's carriage at the Haymarket Theatre, and Bibby's mouth fell open when she realized she was to ride in it.

"Cor lummy," she muttered, clambering in. A hint of cynicism had entered her eyes. "What I got to do for this, ma'am?"

"What did Janey tell you about my establishment?"

"That she don't whore no more. I can't make up my mind whether you's a reformer or a real madam. If you're the madam that can afford this, then I don't know what you're doing with me. I never been anything special."

"You are," Constance said firmly. "As for me, I am both and neither. Our trade is as old as man or woman and nothing will shut it down. I don't judge and I don't blame, but I do believe in choice. My establishment is safe and our clients are wealthy and generous and know what behavior is acceptable. If you choose to entertain them, you contribute to the running of the business with a percentage of your earnings. You keep the rest. If you'd rather do something else, we can help educate and train you, either inside the establishment or out."

"What sort of something else?"

"Domestic service, dressmaking, millinery, teaching, bookkeeping, baking... We have former residents of the establishment in all of these positions and more."

Bibby was frowning. "What d'you get out it, then?"

"The membership fee of our clients." Constance shrugged. "Also, friendship, as a rule, and the guilty feeling of perhaps doing some good in the world."

Bibby laughed, which lightened her sharp face and lent her a moment's appeal. "You're funny. Not like any reformer I ever met."

"Well, we avoid those, too."

Bibby's eyes began to widen as they moved through Mayfair toward Grosvenor Square. "Lummy... Look, ma'am, I don't know what to do. I never lived anywhere like this, never thought I'd... Well."

"What do you dream of, Bibby?" Constance asked softly. "What do you long for when times are bad?"

"My locket."

Reprehensibly, Constance almost laughed. "Nothing else?"

"Lots of things," the girl whispered. "But none of it's real."

"Look, stay with us a few days and see how things suit you. You needn't decide right away. When you're well enough, you can just muck in with the housework. Here we are…"

Having deposited Bibby with Sarah, who was her lieutenant of the establishment, and ordered a square meal for their newest recruit, Constance went to her own private rooms to change into something more suitable for a morning call on the Devine household. At times like these, she missed Janey, who had been her lady's maid, because she had to shout for one of the other girls to close the fastenings of her gown.

Aware she was early for a morning call, she prepared to be turned away at the door, while leaving her card. What she did not want was to be intercepted by Ben Devine's mama, for she had no intention of inflicting her scandalous person on the unwary. She had already done so on the Lloyds, of course, but still…

The maid who opened the door of the Devines' modest townhouse curtseyed but said at once, "Mrs. Devine is not at home, ma'am."

"Actually, it is Mr. Benjamin Devine I am hoping to see." Constance presented her card and walked inside before the maid got over the surprise and shut the door in her face. The girl bridled, but Constance's cool assumption that she would be obeyed—entirely assumed—appeared to work.

"Please wait here, ma'am," the maid said, indicating the hard chair in the hallway.

Constance did not have long to wait.

Benjamin Devine came clattering down the stairs less than a minute later. "Mrs. Silver! Please, come inside and tell me how I might help you."

He led her into a pleasant room where the fire burned and the low sun shone through the window to give an impression of welcome. He did not close the door, but conducted her to a chair far enough away from it that they would not be overheard by lurking servants. Or parents.

He looked a trifle anxious as he brought a chair over to join her.

"I'm sure you know," Constance said, "that Mr. Grey and I are inquiring into the disappearance of property from Mr. Lloyd's strong room. At the moment, I am merely collecting observations from those who were in or around the house that evening."

His expression of polite, slightly worried interest never changed. He was a better actor than he looked.

Constance sighed. "Perhaps it will save us some time if I tell you that I am already aware of your assignation in the garden with Miss Jemimah."

Devine's shoulders relaxed. "Not the sort of thing a gentleman wants to bandy about."

"Certainly not in front of her father."

"I assure you, my relationship with Miss Lloyd is everything that is proper and respectful."

"Aside from clandestine meetings."

"That was only the once," Devine said hastily. "Because of her father's return that day, everyone thought it best that I should not call at the house. But we wanted to meet, so…"

He trailed off and Constance left it there, hoping she had made her point. "As I said, I am only interested in your observations. While you were in the garden, did you see anything at all unusual? Anyone lurking in the mews lane beyond the garden? Strange sounds? Any lights on in the house that should not be?"

"No," Devine said. "I saw nothing unusual at all. Though, of course my attention was all on Jemim—Miss Lloyd."

"Could you see the back door from where the two of you met?"

He frowned. "Yes, I could, most of the time."

"Did anyone go in or out of the house while you were there?"

He shook his head. "The servants had all gone to bed. Jemimah had to unbolt and unlock the back door to get out. Most of the place was in darkness, though there was a light in Sydney's room and in one of the others—Jemimah's, possibly."

"What time was this?" Constance asked.

"Midnight," Devine said sheepishly. "It was her idea."

"And how long did you stay?"

"Maybe twenty minutes? Half an hour at the most. It was cold."

"Were you aware that Mr. Lloyd had brought back a treasure chest from his travels?"

"Not until Jemimah told me."

"Did she describe the treasure?"

"No." Devine frowned. "Actually, that's odd, now I think about it. I thought it would be the sort of thing girls loved to chatter about. But I expect her father's return seemed more important than his loot."

"Loot," Constance repeated thoughtfully. "That is an odd word to use. It implies theft."

"Well, we British are not above plundering the foreigners," Devine said defiantly. "Look at the Elgin Marbles! However, I never meant to accuse Mr. Lloyd of any such thing. I am aware this treasure was taken from somewhere else within living memory and only buried on that island. Even if it was stolen in the first place, Mr. Lloyd only took it from another thief."

Interesting. A conscience and a backbone. Maybe. Perhaps Jemimah could do worse—in a few years when she was grown up and so was he.

"How serious are you about Jemimah, Mr. Devine?" Constance asked.

"Serious? What do you mean?"

"You appear to be courting her. Is it your plan to approach her father for her hand in marriage?"

"Not until I have some means of support," he said, flushing slightly.

She couldn't tell if it was shame or anger. Though it struck her that the treasure, properly disposed of, could supply a considerable means of support. "What do you know about Mr. Lloyd's strong room? Have you ever seen it?"

"Lord, no. I'd never even heard of it until the treasure went missing."

He looked and sounded sincere, but she had already established that he could act when he chose.

"You've run tame around their house since you were a boy, have you not?"

"Yes, I stayed with Sydney often over school holidays, both in Town and at their country house."

"Did you ever play in their parents' bedrooms? Dressing up? Tag?"

"Oh, no. The Lloyds were never as relaxed as that! Even when he was away, parents' rooms were out of bounds. Sydney never broke that rule, or at least not when I was around."

Constance frowned as though deep in thought, then asked suddenly, "Where did Mr. Lloyd keep his strong room key?"

"On a chain around his neck or under his pillow for all I know."

She couldn't work out if his flippancy was studied. In fact, there was quite a lot about him she could not quite work out. He might well require further study.

Only as she was about to rise did another question strike her. She sat back. "Mr. Devine, did you wait in the garden until Jemimah had gone back inside?"

"Of course."

"Did she lock and bolt the door behind her?"

SINCE MRS. LLOYD was convinced that her husband meant to eat a midday meal at Barker's Club in St. James, Solomon elected to beard him there rather than kick his heels at the house for several hours.

At first glance, there was little to make it stand out from the surrounding buildings. Solomon was surprised that Lloyd was not a member of some more imposing club, such as the Athenaeum or White's. Until he considered the fees and Lloyd's apparent shortage of funds.

"Good morning, sir," the porter greeted him with frosty politeness. "May I help you?"

"I hope so. I'm looking for Mr. Barnabas Lloyd."

"If you will take a seat here, sir, I shall inquire."

"You needn't trouble," Solomon said. "If you don't know where he is, I shall find him myself."

The man's eyebrows flew up. He had clearly perfected the art of gazing down upon undesirables in a superior manner that drove them from the door. In this case, the effect was spoiled somewhat by the fact that he had to tilt his head backward to do so, Solomon being several inches taller than he was. "Are you a member, sir?"

"Yes," Solomon said, meeting the glacial stare.

"Your name, if you please, sir."

Solomon sighed and produced one of his cards. The porter made a fuss of checking through his membership book under the letter G. Quite clearly, he did not expect to find the name in front of him, but in fact, although he had never before set foot in the place, Solomon had been elected a member more than a year ago, having been proposed for membership by a gentleman he had once done lucrative business with, and seconded by Sir Nicholas Swan.

Flummoxed by this discovery, it took the porter some time to lift his gaze from the name written quite clearly on the page.

"You needn't take my coat," Solomon said pleasantly, already pushing open the inner door to the hallowed halls. "I shan't be long."

The club held few surprises for him. He discovered several men snoozing over newspapers in one room, a few more silently poring over worthy tomes in the library, and an enthusiastic group having a political argument in one of the meeting rooms. It was in the next door meeting room that he finally found Barnabas Lloyd.

Lloyd had clearly been holding court about his adventures to several interested gentlemen of all ages, a few of whom were studying the photographs on the table.

Lloyd, in the middle of answering a question, noticed Solomon immediately and broke off to exclaim, "Grey! Excuse me, gentlemen." He strode straight toward him, hand held out. "What brings you here? Have you news? Have you found it?"

"I have not," Solomon said, briefly shaking the man's hand. "I do, however, have questions."

Lloyd glanced around the room, clearly reluctant to leave. "Come, then, we can speak undisturbed for a few minutes…" He led Solomon to the far corner of the room, dragging a couple of chairs with him.

"What is on your mind?" he asked, as they sat.

"First of all, that if you actually expect us to have any chance of finding your treasure, you must be completely honest and clear in the information you give us."

Lloyd sat up. His nostrils flared. "In what way have I ever been dishonest?"

Solomon met his haughty gaze without difficulty. "You led us to believe that you had shown your family the treasure on the night you came home. Instead, you allowed them to stare at a closed chest for several hours before you locked it away."

Something like chagrin might have flickered in Lloyd's eyes. But he remained outwardly offended. "Whatever you might have interpreted from my words does not make me a liar, sir."

"Technically not, but frankly, if we cannot take your words at face value, it makes you damned difficult to do business with."

Redness suffused Lloyd's weather-beaten cheeks—temper, not shame. Interestingly, he wrestled it back. "I fail to see how this makes a blind bit of difference to your task of locating my property."

Was he really so lacking in imagination? Or merely pointlessly defensive?

"Why did you not open the chest for them?" Solomon asked bluntly.

Lloyd jerked his arm in an instinctive gesture of dismissal. "I assure you it is of no account."

"From what I hear, they were all eager to see it. Were you teasing them? Or was there some other reason?"

"Oh, teasing them, of course," Lloyd said with impatience. "It was my little joke, which rather turned against me—against all of us—when everything was stolen."

"You must see that this throws up several possibilities."

Lloyd scowled. "Such as?"

"Such as the treasure never left the ship, only the chest full of the rubbish you found in it the next morning. Such as one of your own family was irritated enough—or just as teasing in nature as yourself—to play a trick on you."

"Oh for the love of—" Lloyd scrubbed at the back of his neck and dropped his hand, glaring at Solomon. "Of course it left the damned ship! The weight alone told my son, my seamen, and my servants that. Secondly, none of my family would ever do such a thing."

"Why not?" Solomon pressed. "From what I have seen of them, all three of your children are spirited and intelligent and could easily learn from your example."

"I have their respect, sir! They would not dare. Besides which, no one could have taken the strong room keys without waking me."

"Why is that?" Solomon asked. "Did you not spend all night in your wife's room?"

He was being deliberately provocative because it seemed the only way to get to the truth, but he more than half expected an explosion that would not only dismiss Silver and Grey from the case, but force him to defend himself.

Lloyd stared at him, as if flabbergasted. Then a boyishly proud grin spread over his face. "I might have done. I'd been away from home for a long time."

Solomon took a slow breath. "So, in effect, any member of your household who knew where to look could have taken the keys from your bedside drawer, opened and closed the strong room, and returned the keys, all without your hearing a thing."

Lloyd's smile faded.

"You take my point about telling us the whole truth," Solomon said. "It makes a difference."

"Oh, pshaw! My family would not steal from me! It would be stealing from themselves."

Solomon did not mention Sydney's photographic ambitions or his daughter's possible marital ones. "As I say, they might play a joke on you, although I'll grant you, it has gone rather far for that. Who *would* steal from you? Mark Terrance?"

Lloyd blinked. "Don't be ridiculous. Silly old windbag hasn't got it in him."

Oddly, it didn't sound like a compliment. "Then who? Who dislikes you enough, or is desperate enough to steal? It has to be someone acquainted with you or your family, who would know where the strong room and the keys were located."

Lloyd did him the courtesy of appearing to think about it. "I honestly don't know anyone that...*ungentlemanly*. If I had suspected anyone, I would have acted already without consulting you."

"What *did* lead you to consult us?" Solomon asked, genuinely curious.

"Impulse."

Lloyd sounded so rueful that Solomon said, "Do you wish us to continue with the case?"

The client's lip twitched, his eyes suddenly direct. "Would you end your inquiries if I did?"

"No," Solomon admitted. "Once begun, I follow a puzzle to the end."

"Then I am glad I employed you. Find my treasure, Grey. I need it, and so does the rest of my family."

Solomon took Juliet's list from his pocket once more. "Are you acquainted with any of these gentlemen? Or their families?"

Lloyd took the folded paper and cast his gaze down it. "We

know the Graftons. Can't think of the others."

"Not Arthur Fenwick?" Solomon said, pointing to the name Sydney had picked out earlier.

"Not to my knowledge, no. Who is he?"

"A collector of antiquities. Tell me, who knew the purpose of your expedition? Everyone in the club here?"

"And several others. All my friends. It wasn't a secret."

"And who was this sailor who gave you the map in the first place?"

"Old Cauley? He sailed with me often in the early days, before I had my own ship. Arthritis got him in the end, though—he couldn't work, so he never could get back to his treasure. He asked me to do it for him."

"Then the treasure is his?"

"It would have been, but he died long before I sailed. No family."

"Why did it take you so long to sail? Were you collecting subscriptions?"

"Lord, no. To be honest, though I thanked old Cauley for his map, I thought it was a load of old rubbish and had no intention of taking it further until I came across another old salt in a Bristol alehouse. When we discovered Cauley was a mutual acquaintance, he asked me if Cauley had ever gone back to collect his treasure. 'What treasure?' I asked. And the answer came back, 'The stuff he found in the West Indies and buried on a deserted island when their ship was wrecked.' He was ill when he was rescued, so he couldn't dig it up and he didn't trust his surviving shipmates.

"Anyway," Lloyd continued, "It was enough to send me back to old Cauley for more details, but he had, sadly, died in the interim. All I knew was that the island was off East Africa, so we sailed round the Horn of Africa and anchored at every island that looked remotely the same shape as Cauley's map. We found the right one eventually, some two hundred miles north of Madagascar."

"It must have been like finding a needle in a haystack."

"It was," Lloyd said fervently. "But I needed something big like this, to cover not only the huge costs of the expedition, but also to replenish the family coffers. Expensive business, adventuring, and I can't let my family go short."

He *would* let them, though, Solomon felt, rather than give up the adventuring and take to farming the acres of his ancestral home instead.

"Do you still have the map?" Solomon asked.

"It's on the table, with the photographs."

Showing just how clever he had been, Solomon thought cynically, though he rose and followed Lloyd with some interest.

The map was aged, creased, and frail through being folded so often, but its shape seemed to have been drawn with attention to detail. Nothing was named, but pictures identified trees, pools, reedy grounds, and hills. A chest marked, presumably, the burial place of the treasure, with feet shapes drawn from a crooked tree through the reeds.

"Here's the spot," Lloyd said, picking up a photograph and pushing it in front of him. It showed the tree in the background, a lot of reeds, and several people, including Lloyd and Sydney, clustered about an open chest. Solomon thought he could make out a coin at the top of what appeared to be a sizable heap inside.

"Keep it," Lloyd said generously. "In fact, if everyone's finished looking, take any you like. I have several copies at home."

This caused another stir of interest among the other men present, many of whom seemed very interested in the processes of photography.

Solomon chose a few that were similar to others and promised to return them.

"Join us for luncheon," Lloyd said amiably, apparently forgetting his earlier annoyance.

Solomon glanced at his watch. "Sadly, I have another appointment. My thanks, sir. Gentlemen, good day."

CHAPTER SEVEN

CONSTANCE ARRIVED AT the office only minutes after Solomon.

"Run and fetch us all something to eat, Janey," she said in the hall. "And then you can go about Bibby's business. She's at the establishment, by the way."

"Bless you, ma'am," Janey responded with unusual warmth, and the front door opened and closed even before Constance blew into his room like a whirlwind.

"The back door might not have been locked," she said without greeting or introduction. "We need to speak to the servants again, and to Jemimah."

Solomon caught her hand as she breezed past his chair and pulled her onto his lap. Before she could protest, he kissed her lips. She yielded without thought, kissing him back with enthusiasm.

"What was that for?" she asked breathlessly at last.

"We have not quite established the affectionate greetings of an engaged couple. I thought I would try this to see if you liked it."

"You know I do." Her color was heightened. She gave him another, quicker version, then slid off his lap. "It is not, however, suitable in public, and we are right in front of the window."

"I'll work on the public one," he said. "What makes you think the back door was not locked? I presume you mean the night the treasure was taken?"

"I do." She sat in the chair beside him. "Ben Devine watched Jemimah go safely back inside, but he did not hear the key turn in the lock, nor the bolts being shot."

"That doesn't mean she didn't do either."

"No, but it's something to pursue. Think about it, Solomon. She has lived all her life with servants. She is not used to locking up at night. She's had a daring and no doubt agreeable half-hour with Ben. She's elated and very probably distracted. The chances are, she sailed through the door, closed it, and went off to bed in a romantic dream of her own."

Solomon's lips twitched. "Is that what you do?"

"No," she said crossly, "but I am not a sixteen-year-old girl in the throes of her first love."

"Are you sure *she* is?"

"Well, she's sixteen. But she probably thinks she's in love. So does Ben." She shifted restlessly. "Mind you, even if she did leave the door open, we're not much further forward, are we?"

"We might be. Lloyd spent all night in his wife's room. He probably wouldn't have heard anyone swiping the keys. Also, a couple of your mother's collectors are known to the Lloyds. Grafton and his wife dined there both before and after Lloyd's departure, so one of them could have borrowed the keys at some stage. Sydney recognized Fenwick's name, and there's another collector called Terrance…"

He told her what he knew of Lloyd's quarrel with him, then said, "There's something else I don't like. Lloyd keeps telling us half-truths. None of the household saw inside the treasure chest."

Constance listened, frowning to that story too. "It's control," she said abruptly. "Reasserting his position in the family by controlling who gets to know what or is entitled to which rewards."

"It does seem to be habitual with him. His family seems to regard it as his teasing sense of humor."

"And yet it can amount to cruelty," Constance said. "It's why he didn't warn any of them that we were investigating for him."

"And why he doesn't always tell us everything there is to know. I do think he genuinely wants the treasure back, though. He isn't just going through the motions. Apparently, he went into a real rage when he discovered the theft and went storming through the house in search of it."

"Then he *does* suspect his own household…"

"It certainly crossed his mind. Oh." He reached for his satchel and took out the battered map of the deserted island and the photographs.

"Goodness, these are remarkably clear." Constance picked up one of the photographs.

"The photographer utilizes a new process that combines the clarity of the daguerreotype with the ability to print unlimited copies from a negative. Sydney seemed rather interested in it all. He plays the dilettante, but I'm not sure. He told me he'd had an idea of spending his share on photography equipment and setting up a business. Although wine and women were apparently an equally pleasing alternative."

"I suppose that gives him a motive for taking all the treasure rather than just his share. He could do both, then."

"Not while his father's holding what purse there is," Solomon said wryly, "*and* watching him like a hawk. He'd have to flee the country."

"Well, he has the experience now. Why not live abroad? Perhaps Jemimah and Ben Devine had similar thoughts. He told me he would not propose until he could support her."

"Not sure stealing from her father is the way to her heart," Solomon said. "Although it might be. What did you think of Devine?"

"I'm not sure. He acts. And he can lie while looking you in the eye if it serves his purpose. So can I, of course, when it matters, so I don't hold it against him. Yet."

"Perhaps the three of them took it," Solomon said thoughtfully. "Perhaps Jemimah's assignation was really to give the treasure to Devine, so that Lloyd wouldn't find it should he tear the house apart looking."

"They all knew each other from childhood," Constance allowed. "Only…"

"What?"

"Why did Ben not stay away the day we were there? Why risk drawing Lloyd's ire? And I'd swear Sydney was surprised to see him."

"He certainly didn't leap up to greet him," Solomon said. "Because they had already met since Sydney came home?"

"Or because Jemimah barely gave him the chance," Constance said.

"Or because he knew Devine's casual arrival would annoy his father. It's all speculation. We have no evidence of any of it."

Janey returned then, with some warm, thick soup and bread from the public house down the road. The three of them ate together, continuing to discuss the Lloyds' case and Bibby's, after which Janey, who had bolted through her meal, ran off with a list of questions for her friend.

"She won't get herself into trouble, will she?" Solomon said with sudden unease. "Asking questions of the wrong people in the wrong places?"

"Janey can take care of herself. Her tongue alone can blister most ruffians at twenty yards. And to be honest, a trinket of no value is really not going to ruffle many feathers. What should we do next? Find out about the back door?"

"I think so," Solomon replied. "We'll try the servants rather than land Jemimah in the soup with her parents. And then we could call on these rogue collectors."

Her gaze fell back to the photographs. "Who are all the other people here? Lloyd's sailors?"

"I presume so."

"Most of them are looking at the camera, as though it's more fascinating than the treasure."

On impulse, Solomon rose and fetched the magnifying glass from his desk drawer. Although he offered it to Constance, she passed him back the photograph and he inspected the treasure more closely. The coin at the top of the chest sharpened, as did the shape of something like a candlestick with a jeweled necklace wrapped around it. As far as he could tell from the angle of the photograph, the chest was pretty full.

He shifted the glass upward to Lloyd's face. Due to the length of time subjects had to remain still before the camera, most expressions tended to be a trifle wooden. Lloyd, however, looked entirely satisfied. His teeth showed in his smile, and his eyes looked bright with excitement.

Solomon moved the glass to Sydney, whose excitement might have been tempered with cynicism. Or surprise. It was difficult to tell. Gradually, he moved the glass across the other faces, those in front, and then the two at the back, lurking behind Lloyd.

And the whole world seemed to halt.

CONSTANCE, WATCHING SOLOMON with something like wonder— as she often did when she thought he wasn't looking—saw the instant of change.

"Solomon? What do you see?"

He set down the magnifying glass and turned away. "Excuse me. I need to wash my hands before we go out."

He walked across the room with his usual, unconscious grace, not in any particular hurry, and yet she knew something was wrong. As she reached for the photograph, she was distracted by the postman passing the window, and went to collect the lunchtime post.

By the time she had cast aside a couple of tradesmen's accounts and opened a letter from a lady who had lost her cat, Solomon returned to the room with his hat and coat on.

"Are you ready to go?"

She jumped up, dropping the letter into his hands. "Just the case to make our fortune. Give me a minute."

Since they had a few calls to make, they again made use of her carriage. Whatever had annoyed or upset Solomon, she decided to wait for him to tell her. He did not. On the other hand, he appeared to be back to his usual self, talking about the current case—and the cat—with his usual mixture of insight and wit.

They alighted once more at the Lloyds' house, but this time descended the area steps to the tradesmen's entrance.

The kitchen maid Rosie answered their knock. Although her eyes widened with alarm, she let them in without fuss.

"We're looking for Garrick," Solomon said briskly.

"In his pantry, sir. I'll take you."

She led them through the kitchen, past the servants' hall to another room near the baize door that led to the family's part of the house. She knocked timidly and opened the door.

"Mrs. Silver and Mr. Grey to see you, Mr. Garrick," she said in a rush, and fled.

Garrick was already on his feet. Constance thought he would have liked to sit back down again to show his contempt but didn't quite dare.

"Yes?" he said wearily.

"You stated that you locked and bolted all the doors the night of the theft," Solomon said without preamble. "And unlocked them at seven o'clock the following morning. Was the back door just as you left it? Or was it actually not locked?"

Garrick's lips curled, almost into a snarl.

"Don't say what you'll regret," Solomon snapped, giving Constance a rare glimpse into the icy authority that must have either trained or dismissed any number of unruly employees. "We already know someone opened the door after you locked it. Our aim is to find out if they locked it again behind them."

In anyone else, Constance would have called it a sag. Garrick was much too stiff to do so, but she was sure he sagged *inwardly* with relief.

"I found it locked," he said. "But the key was still in the key-hole and the bolts had not been shot."

And he hadn't said so before because he was afraid he might have had an aberration and forgotten to do it as he always did.

"May I see that key?" Constance asked.

Without a word, Garrick led them back through the kitchen to the garden door and took the large key from the hook on the wall. He offered it to Solomon, who merely passed it to Constance. She opened the door to let in the daylight and inspected the business end of the key for signs of tampering.

Finding none, she shook her head and politely returned the key to Garrick. "Thank you. That will be all for now. We'll show ourselves out the way we came in."

"Unlikely, then," Solomon murmured as they returned to the carriage.

"But not impossible. Let's see what we can discover from your Mr. Terrance."

⁂

MARK TERRANCE WAS dusting his cabinets and their precious contents. The maids were not allowed to clean those, and he prided himself on keeping them as beautiful as they had always been. No fine dust dulled the rims of his porcelain; no tarnish touched his silver. His jewels glittered and his gold gleamed.

Some of his fellow collectors were stunned that he chose to do all this tedious work himself when he had a house full of servants, but in truth he was at his happiest among his treasures, pottering, cleaning, arranging.

It gave him plenty of time to think. And brood, of course, though he had resolved to do less of that. It would be a difficult resolution to keep now that the wretched Barnabas Lloyd was home with the treasure everyone had been so sure was mere legend.

He replaced the exquisite porcelain bowl in its rightful place at the center of its glass cabinet and was just closing it when a knock sounded at the room door. He growled something that was clearly taken as permission, for the maid came in bearing a small silver tray.

"I said I was not to be disturbed, Becky," he said irritably.

"No, sir, but the callers at the door asked for you, sir, not the mistress, so I said I'd take in their card."

Terrance grunted and snatched the card off her tray.

Silver and Grey, it proclaimed, and in smaller script beneath, *Inquiries, C. Silver & S. Grey*, with a respectable business address.

Intrigued in spite of himself, he said, "Show them in here, Becky. I'll ring if I want anything else." After all, one did not drink tea with the representatives of firms in one's own home.

A moment later, his beautiful room was invaded by two dazzling people. The woman was exquisite—young, not very tall, but extremely well formed. Beneath her fashionable hat, her hair shone red and gold like a sunrise, and her features, although perhaps not perfect in themselves, were somehow perfect together. Her eyes were brilliant, and her mouth…

Hastily, he transferred his attention to his male visitor, a tall, dark, slender man with short black hair and skin made bronze either by hotter sun's than England's or by birth. He was handsome enough, but it was more than his looks that seized the attention. He had an air of authority, of presence. And although Terrance hadn't really intended it, he bowed in civil response to his visitors' courtesies.

Fashion was lost on him, but he had the impression that both were extremely well—and expensively—dressed.

"I'm Terrance," he said abruptly. "How can I help you?"

"Grey," the man said, inclining his head. "This is Mrs. Silver. Our apologies for intruding, but we are inquiring about certain valuable items that were stolen recently. As a fellow collector of antiquities, you might well hear whispers of unusual items for sale or perhaps even recently acquired."

"Not much of a man for whispers," Terrance said, staring at him with some hauteur. "I have reputable dealers who inform me. And occasionally, I tour the curio shops and pawnshops on the off chance of discoveries. What exactly are you looking for?"

The lady, Mrs. Silver, drew from her large, embroidered bag several sheets of paper, which she presented to him.

"Please, sit down," he said, although he hadn't meant to offer that courtesy either.

While they ensconced themselves in the chairs by the fire, from where he usually liked to sit and read and admire his collection, he glanced at the extensive list of items. There was not much in the way of porcelain, but a lot of solid gold items, jewelry, coins, carved statuettes of several eras and materials.

Terrance felt a surge of excitement.

Without raising his eyes from the paper, he found the back of the third chair by feel and maneuvered himself into it. Behind the thrill came laughter he could not prevent, though he tried manfully for several moments.

"This is Barnabas Lloyd's hand," he said, raising his eyes at last. "So he found his treasure after all—and managed to lose it again!"

The laughter wouldn't stay in after that, so he gave it free rein. His visitors did not seem surprised to see him hold his sides with mirth at the misfortune of his fellow collector.

"You do not find it alarming that so discerning a thief is at large?" Mrs. Silver asked, gazing around the cabinets full of his own treasures.

"No, I don't," he said frankly. "My collection is known only to a few fellow appreciators of art and beauty. Lloyd goes out of his way to seek adulation and publicity for his exploits as much as his acquisitions. The man is an *un*discerning philistine who merely masquerades as a collector to the masses. I imagine all the villains in London were lining up to rob him."

Grey raised one eyebrow. "Is that not a trifle unjust? I understand he arrived back in England with very little fanfare. Did *you* know he was home, for example?"

"I believe I did."

"When and how did you hear?"

Terrance pretended to think about that, although jubilation still threatened to burst out of him. Examining Grey's face, which was by no means foolish, he decided to admit freely to what the man probably knew already.

"I have an interest in a quite different ship. I was looking for any news of it when I came upon the expected arrival of Lloyd's. In fact, I went down there, watched him disembark, just to see what he unloaded. I saw his seamen carry off an old chest, held shut with ropes. It might as well have had *Treasure* inscribed on the front in gold lettering."

"I see," Grey murmured, holding his gaze. "Did you also know the treasure was put straight into his strong room at home? From where it was stolen that very night?"

"No. No, I did not know that. There has been nothing about the theft in the newspapers. In fact, I heard he was giving talks and exhibitions of his photographs round all his clubs. Even the Athenaeum!"

"Did you not attend any of his meetings?" Mrs. Silver asked.

She really was a stunning creature. "No. I would not give him the satisfaction."

"Even though you had the pleasure of dining recently at his home?"

Terrance felt a twinge of guilt. More than Lloyd himself would suffer from this loss, and he had no quarrel with Christine Lloyd. "My wife and Mrs. Lloyd are friends. Lloyd and I are not. The invitation came from Mrs. Lloyd while he was away, and my wife wished to go."

"Was that the only time you were ever in his house?" Mrs. Silver asked.

"No," Terrance said reluctantly. He was still angry about those days. "In the past, I visited there often. Lloyd and I used to be friends. Of a sort."

"What sort?" Mrs. Silver asked.

"The one-sided sort," Terrance retorted. "I passed on tips to him about collectible items and sales, and he kept his information to himself so that I would spend a fortune on a vase worth less than the kitchen sugar bowl."

"Was that not your mistake rather than his?" Grey asked.

Terrance narrowed his eyes. Was the man trying to rile him? To see how angry he truly was with Lloyd? *No chance!* He shrugged. "Lloyd clearly rejoiced in my misfortune. But yes, the mistake was mine. I wanted it to be genuine too much and failed to see the signs. Admittedly, it was a dashed good fake, but still… I thought I had bagged a bargain treasure, while Lloyd kept to himself a tip that the vase was a mere copy of one in Blenheim Palace. I never spoke to him again."

"What did you think of the security at his house?" Grey asked.

Terrance allowed contempt to curl at his lip. "What, his strong room? Excessive and showy, like the man himself."

"What makes you say that?" Mrs. Silver asked. "Could you see some flaw in it that Lloyd himself missed?"

She was clever, indeed, much more, as it were, than a pretty face. "I never saw it, ma'am. He merely told me about it. Do you mean all this stuff"—he waved the list still clasped in his hand—"was really taken from the strong room? Ha! Knew it was a waste of time. I hope he was properly insured."

If he wasn't, Terrance thought with another twinge of shame, poor Christine and the children were done for too. He'd have to sell what was left of his collection and even that… Mind you, there were a couple of items Terrance would be prepared to take off their hands for a reasonable sum. That would help.

"To assist us with our observations," Mrs. Silver said, "could you tell us which rooms you visited when you and your wife dined with Mrs. Lloyd? Did they look the same as before?"

"They hadn't been redecorated, if that's what you mean. We were only in the drawing room and the dining room."

"You did not use the retiring rooms at all?"

Terrance blinked at such unexpected bluntness. Oh yes, they suspected him. Which meant Lloyd did too. That pleased him rather than worried him unduly. "The one on the ground floor."

"And your wife?"

"Likewise. Young woman—"

"Were you the only guests on that occasion?" Grey interrupted, distracting him so that he forgot to be offended.

"No—the Graftons were there, as I recall, with their daughter and several young men I imagine were there to admire Jemimah Lloyd and the Grafton chit."

"I don't suppose you noticed," Grey said, "whether any of the other guests left the company for any length of time?"

Terrance stared at him. "You suppose rightly."

"From your knowledge of this world of discerning collectors," Mrs. Silver said, "are you aware of any who might be unethical enough to steal or cause to be stolen?"

"Of course not," Terrance said, genuinely shocked.

"Well, thank you for your time," Grey said, rising. "Might I ask you to inform us should you see or hear of any such items as are listed there?"

Terrance rose with Mrs. Silver, to whom he returned the interesting list. "Of course." He rang the bell beside the fireplace. "Becky will show you out."

CHAPTER EIGHT

"WELL," CONSTANCE SAID, as the carriage rolled through the gracious Mayfair streets, "he could hardly contain his delight at Lloyd's misfortune."

"Did it seem unalloyed delight to you?" Solomon asked, for in truth he was having difficulty concentrating. He owed Constance and their client his best efforts, and under normal circumstances he was good at locking away matters that had no bearing on the task in hand. But this—this was no normal circumstance. In fact, the hugeness of his discovery overwhelmed him. He needed to be pursuing it instead of fulfilling lesser obligations.

Only the knowledge that a couple of hours could make no difference, and that his time was already promised to the case, kept him in the carriage.

Constance was considering his words. "He might have been a little ashamed of his instinctive reaction."

"Or guilty?"

"He is very single-minded," she allowed. "And it's interesting that he actually went to the docks and saw the treasure chest being unloaded. But I can't imagine his creeping about the Lloyds' house in the dead of night. Even less, dealing with the criminal underworld to arrange the burglary. Perhaps we should have spoken to his wife as well."

"She clearly has no interest in his collection. It's all banished to the one room, along with Terrance himself."

She sighed. "We did not learn anything new, did we?"

"I think we learned not to rule him out of this crime. The *how* may not be immediately obvious, but the *why* goes very deep."

"Perhaps the Graftons will prove more useful."

She lapsed into silence, which left his mind too much space to veer off course. He held it to the case almost desperately, going over Terrance's responses and expressions, speculating on how he might have done it.

Constance was gazing out of the window. She might have been thinking as he was. Or she might have been waiting. She was nothing if not perceptive, and she would have noticed his reaction to the photograph. He didn't have the words to explain just yet. Soon, he would find them, one way or the other.

In the meantime, there were Mr. and Mrs. Grafton.

Judging by the number of carriages waiting outside the Grafton house, its mistress at least was at home. This was, after all, one of the prime hours for morning calls. Solomon again asked at the door for Mr. Grafton, hoping that the man might well welcome a respite from tea and feminine chatter.

"We don't need to disturb Mrs. Grafton when she is entertaining," he added.

The footman took him at his word and ushered them into a small reception where, in due course, Mr. Grafton himself joined them, the Silver and Grey card in his hand.

"Sir. Madam." He bowed so minimally that he might as well not have bothered. "I confess I am at a loss as to the reasons for your visit. I don't believe we are acquainted, and *Inquiries* gives me no clues except ones I dislike."

"Forgive our intrusion, Mr. Grafton," Constance said with a winning smile. "It must seem unforgivable on our part. But the truth is, we come on behalf of a friend of yours, Mr. Barnabas Lloyd."

"Mr. Lloyd is perfectly capable of speaking to me without intermediaries. In fact, I believe we are dining with them this week."

"It is not a social call, sir, but a matter of business. Mr. Lloyd has engaged us to uncover the truth of his missing treasure."

Grafton's eyes widened in what seemed to be genuine astonishment. "Missing treasure? I thought he had brought it home—against all the odds at White's, I might add."

"Oh, he did. His house seems to have been burgled that very night. We were wondering if you—a fellow collector, we understand—might have come across anything like these items in sale rooms of any kind, or even heard a whisper of their availability?"

Grafton took the list from her, his eyebrows rising spectacularly. "Quite a haul. No, the only whisper I heard was that Lloyd himself would sell most of it, and that came from his wife."

"When did she tell you that?" Solomon asked.

"Oh, last month, I think, when they dined with us."

"I believe you and your family also dined with Mrs. Lloyd recently."

Grafton stared. "We are old friends."

"Yes, I know, that's why we wanted to ask your opinion of his security measures in his house."

"You mean the strong room? Knew he had one. Never saw it. Never told me how it worked or what made it so damned strong. I suppose it was like those in a bank or a solicitor's office."

"Have you seen any of the Lloyd family since the return of Mr. Lloyd and his son?"

"I have not. Keep missing Lloyd at the clubs."

"May I ask how you knew he was home?"

"My wife told me. She had been due to meet with Mrs. Lloyd that afternoon, and Christine sent a note putting it off because the ship was expected and Lloyd had apparently found what he was looking for. Good for him, I said, though someone should invest it for him this time rather than letting him spend it on other damned expedition to Timbuktu or wherever."

"Is your wife also interested in art and antiquities?" Constance asked.

"Of course," Grafton replied frostily.

Solomon and Constance departed only a few minutes later.

"I'd say his wife knows Mrs. Lloyd well enough to have spent time in her bedchamber," Constance said, walking up to the waiting carriage.

"Doing what?" Solomon asked, bewildered.

"Talking, trying on gowns and hairstyles—women's things. I think we need to speak further to Mrs. Lloyd."

"Possibly." Solomon handed her into the carriage before following and sitting beside her as usual. Even with all the turbulence in his mind, her nearness was oddly calming. Like an anchor in a world that might be about to change forever. He shifted restively as the horses walked on. "Even if Mrs. Grafton managed to borrow and copy the strong room keys, I still don't see how either of them could have broken into the house."

"I admit he doesn't seem the type to know or employ a tame burglar, but one never knows. So where do we find this Fenwick character?"

"He has rooms down toward Westminster."

They alighted at the address provided by Juliet. Solomon had just raised his hand to the knocker when the door flew open and a man barged out with such energy that Solomon had to step back to avoid him.

"Beg your pardon," said the man, reaching back to slam the door.

"We beg yours," Constance said, stepping forward so that the man was temporarily dazzled. He was perhaps Solomon's own age, or a few years older, thin featured, and with a definite sparkle in his shrewd eyes. "We wish to go inside in search of one Mr. Fenwick."

"Do you indeed? And who might you be?"

"I am Mrs. Silver. This is Mr. Grey."

"Never heard of you," the man said cheerfully.

"*You* are Mr. Fenwick?" Solomon asked.

He clearly was, although he seemed reluctant to admit it in so many words. "And what is your business with Mr. Fenwick?

Can't let just anyone in, you know. Even a lady as beautiful as you, madam."

"We come on behalf of Mr. Barnabas Lloyd," Solomon said. "His son, Sydney, gave us your name as a collector of art and antiquities."

"Did he now? Well, I'm Fenwick, and whatever I know about such subjects, I know nothing about any Lloyds." He slammed the door firmly behind him. "Except the insurance people. What are you looking for?"

"Information," Constance said.

"I don't deal in that," Fenwick said, almost regretfully. "And since I don't know your principles, I can't see that we have any business together. Good day!" He lifted his hat politely enough, but then strode straight past Constance, forcing her to step aside to avoid him.

"Well," she said, gazing after him, "he's the most suspicious character we've encountered. Do you believe him that he doesn't know the Lloyds?"

"I think he's the sort of man who denies everything as a matter of course. I'm more interested in how Sydney knows him."

"Perhaps he doesn't. Perhaps he was just throwing you off his own or someone else's scent. Either way, it's suspicious."

Solomon tended to agree.

"Back to the Lloyds' house?" Constance suggested, turning once more toward the carriage.

But Solomon's impatience had reached its limits. "No. The afternoon wears on." He handed her inside. "Go home and enjoy an hour or two of peace. I think you deserve it."

"Then so do you."

"I'm too restless. I'll make a quick call on the locksmith and Lloyd's solicitor on my way home, and call for you as agreed to attend the opera." He kissed the hand he still held, then stepped back and closed the door on her puzzled face. He didn't want to see the hurt there, so he turned away quickly to give the coachman his order and strode off down the street.

SOLOMON HAD MANY contacts at the London docks, and it did not take him long to locate Lloyd's ship, *Queen of the Sea*. In contrast with the hive of activity on other ships, the *Queen* looked lifeless. Its gangway was pulled up and it rocked lethargically, too high in the water to have much weight aboard.

Solomon cupped his hands around his mouth to funnel his voice and shouted. "Ahoy! *Queen of the Sea!*"

After a few such attempts, an old watchman tottered out from below and came to the rail to speak to him. From his gait and his weathered face, he had been a seaman all his life.

"Crew's all paid off and gone home," the old man told him.

"Apart from you?"

"No, sir, I don't go to sea no more. Just paid to mind it till it goes into dry dock."

"Do you know the crew, then? The owner? Mr. Lloyd?"

"Know the captain. And one or two of the boys been around for years."

"Did you know any Africans on the crew?"

The old man scratched his head. "Don't *know* him, but I saw one bloke might have been African." The deep blue eyes scanned Solomon's face. "But then, so might you."

"What was his name?"

"We wasn't introduced. What do you want him for?"

"Nothing bad. He's a friend. I think."

The old man shrugged. "The others called him Johnny."

Solomon's heart twinged with disappointment. "Do you know where Johnny is now?"

"No idea. Went off with the rest of 'em, his bag on his shoulder."

"I don't suppose you know where I can find Captain Tybalt?"

The fact that Solomon knew the captain's name seemed to reassure the watchman, who told him an address not too far away to walk. Solomon thanked him and set off. The first hope of certainty had gone, but this chance discovery was as close as all his deliberate and painstaking inquiries had come in ten years. He would not give it up lightly.

The captain's house was a modest affair, chosen for convenience to the river rather than comfort, Solomon suspected.

A knock brought the man to the door. He was not young, perhaps in his forties. Nor was he tall or particularly imposing in appearance, but his unquiet face bore all the hallmarks of a restless spirit, the kind of man who was only truly happy at sea. Solomon had encountered many such men during his life.

"Captain Tybalt? My name is Solomon Grey." He presented his personal business card, and the man's eyes widened as if he recognized it. Solomon didn't think Tybalt had ever worked for him—he knew most of his sea captains—but perhaps he had heard of him and hoped for another ship. "I'm looking for one of your crew," he said quickly, to avoid false hope. "A man called Johnny something?"

"Johnny?" Tybalt repeated. "What's he done?"

"Do you expect him to be in trouble?"

"Lord, no. Seemed a decent fellow, willing and able and never gave *me* any trouble. But I don't know him well—picked him up at Madagascar when one of our own took ill, and he stayed on. Said he'd never been to England before, let alone to London."

"Then where did he go when he left the ship?" Solomon asked.

"I don't know. A couple of the crew, Jackson and Squibbs, took him along with them."

"Can you tell me where their lodgings are?"

"No, but I suspect you'll find them in the Crown and Anchor."

The Crown and Anchor was not a house Solomon had ever frequented. Nor would he have advised anyone else to risk it, whatever their station in life, especially not someone who had never been in London before. He'd be lucky to get in and out with only his pockets picked.

Also, it was getting dark, and he had to take Constance to the opera. Still, he couldn't leave the matter until he had laid eyes on this Johnny. So he extracted the names of the crew members who had been with him when last seen, thanked the captain, and walked on toward the notorious alehouse.

He was so deep in thought and in so much of a hurry that he almost missed her, even though she stepped out of a doorway on his left, almost bumping into him. She was vaguely familiar, so he touched his hat somewhat mechanically before he realized she was twittering his name.

"Mr. Grey! What a surprise to see you in this neck of the woods, as it were."

It was Miss Audrey Lloyd, his client's maiden sister, all flustered untidiness and kind eyes. "Miss Lloyd. I have to say the same. May I escort you somewhere?"

"Oh no, there is a hackney stand close by. I am quite used to the neighborhood, you know. Charity… Though I would appreciate it if you didn't tell my brother precisely where you met me. He worries so…"

Solomon was not entirely surprised if she frequented areas like these in the dark. Although he really wanted to be elsewhere, he felt obliged to offer his arm and slow his steps.

"So kind," she murmured. "Are you here in search of my brother's lost treasure?"

No. My own. "Something like that." In spite of the search crowding the forefront of his mind, curiosity pierced its way in. He regarded her thoughtfully. "You are a very independently minded lady, are you not? Considering your brother's— ah…caring nature."

"Oh well, a spinster lady has to go her own way if she is not to vanish into the woodwork," she said in a vague kind of way. "I do so enjoy my charities, and one likes to feel useful."

"I'm sure you are and have been extremely useful to your brother's family."

"Oh no. The children are dear, but they always had nannies, you know, when they were very young. And Christine is the most ferocious housekeeper, leaving me nothing to do but eat my head off."

She reminded Solomon of a tiny, starving bird in winter. He could not imagine her eating her head off anywhere at any time.

"Have you not your own conveyance, Mr. Grey?" she asked anxiously.

"Why no, I traveled by hackney also. I shall take the one after you."

"You are welcome to share mine," she offered with the timidity of one used to being refused in all things.

"I have one more errand first."

"Of course you do. Please don't let me keep you."

He saw her into a hackney, doffed his hat, and set off back the way he had come.

The Crown and Anchor was dark, smoky, and crowded, which at least meant he was not quite as noticeable as he would otherwise have been in his smart coat and hat. Having stumbled into the bar counter by accident, he ordered a pint of ale, and when it came, rather than actually drink the foul-looking brew, he asked the tapster if he knew the two crew members from the *Queen of the Sea*, Jackson and Squibbs, by name.

"No," said the tapster without even thinking about it, and went to serve someone less inquisitive.

Solomon picked up his mug and turned to face the room through the fug of tobacco smoke. By accident, his eyes met those of the man next to him.

"Over there," the man said amiably, nodding toward the table in the corner, "which I give you for free, though I'd thank you for a pint."

Solomon almost gave the man his own, but instead set a coin in front of him. "Have two," he said, and took his mug across to the corner.

In fact, there were three men at the table, and one of them

had his back to Solomon. His heart began to beat faster. He sat down on the bench, not so close that anyone could put a hand in his pocket, and set his mug on the table shared by the trio.

"Gentlemen," he said, "is it true you're part of the *Queen of the Sea* crew that brought treasure back to these shores?"

One of them grinned. "So we did, but if you imagine it's made us rich, think again!"

"Wouldn't be drinking here if we was rich," said the man whose face he hadn't previously seen—a weather-beaten face, but not the one he sought.

The disappointment was like a blow. He had to remind himself that of course it was never going to be that easy.

"Which makes us wonder," said the third man, "why *you* are drinking here?"

"I am looking for someone and Captain Tybalt couldn't help me. He said you fellows might know where Johnny is lodging."

"Johnny? Too cold for him in these parts. Got aboard another ship, didn't he?"

→≫≪←

THE DISAPPOINTMENT WAS so crushing that he arrived back at the Silver and Grey offices with no clear recollection of the journey. He was only there to close the shutters and make sure the fires were safe, but he was running out of time for the opera.

He lit the wall light in the hall and the lamp on his desk, then moved around, completing his mundane tasks. He always kept a few items of clothing at the office, so he splashed some water about his person and changed into a clean shirt and evening dress, abandoning his overcoat, which stank unbearably of tobacco, filth, and old, old grief.

Then, although he knew he was already going to be late, he sat down at his desk and drew out the photograph. Unmagnified, there was nothing to make the African sailor stand out. He could have been anyone. Only hope had made him into Solomon's lost brother. He should have known that. Both Lloyd and his son had spent time on the same ship as this man. He had helped pull up his treasure. Would they not have seen Solomon's likeness to him as soon as they met if this Johnny had been David, his twin? Yet neither Lloyd had reacted to him.

He had wasted half his afternoon on a wild goose chase. Still, he had done the right thing. There was no point in having agents around the world looking out for David if he failed to follow up on tracks and traces that came his own way. He would have liked to have met this man. There was even that small, lingering chance that he *was* David. Which was why he had given this address to the sailors to pass on to him, should they run into him again.

He had lived all his adult life alone. It had never been impossible. And now there was Constance, his totally unexpected joy... For whom he was going to be late.

He touched the face in the photograph, then swept it into the drawer below and left the office.

Miss Audrey Lloyd sat on her bed, rummaging through her bag in search of her missing key. She brought out three mittens, a few coins, a screwed-up piece of paper, several handkerchiefs—all used—and a piece of pastry that made her wrinkle her nose in distaste.

Hastily, she wrapped the disgusting fragment of pie in the paper and threw it in her wastepaper basket before she swept the handkerchiefs into the laundry. Then she sat back on the bed, and had just drawn out the missing key with some triumph when abruptly her bedchamber opened and Christine walked in.

It was all Audrey could do to force a vague, silly smile to her lips. She had thought she would be free of all visits tonight—she usually was, to be fair—for the entire family apart from herself and Rachel were going to the opera.

Christine was in all her finery, looking both beautiful and regal.

"How lovely you are," Audrey said admiringly.

Although Christine liked to be complimented—even by her sister-in-law—she would not be distracted.

To Audrey's dismay, she closed the door softly behind her. "What key is that?" she demanded in a hard voice that was entirely free of fear.

"Oh, just the back way into the church. I think. To be honest, I have been trying to remember myself…"

"Don't lie to me, Audrey! Please tell me you are not still going to that—that…" Words seemed to fail her, and she broke off and just glared. "You promised me. And you must keep that promise now Barnabas is home."

"Did I promise? I'm afraid I shall continue going to the church. The vicar does *such* good in the community…"

Christine regarded her with dislike. "Give me it." Audrey gave it up without a fuss, and Christine hastily hid it in her own reticule. "You're putting me in a horrible position, Audrey. Don't you care? Have you forgotten I know everything?"

Of course she didn't, which was amusing in its way. Audrey tried a placating smile, but Christine was too rattled to respond, not least because Barnabas could be heard from the hall downstairs calling for his wife to hurry or they would miss the beginning.

"You are a silly old maid, Audrey," Christine snapped. "And it's well past time you realized it."

She swept from the room, leaving Audrey gazing after her. Once, such words had hurt her, not for their truth but for the spite with which they were spoken. Christine had never wanted her here, which Audrey could well understand.

She blinked as Christine left, even called, "Enjoy the music," after her.

When the carriage had gone, she'd go and find Rachel and they could play some game or just chatter a bit. Rachel was a sweet child.

As for her purloined key, it didn't matter. She had another. Somewhere.

CHAPTER NINE

F OR THE FIRST time since Constance had known him, Solomon was late.

At least she could laugh at herself, in all her opera finery, watching anxiously for him, like a neglected wife who knows her husband has strayed to a woman like Constance. At least she knew that was not true. But she also knew something was bothering him and he had excluded her from helping.

She could be miffed at that. And she couldn't deny it hurt. But mostly, she was worried.

By the time she saw his carriage approaching, it was really time for the arrival of the house's first guests. Constance ran down the back stairs to the kitchen area and left the house by the area steps.

By then, a couple of gentlemen were mounting the steps to the front door, politely ignoring Solomon, who stood by the carriage. The sight of him with the lamplight flickering over his uniquely handsome face made her heart lurch, as it always did. There was no sign of distress, so perhaps he had resolved whatever had disturbed him earlier. Or perhaps he was still hiding.

She took his hand and was assisted into the carriage like a lady. He followed, closing the door behind him, and they set off at a fast clip.

"I'm sorry to be late," he said, so politely that her heart sank.

"Only by a quarter of an hour. We shan't disturb the opera

itself, though you might deprive yourself of some excellent dancing. Did you learn anything useful from the locksmith or the solicitor?"

"No," he said, "but let's not talk about the case tonight. This evening is ours."

She slipped her hand into his and his fingers closed around her, firm and strong. Her heart eased once more, especially when he raised her hand to his lips and kissed it.

The new Italian opera house at Covent Garden had been opened only a few years ago and was a magnificent theatre. Constance had attended many times before, for she loved music, and, professionally speaking, it helped with discussion in the salons of her establishment. The men who frequented them often attended the theatre too, although they rarely acknowledged her.

She was glad that their entrance to the private box created little notice, for Solomon would not permit her usual discretion. They sat at the front of the box, with the best view of the stage, lit up for all to see, if they cared to. But the rest of the audience were too busy either watching the dancers or gossiping.

For the first time, she felt exposed. Worse, she felt Solomon was because of her. But she met the challenge head-on, lifting her gaze from the stage to the boxes and gazing around them.

She almost laughed, and touched Solomon's arm. "The third row, almost directly opposite."

He followed her gaze to the Lloyds' box, murmuring wryly, "So much for being *our* evening. I see Grafton is with them."

"That must be his wife beside Mrs. Lloyd. And there is Ben Devine with Jemimah and Sydney... Interesting who isn't there."

"Who?" she asked. "Fenwick?"

"Miss Lloyd."

"Perhaps she does not care for opera."

"And perhaps she is never invited."

Constance glanced at him curiously. "Why should you think that?"

"Just an impression I had. I ran into her this afternoon when she was devoting herself to her good works. Am I unkind to think she would just make their box untidy?"

"She would not be untidy if she had a decent gown and a maid to dress her hair," Constance said thoughtfully. "But then, if the family is so short of money that they let the child's governess go, then a maid for the spinster aunt would be unthinkable. And perhaps the price of her opera ticket."

The curtain went up then on the main opera, and Constance lost herself in the music and the tragedy. It was almost the end before she realized that Solomon had positioned himself so that he could easily see her face and the stage. And at the moment, he was focused on her.

He must have seen the play of emotions in her expression, known how it moved her. Oddly, she didn't mind this invasion. It added a strange new intimacy to their bond. Did he know that it was all so much *more* to her with his presence at her side?

Perhaps he did, for as they drew into the shadows at the back of the box, he bent and kissed her lips before he opened the door and they joined the throngs in the corridor leading to the staircase. The flickering gas lamps and the babble around them seemed very distant compared to the man whose arm she held, who guided her through the crowd as though she were the most precious and respected of women. And yet he had no illusions about her...

Or did he? The attraction, the inexplicable bond that had sprung up around them, was inconvenient to them both. Had he endowed her with some illusion of purity to make their relationship bearable? Somewhere in his heart, did he know that, and that was why he had told her nothing of his new concerns this afternoon?

These were thoughts to analyze later. Right now, she was content only to feel, to enjoy his attention and the comfort of his town carriage, which rivaled her own. Neither of them had put on their gloves, and when he took her hand, the sparks played between them. She rested her head on his shoulder, and loved the caress of his thumb against her palm.

"Thank you for tonight," she said softly. "It has been wonderful."

"For me too."

"Then it helped?"

It was the only reference she had made to the trouble he was keeping to himself. And for a moment, she thought he would ignore even that. But he kissed her hair and her hand, which clung to his.

"You always help."

She waited, her heart beating curiously fast in the silence. But when he spoke, it was about the performance, about the singers and Verdi's stunning music, all subjects she was happy to discuss with enthusiasm.

But she had entered the front door of her establishment, and his carriage had driven on before she recognized the desperation with which he had avoided the opportunity to include her in his trouble. Even while he kissed her with such passion and such need.

I am not helping, not this time. But damn it, I will…

SHE MADE SURE to arrive early at the office the following morning.

"Himself isn't here yet," Janey told her cheerfully, and chattered about the lack of progress on the case of Bibby's locket. But she still had a few people to speak to, and Constance encouraged her not to give up hope.

As soon as Janey had gone, leaving a couple of letters behind, Constance rose from her desk, went into Solomon's office next door, and opened the desk drawer where he had put the photographs. The one that had disturbed him lay at the top. But she took all of them and the magnifying glass back to her own room.

What exactly had he been looking at when the change in him occurred? Presumably the treasure. She focused on the chest first, particularly on the treasure within, which was a little clearer beneath the glass, though she could see nothing that had not been described. She moved to the second photograph in which the chest was closed and the metal catch locked in place. The wooden chest itself and the metal catch revealed nothing she had not seen before except clearer dark patches of ingrained dirt. And faint, small letters carved into the front of the chest, just beneath the fastened catch. They looked like a J and a W—no doubt the initials of its original owner.

But she could see nothing that should have disturbed Solomon. Turning back to the first photograph that had seemed to the one troubling him, she raised the glass to the faces of Lloyd, poised over the chest, and those posed behind them and crouched around—ordinary-looking seamen who might have come from anywhere, their faces weathered by wind and sun and constant work. The last in the line, his face, slightly out of focus, looked no different until she held the glass over it.

She was looking at Solomon Grey.

The glass dropped on the desk with a clatter. For, of course, she was not looking at Solomon, who had been in *this* country when the photograph was taken.

"David," she whispered.

IT WAS ANOTHER hour before Solomon arrived at the Silver and Grey office, unprecedentedly late. By that time, she had written replies to several letters and added a prospective client to the appointment book for the following week. She had also begun writing down everything they knew about the theft of the treasure and the whereabouts of all who could conceivably have been involved or had access to the keys. Not that she did not remember these things, but sometimes writing it down and drawing the connections between facts and people helped her to see patterns she had not discerned before.

At the sound of Solomon's voice in the hallway, she pushed her chair back, replaced her pen in the stand, and picked up the photographs and the magnifying glass.

She marched into his office and threw them down on the desk where he was just about to sit. He rose again, took her in his arms, and kissed her, which distracted her momentarily.

"I approve of our new habit of greeting," she said a little huskily.

He smiled. "So do I."

She slipped free. "*However*. Don't you *dare* tell me we are partners in business and in life when you keep such vital things from me. If you don't trust me, say so and we end it now. All of it."

She knew him now, the man with the direct and yet fully veiled eyes, and he was feeling his way.

"Silver and Grey?" he hazarded.

"Silver is fine alone."

"Our engagement?"

"Over. You can go off around the world as you always intended. I will even wish you well on your quest and hope you find who and what you're looking for."

"I have found her," he said evenly.

She shook her head. "No you haven't, Solomon. If you had, you would not keep things as important as this from me. You would not dissemble and lie to me."

"I did not."

"But you did. You told me you were going to the locksmith and the solicitor yesterday afternoon, but in reality you went this morning, didn't you? That's why you were late."

A gleam of something very like amusement lightened his serious, dark eyes for an instant, and then vanished. "It is. I...I don't know why I didn't tell you, but I do know it was nothing to do with trust, or anything to do with you, in fact. It is my…habits, if you like. I am used to being alone, to finding my brother always being my first priority, however weak the clue to his whereabouts. I managed to keep my mind on the Lloyd case for much of the afternoon, but only if I did not speak of David."

"It did not once enter your head that I could help?"

He looked bewildered by that. "But you did. You do. Your very existence is my anchor, my salvation."

"But not as your partner. We have been here before."

"*Yes*, as my partner! Damn it, Constance, how could I take you to a place like the Crown and Anchor?"

"Sol, I cut my eyeteeth in festering holes like the Crown and Anchor. And worse. It is pleasant to be treated as precious and delicate sometimes, but I am not."

His arm slipped around her waist. "You are to me. I am flawed, Constance. I would be the first to admit it. In my shock, David was my business, not ours, not anything to do with the case."

"Only he is, isn't he? He's in the photograph, one of Lloyd's crew."

"They took him on at Madagascar and he seems to have remained in London a bare couple of nights. He has already sailed and I don't even know if he was David. They called him Johnny, and his features are not so very clear in the photograph. On top of which, neither Lloyd nor Sydney looked twice at me. Wouldn't they if I had truly looked like this Johnny?"

"I don't know. It strikes me that neither of them pays a great deal of attention to anyone but themselves. Not to a lowly, mixed-race sailor, and not even to you or me."

"Oh, they pay attention to you," Solomon said cynically.

"They don't *see* me. They could walk up to me in my establishment and see only my figure, the supposedly beddable female, not the woman helping them find their blasted treasure."

A frown tugged his brow. "Do you believe that?"

She waved one warily dismissive hand. "Up to a point. How

do you know Johnny-possibly-David has sailed?"

"I found the ship's captain and he directed me to the Crown and Anchor, where I found two of the sailors who had disembarked with him. They told me he'd sailed the previous day."

"And you believed them?"

He blinked.

"Solomon, people who drink at the Crown and Anchor are not the sort of people who always want to be found. The men you spoke to might have been from a different ship entirely. They might not have even met Johnny. They just clam up or tell you a bunch of nonsense in the hope you grease their palms. Which I presume you did."

"I did leave our address with them, too. At least they didn't throw it away in front of me. Are you saying I should go back to the docks?"

"I'm saying *we* should. And that we could do worse than speak to Lloyd, father and son, about *all* the crew, including Johnny-possibly-David. He was with the treasure chest in—"

She broke off as a vision of the real chest flashed through her memory, lying on the strong room floor, open and empty. And before that, closed and empty. Her eyes widened as she stared at Solomon.

"Oh, Sol…"

"What is it?" he asked, clearly unsure whether to be excited or alarmed.

"It's a different chest," she blurted. "The original has initials carved beneath the lock. The one in the strong room doesn't."

Solomon caught his breath, staring back. "Are you sure?"

"No, but we really, *really* have to look at it again."

INEVITABLY, GARRICK GREETED their request to see inside the strong room again with haughty skepticism.

"Mr. Lloyd is not at home and left me no instructions about making the strong room available. Come back this afternoon."

"No," Solomon said frostily. "We shall see Mrs. Lloyd. Now."

Reluctantly, the butler showed them into the morning room, where Mrs. Lloyd was writing letters.

Solomon repeated their request to Mrs. Lloyd, who also looked somewhat doubtful.

"The strong room?" she repeated. "Do you think it will help?"

"We think it will. We want to examine the chest."

"Well…I shall have to come with you."

"Of course."

Mrs. Lloyd led the way across the hall to the staircase under Garrick's expressionless gaze. Childishly, Constance wanted to stick her tongue out at him.

"Wait here," Mrs. Lloyd said, abandoning them outside the strong room door, while she continued up the next flight of stairs.

Beside Constance, Solomon flexed his fingers, a sign of excitement she recognized. She brushed her knuckles against his and he smiled. Mrs. Lloyd was not long in returning with the familiar ring of keys.

"I have just realized I cannot help you," she said. "Only my husband and my son know how to open the strong room, or even which key to use."

"If you will allow me, I believe I can remember," Solomon said.

"He showed you?" The words seemed involuntary, blurted in sheer surprise.

"He did."

Solomon found the large, complicated key and turned it the requisite number of times before finding and lifting the flap that revealed the second lock. Constance glanced at Mrs. Lloyd, who seemed to gazing everywhere except at the door.

Because in fact, she already knew how? Or because she genuinely wasn't interested? Perhaps Lloyd had somehow trained her to be so, with his humiliating withholding of treats and information.

Solomon swung the door open and Constance walked in, deliberately ahead of Mrs. Lloyd. She crouched down, feeling the rough old wood of the chest, repeatedly fingering the wood beneath the broken iron flap of the fastening.

She raised her eyes to Solomon's. "Nothing is carved there. No initials. Nothing."

CHRISTINE LLOYD WAS sure she had done the wrong thing admitting strangers to the strong room. She'd known it as soon as she walked into her husband's bedchamber. On the other hand, since he had made it clear that the entire household should co-operate with Mrs. Silver and Mr. Grey, she didn't see what else she could do. For a few moments, she hoped she might be saved by the fact that no one except Barnabas and Sydney knew how to open the door. But she was wrong in that too.

Squashed into the strong room with them, she could almost feel her sense of superiority slipping away. She looked from one to the other.

"What does it mean?" she asked. "Whose initials do you expect to see on a chest dug out of an island swamp?"

Mrs. Silver rose to her graceful feet.

Mr. Grey said, "In your husband's photograph, taken on the island, the initials are clear. And they are just as clearly absent from *this* chest."

"Someone rubbed them off?" she hazarded. "Why would anyone do that?"

"I can think of no reason," Mr. Grey said. "I think this is a different chest."

"But…how can that be?" She frowned with incomprehension, floundering. With relief, she heard Sydney whistling casually as he sauntered downstairs from his own room.

When he saw them, he staggered back theatrically. "Aha! The burglars are it again! I shall send for a policeman forthwith. Stop, thief!"

"Oh, be quiet, Sydney," Christine said, not quite able to laugh. "Mr. Grey believes this to be a different chest."

"Different from what?" Sydney asked, apparently as mystified as she, although his mother doubted that he was.

"Look at the chest," Mrs. Silver invited him. "Is this truly the one you dug up on the island?"

"Of course it is." Sydney glanced in some amusement from her to Mr. Grey. "What on earth makes you think it isn't?"

Mrs. Silver explained about the initials in the photograph and Sydney scratched his head.

"Well, that's odd," he admitted, squeezing inside the room in place of Christine and inspecting the place on the chest where the initials were, apparently, meant to be carved. He glanced up again. "I don't recall any initials. I just recall a dirty old chest full of sparkly things. Could the chest have been rubbed so hard in cleaning it that layers of the wood came off and obliterated the carving?"

"I don't see how. We believe the original chest never left the ship."

Sydney's eyebrows flew up. "Do you, by God?" He met Christine's gaze and laughed. "Lord, no wonder the old devil wouldn't open the chest for you and the girls!"

"Sydney!" Christine exclaimed. "What on earth do you mean? That your father put the treasure somewhere else? They why employ Mrs. Silver and Mr. Grey to find it?"

Sydney shrugged. "Because he never thought they would? I don't know how his mind works. Perhaps he thought it was a safety measure. Or something." He frowned down at the chest. "But are you absolutely sure about this? It looks like the same chest, right down to the grubby old wood. You can even see where it was cleaned."

Mr. Grey moved, bending to rub his fingers over the wood,

inhaling, almost like a sniffing dog.

Sydney's dancing eyes met Christine's.

"Salt," Grey said. "I can smell the sea and must off this chest. The wood has been damp, but…"

"The nails are old too," Sydney said, rubbing at one or two. "And dirty. How can they be exactly the same, apart from the damned initials—sorry, Mama, Mrs. Silver."

"Because someone went to a lot of trouble to copy the shape and materials of the first," Mr. Grey said. "Who would have had opportunity to do that? Or the skills?"

"No one," Sydney said. "The treasure stayed with my father in his cabin. But I suppose we had all seen it. I still don't understand how anyone could have swapped the chests, though. I saw Papa open it for customs before we left the ship, and the treasure was definitely in it at the time. Good Lord, do you mean the treasure *stayed* on the ship for anyone to steal, while we brought back an empty chest?"

He scowled. "Wait, though, it *wasn't* empty. Harry and I had to heave it up here from the drawing room, and I can assure you it weighed a great deal! None of this makes any sense."

Mr. Grey kicked at the little pile of rubbish that Barnabas had raked out of the trunk on opening it for Rachel the morning after he had come home with it. Could that have been what Harry and John had carried into the house inside the chest? What Harry and Sydney had carried up here before dinner?

Unease tugged at her chest. Something more complicated than simple theft was going on here, and her mischievous son was a little too amused…

"Sense?" Mr. Grey said calmly. "No, not yet. I suggest we repair to the *Queen of the Sea* as soon as possible."

"You truly believe the treasure is still there?" Christine asked in astonishment.

"No," Mr. Grey replied. "I'm sure it has long gone, but some clues might be left behind."

Christine's mind was swirling with alarm. Somehow, this

would be her fault. She really needed to speak to Sydney before they went haring off to the ship.

"You had better collect your father," she said instinctively. Surely it was *his* devious hand, not Sydney's, that she sensed in all of this, whether a secret insurance cheat or some other, more Machiavellian maneuver. He would have to get himself out of it.

She had never seen the so-called treasure. For all she knew, it could have been glass beads and base metal that would never revive the family fortunes. Barnabas had gambled everything on this trip that everyone else had told him was foolish.

As his inquiry people and Sydney went rushing out of the house, she stood still on the landing, deep in thought.

"What on earth is happening, Mama?"

Jemimah and Rachel stood on the stairs above, leaning over the banister.

"I really don't know. It seems someone might have played a trick on us. Your father's clever detectives believe the treasure was never in our house."

Jemimah's eyebrows flew up. Then she laughed. "No wonder we weren't allowed to see inside the chest," she said cynically.

Like Christine, she assumed the trick was Barnabas's. *Was it?*

"Oh, no, it wasn't Papa who tricked us," Rachel said. "Don't you remember how furious he was? He really *did* mean to show me the treasure that morning."

"Of course he did, dear," Christine said hurriedly. "I'm sure it's Mr. Grey and Mrs. Silver who have misunderstood everything. To the schoolroom with you, Rachel. I shall be along in a moment. Jemimah…"

She waited until Rachel had dragged herself back to the top of the stairs and Jemimah stood beside her on the landing before she continued in a low voice, "Don't go telling people all this."

"As if I would," Jemimah said innocently.

But there was a spark of mischief in her eyes that was almost excitement. And God help them all, she was Barnabas's daughter.

Christine caught her arm. "Jemimah, you're not playing some

kind of foolish trick on your father, are you? Imagining you are avenging some other trick, or out-tricking him?"

"Of course not!" Jemimah laughed, more amused than shocked.

"Because if we don't get this treasure back, it affects *all* of us. Do you understand?"

Jemimah tugged free. "Talk to Sydney, not me."

CHAPTER TEN

"TELL US ABOUT the ship's crew," Constance said to Sydney, as much for Solomon's quest as for the resolution of this increasingly bizarre case.

They were in her carriage, en route to one of Barnabas Lloyd's lesser clubs to collect him before going to the ship.

"The crew?" Sydney said. "I don't really know anything about them. Captain Tybalt dealt with them."

"Your father gave Tybalt free rein to pick his own men?" How odd, when he went to such lengths to control other aspects of his life. "He must place a lot of trust in this captain."

"Oh, they've sailed together for years, off and on," Sydney said without much interest.

"Is he ever a guest in your house?" Solomon asked.

Sydney looked at him as if he had grown horns. "Of course not." He was silent a moment. "Come to think of it, I don't believe he's ever been in the house for any reason. I've certainly never seen him there. My father contacts him when he needs him for expeditions, and he sees to the seaworthiness of the *Queen* and engages the crew."

"Always the same crew?" Constance asked quickly.

"Don't know, to be honest. Old Silas Cauley—he of the treasure map—had certainly sailed with Tybalt and my father several times before ill health caught up with him."

"How many men were there on the crew for this last expedition?"

"Lord, I don't know," Sydney replied without much interest. "A handful."

"Did you change crew members at all during the journey?" Constance asked, mostly to see if Sydney was honest in his ignorance.

The young man considered. "One of them took ill. We left him in Madagascar and took up another fellow, I think."

Constance did not look at Solomon. "What happened to the sick sailor you left on Madagascar? Did you pick him up on the way back?"

"No idea," Sydney said. "Captain Tybalt will know."

"What of the replacement sailor you took on at Madagascar?" Constance pursued. "Can you describe him?"

"Not really," Sydney said. "Just another sailor. Young-ish, I think."

The carriage halted outside the club and Sydney dashed out to fetch his father, leaving Constance and Solomon to exchange a long, meaningful glance.

"I wonder if he could describe you or me?" she said wryly.

"I shan't argue the point any further. He is a singularly self-absorbed young man."

"Or he just doesn't notice the lower orders."

Barnabas Lloyd was clearly not best pleased to have been winkled out of his club at this hour for a jaunt to the docks. Nor did he think much of their theory that the chest they had taken off the ship was a copy.

"Utter rot," he said angrily. "A mere excuse for your own incompetence."

"Be reasonable, Papa," Sydney drawled. "It wasn't they who lost the treasure in the first place."

His father glared at him. "We did not *lose* it. It was stolen from us. There is no point in my even being with you. Tybalt is the man who knows the ship. And the crew."

"Did you recognize any of the crew?" Solomon asked. "Had any of them sailed with you before?"

"Don't think so," Lloyd growled. "Ask Tybalt."

At the dockside, an urchin was dispatched to fetch Captain Tybalt, while Lloyd stormed along to his ship, yelling for the watchman. With the gangway lowered, they followed him on board. Constance was glad not to have worn one of her more fashionable gowns, where the crinoline would have made it next to impossible to climb down the ladders and negotiate the narrow passages.

She had only ever been aboard pleasure boats on the Thames before, and she was fascinated by her glimpses into a working, seagoing vessel. Not that either of the Lloyds seemed to know a great deal about it beyond their own cabins. What on earth had they done during such long voyages?

The rooms meant to be the captain's cabin had apparently been taken over by Lloyd himself, while the captain slept in the first officer's accommodation. Sydney had been given a tiny cabin next to his father's, the main benefit of which seemed to be that he would not need to share.

They began with Lloyd's cabin, where the treasure had been stored, the chest secured to a wall hook by rope. There seemed to be no bolts on either the cabin door nor the bed alcove.

"Did you have a servant with you?" Solomon asked.

"No, no. One of the crew served meals in the main cabin. Tybalt joined us."

"Always the same crewman?" Constance asked.

"Generally," Lloyd said.

Fortunately, Captain Tybalt did not take long to arrive, looking somewhat harassed. He bowed to Lloyd and Sydney, nodded to Solomon, and widened his eyes at Constance before adding another hasty bow.

He took them down to the crew's deck, where they had all slept in hammocks in the same space. A smaller cabin had been set aside as a sick bay—the captain being the nearest thing to a medical man. Other cabins were used as workshops for various necessities like mending sails and ad hoc carpentry work. Then there was the galley kitchen, which, although apparently clean, still smelled of old onions and stale rum.

There was no direct means of getting from the crew's quarters to the owner's and captain's. The men would have had to go up through the hatch to the open deck and then down again. Experienced sailors like Captain Tybalt could dash with great speed and ease up and down those ladders, though.

"What do you do during long voyages?" Constance asked Lloyd.

"Read," came the reply. "Write my journal. Plan. Sometimes I sketch a little, though I am an indifferent artist. We'd play cards some evenings, though three is not a great number!"

"Where did you play?" Solomon asked.

"In my cabin, usually. Sometimes in Tybalt's."

Which certainly gave all the crew opportunity to go and inspect the chest in Barnabas's quarters, but how on earth was it copied, and how had it been replaced?

Solomon clearly had the same idea, for he turned to Tybalt. "Captain, did you have a carpenter aboard?"

"Yes, we did. Very handy he was, too, replacing rotten planks and repairing cabinets."

"Was he one of the crew you already knew?" Constance asked.

"No, actually. He was a bit older but happened to be around when I was recruiting. We were still short, so I took him on."

"Did you know all the others?"

"Yes, I'd sailed with all of them before. Good men." He glanced at Solomon. "Apart from Johnny, of course, who we picked up at Madagascar."

"Maybe we should be looking more closely at *him*?" Lloyd said, scowling.

"Oh, we are," Constance assured him.

AS A GESTURE of courtesy, Constance instructed her coachman to convey the Lloyds back to wherever they wished to be. Tybalt, who had been instructed to help them as though he were an old retainer, hovered uneasily on the dockside.

"Would you mind accompanying us to interview the sailors?" Constance said, bestowing one of her smiles upon him. It had its usual effect. "We believe their trust in you will incline them to answer our questions with truth."

"I'll come with you, of course," Tybalt said, "but I really do not suspect any of them." He cast Solomon a look of dislike. "Is that the real reason you were looking for Johnny yesterday?"

"Actually, no. I was told he'd sailed."

"He might have," Tybalt said neutrally. He led them through a warren of filthy, busy back streets east of the dock until they came to a row of crumbling old tenements, where he hesitated, glancing at Constance. "Shall I bring them down?"

"I am happy to go up," Constance said at once. Like Solomon, she wanted to catch the sailors unwarned.

Since he had told her the truth this morning, Lloyd's case seemed to have merged more calmly in Solomon's mind with finding David—if Johnny was indeed David. He had always known Constance could be more easily hurt than she pretended, but until now, he had not realized how much pain he could cause her by sheer thoughtlessness, by chasing his own agenda without her. On top of which, she had reminded him of what he should have known—that men frequently lied to anyone in apparent authority, assuming they were always in trouble.

It was a good idea to bring Tybalt, as he realized as soon as they bumped into Jackson on the stairs.

He grinned in friendly surprise. "Captain! What brings you here? You're not looking for crew again already, are you?"

Over Tybalt's shoulder, he took in Solomon with irritation, and Constance with astonishment.

"Not yet. Any of the others here, Jackson?"

"Not just now. Kelly's found a woman, God help her. What

can I do for you?" He made way for a woman coming downstairs with a huge bundle of washing, and then for two arguing men coming up.

"Shall we talk outside?" Tybalt suggested.

They trooped back down again, and Jackson led them over to some disused steps. Constance perched on a low wall, with Solomon leaning beside her. Jackson and Tybalt sat on the steps.

"You told me Johnny had sailed," Solomon said mildly.

Jackson grinned. "Figure of speech. Don't know you from Adam, do I? A man's got a right to choose who he talks to. I gave him your card. If he wants to, he'll find someone who can read it."

The air left Solomon's lungs. "He can't read?" Was this worse or better? Either seemed unbearable. And yet it wasn't.

"Course he can't read," Jackson scoffed. "He's African."

"So am I," Solomon said. "Can *you* read?"

Jackson's gaze flickered over his face. He was too wily to betray any likeness of features he might have perceived. Or perhaps there was none, except in Solomon's imagination.

"Nah," Jackson said indifferently. "Never needed to read. You ain't do-gooders, are you?"

"No, I told you yesterday. I work for Mr. Lloyd. And I need to know where everyone was during that last afternoon, from when the customs men came aboard until Mr. Lloyd stepped into his waiting carriage."

"Blimey," said Jackson. "He going to dock our pay 'cause we weren't busy enough while waiting for the revenue men to poke about?"

"You've already been paid," Tybalt pointed out. "I doubt we could get much of it back if we tried. You were on deck some of the time, shouting insults at old friends."

"I was," Jackson admitted. "Showing Johnny some landmarks, too."

"Then you didn't see the revenue men inspecting the treasure chest?" Constance asked quickly.

"Nah. Seen it before. So'd Johnny."

"I saw it," Tybalt said. "There was only Mr. Lloyd and me and a couple of revenue men, one to poke about and write everything down. Presumably they'll send Mr. Lloyd the bill when they've worked out what it is."

"Was this all in Mr. Lloyd's cabin?" Constance asked.

"It was."

"Was young Mr. Lloyd not there?"

"To start with. Then he wandered off," said Tybalt.

"And when the customs men left the ship, did you escort them?" Solomon asked.

"I did."

"What did Mr. Lloyd do? Did he come up on deck with you?"

"No, he stayed with the treasure, as far as I know. In fact, he got Samuels—the ship's carpenter we spoke of—in to tie it closed for transporting."

"When did either of you next see the treasure chest?" Solomon asked.

"Quarter hour later?" Jackson replied with a shrug. "Whenever it was, Johnny and Squibbs lugged it up on deck. Which was when the gents got off the ship. His nibs—Mr. Lloyd—supervised its journey into his waiting carriage. Then we went off to the pub, me and Squibbs and Johnny."

"Where were the rest of the crew?"

"Already disembarked," Tybalt said. "I shook hands with the Lloyds, watched them leave, and then took my own trunk and went home."

Solomon frowned. "Did Mr. Lloyd—either of the Mr. Lloyds—come up on deck with the treasure chest?"

"They were already on deck," Jackson said. "Arguing about something. They did that a lot."

Tybalt frowned at him but didn't tell him off. The man was considerably more forthcoming than yesterday.

"How long before the treasure chest were they up on deck?" Constance asked.

"Couldn't say precisely," Jackson said. "More interested in getting to the Crown and Anchor."

"You carried Squibbs's and Johnny's kits off the ship as well as your own," Tybalt said. "You must have been in a hurry indeed."

"Had quite a thirst," Jackson admitted.

"So there were other chests or trunks standing on deck at the same time as the treasure chest?" Solomon asked.

"There were the Lloyds' own trunks and mine," Tybalt said, puzzled. "Why is that important?"

"Were any of them close to the treasure chest?" Solomon asked without answering the captain's question.

"Mine wasn't. I kept it well out of the way of the Lloyds' baggage, which was piled up just at the gangway. Squibbs and Johnny took that first, didn't they? Then came back for the treasure chest, which was when the Lloyds themselves finally disembarked."

"What about *your* kit?" Solomon asked Jackson. "And your shipmates'?"

Jackson regarded him with derision. "In seamen's kit bags? Couldn't have crammed a lot of treasure in there however hard I tried."

"I'm not accusing you," Solomon said mildly. "Just trying to find a way for the impossible to become possible. Was all this baggage under your eye the whole time? You didn't go off below for any purpose?"

"Too keen to get going," Jackson said. "And no, I didn't see nobody tamper with 'em neither."

Solomon cocked an eyebrow at Tybalt, who shook his head.

"From the way Squibbs and Johnny carried the treasure chest," Solomon said, "would you guess it to have been as heavy as before?"

"Oh yes," Jackson replied. "Squibbs said it were like carrying a box of bricks."

Perhaps it was.

"Squibbs does like to exaggerate," Tybalt put in dryly.

"Going back a few weeks, to the island where you found the treasure," Solomon said, "did the entire crew accompany the Lloyds ashore, or did some of you wait on the ship?"

"Samuels and I remained on board," Tybalt said. "The rest went off with Mr. Lloyd."

"Why Samuels?" Constance asked.

Tybalt shrugged. "He's older. And we needed some repairs to the ship."

"Didn't you mind being excluded from the treasure hunt?"

Tybalt smiled. "Not really. I didn't honestly think they'd find it. Between ourselves, I thought Mr. Lloyd was pinning too much on the ravings of a dying man."

"Did you know this Silas Cauley who gave him the map and the story?" Solomon asked.

"I did." Tybalt hesitated. "Look, he was a good man in his day. Bit of a rogue, I suspect, long before I came across him. He was still fit enough in his body, but he was forgetting things, often at just the wrong time. I couldn't send him up the rigging in case he forgot where he was and fell. If I gave him an order, he forgot it before he got to where he was going. He was a liability because his mind was going. He talked a lot of nonsense. In fact, if I'd known when we set off that Mr. Lloyd's information came from Cauley, I'd have advised against the whole expedition."

Solomon held his gaze. "Did the crew get paid?"

"Yes."

"Did you?"

Again, the wry, flickering smile. "Mostly. But yes, I have a vested interest in your finding Mr. Lloyd's treasure."

"AS FAR AS I can see, the only time the chests could have been switched was about ten minutes between Lloyd coming on deck and Squibbs and Johnny bringing up the baggage."

Constance spoke in frustrated tones as she walked beside Solomon toward the alehouse that was the address Samuels the carpenter had given to Captain Tybalt. Tybalt himself had pleaded an appointment with family, and given that the man was only a few days returned from a long voyage, that was not an unreasonable excuse.

"Which on the face of it," Solomon agreed, "would point to either the captain, or one of the Lloyds themselves. There's no quick or easy way from that part of the ship to the crew's quarters."

"And yet the ship's carpenter is the best candidate for making a replica of the chest. Plus, he was there, helping Lloyd secure the chest with ropes. I just don't see how he can have done it and got the original chest off the ship. All the crew but Jackson, Squibbs, and Johnny had gone by the time the Lloyds disembarked. Surely one of them trundling the treasure chest—or even a large trunk— would have been noticed. The sailors only carry meager kit on board, and that seems to be in soft bags or rolls."

"I can't imagine any of the Lloyds having any knowledge whatever of woodwork," Solomon said. "Which leaves Captain Tybalt. The crew would be too used to his comings and goings all over the ship to pay much attention to him unless he's issuing orders. A mere ten minutes below could have passed Jackson by. And Tybalt *was* quartered in the right area of the ship and was the last to disembark. He could have taken the chest."

Constance nodded. "He *could*, perhaps, have knocked together the replica, hidden it in his cabin, and, once the revenue men were seen off, hastily swapped the chests, waited until the Lloyds were gone with a chest full of rubbish or stones or whatever, and departed at leisure with the stolen chest among his own belongings."

"He doesn't seem that kind of a man," Solomon said regretfully. "From a character point of view, I could more easily imagine it was one of the Lloyds."

"Me too, only we don't actually know Tybalt, do we? And

besides, what possible motive could either of the Lloyds have? If it is not for the insurance? Oh." She took his arm and cast a quick look up at him. "We were distracted. You never did tell me what you learned from the maker of the strong room and the solicitor."

"Sadly, nothing that helps. Lloyd's notes with the solicitor on the subject of the strong room are kept safely, and have never been asked for or disturbed. All Lloyd's contracts and insurance agreements are lodged with him, including insurance for this last voyage, which does not include cargoes of any value, let alone the kind of treasure he found. He loses everything by this theft. So does his family."

"Unless Sydney has it all," Constance said.

"How? I could imagine him finding a time and a way to unload everything into his own trunk—though it would be tight—but the chests themselves were switched. He might have been able to hide a replica in his own cabin, but how the devil did he *make* it?"

Constance considered. "An accomplice among the crew? Samuels the carpenter? It could work. Only…"

"Only his father tore the house apart," Solomon finished for her. "When he discovered the theft. Besides, it seems an unnecessarily complicated way of stealing it when he had full access to the keys. Why not just take them while his parents were engaged that night, swipe the treasure, and flee?"

"Because there would have been a watch for him at every port?"

"Would there? Would Lloyd risk the scandal?"

Constance considered. "He might, to get his treasure back. After all, if he doesn't, he risks a scandal anyway, with bankruptcy, poverty, and disgrace for his whole family."

"And children can always hide things from their parents if they try," Solomon agreed. "Even a parent in a rage. *Especially*, perhaps, a parent in a rage. But the point is…"

"The change of chests," Constance said. "Yes, we really do need to speak to this Samuels—unless he's already in France selling the treasure."

"Can you see Sydney handing it over and trusting a mere ship's carpenter with that?"

"No." She sighed and asked without much hope, "What of the locksmith?"

"It was a one-off set. He destroys the originals."

This didn't seem to surprise her. She lapsed into silence.

They had left the noise and bustle of the docks by this time, but there were still costermongers with their stalls and barrows selling everything from hot tea and soup to flowers, old boots, and fresh meat. The calls of criers and patterers spilling actual news among their made-up stories and songs would have amused Solomon at another time. Just now, he had to concentrate on the wonder of the woman beside him to stop the unbearable, aching thoughts within him.

He wasn't really surprised when she said, "Have you considered that Johnny was the accomplice? Especially if he has already sailed. Or is about to."

"I don't think he has," Solomon said with difficulty. Openness was new enough for him. About David, it was painful. "I think he's lodging with Jackson, or at least in the same building. If he truly doesn't know London, where else would he go?"

Her gaze was a caress, yet seemed to burn a hole into his head and heart.

"And yet you walked away."

"I did." He drew a breath. "Jackson is right. Every man has the right to choose whom he talks to. If Johnny is David, he knows who I am and where I am."

For an instant she pressed her head into his shoulder and gripped his arm more tightly—the only comfort he could bear. For if these roles had been reversed, if Solomon had been presented with *David's* whereabouts on a card, and they had been in the same city, within the hour he would have battering down the door to get to his brother, his twin, his missing self. The boy he had quarreled with the very day he'd disappeared.

However stupid, he had never shaken off his fear that whatever he had said or done was the reason David was lost, had run away, had never come back. And now it seemed he might well have been right.

Desperately, he wanted something else to focus on, anything until the pain receded. As always, Constance gave him what he needed. "Is that the alehouse Tybalt spoke of?"

"Yes," he said gratefully. "That's it." Now he could shove the ache aside, slam the door, and concentrate on the matter in hand. "I don't know whether it's worse to leave you outside alone or take you in there."

"It's a step up from the Crown and Anchor. And I was never really a lady." She shoved her charming hat to the back of her head, ruffled her hair, and changed before his eyes.

Her smile was bold and inviting. Her hips rolled temptingly as she walked. Not a professional woman of the streets, but what one might call an enthusiastic amateur. He didn't know whether to laugh or groan until her dancing eyes gave him no choice. She really was rather wonderful.

The public house was a definite step up from the Crown and Anchor. The barmaid was polite, for one thing.

On the other hand, she denied knowing anyone called Samuels.

"I believe he lodges here," Solomon said.

"Does he?" The girl looked surprised and called, "Alf! You got a new lodger?"

The landlord himself loomed up to the counter. "Lord, no. Who you looking for, sir?"

"Arthur Samuels," Solomon said patiently. "I was told he lodges here."

"Not unless he's changed his sex," Alf said with a wheezy laugh. "It's old Mrs. Simmonds what lodges with us. Has done for ten years."

Constance laughed. "It'll have been his little joke," she said, in an accent much closer to those she had grown up with. She even nudged Solomon as she spoke. "I'll bet he's here so often he seems like your lodger. Seafaring cove, ship's carpenter by trade. Not as young as your fine self."

Inevitably, Alf responded, holding his sides and laughing. The maid smiled perfunctorily but still looked mystified.

"We don't know anyone like that, do we, Alf? Unless it's an occasional drinker. Here, what about that quiet cove what sits over there by the window when he comes in?"

"Haven't seen him for months," said the landlord. He grimaced. "Reckon he's dead. Or moved house."

"Gentle soul. Always polite, with a cheery word," the maid mused. "Sad eyes, though. Hope he ain't dead."

"Actually, he might be a carpenter," Alf reflected, raising Solomon's hopes momentarily. "In fact, he is. Heard someone talking business in here with him once. Never heard of him going to sea, though."

"I don't suppose," Solomon said, his buoyancy seeping away again, "that you know where he lives?"

CHAPTER ELEVEN

A LF'S DIRECTIONS TOOK them via a route Solomon did not recognize to a house and a blue door that he definitely did.

When Constance would have stopped in front of it, he drew her on.

"Not yet. This is interesting. That's where I saw Audrey Lloyd. Coming out of that particular door."

Constance blinked at him. "So Alf saw a carpenter who might be Samuels go in there. And you saw Miss Lloyd come out? Since she doesn't live there, perhaps *he* doesn't either. I'll tell you what, though, it doesn't look like the house of someone particularly poor and deserving of charity. And if it *is* Samuels, we know he's healthy enough to work a long and arduous voyage."

"And why did he give the alehouse address rather than this one to Captain Tybalt?"

"Well, let's go and see who is there now…"

Constance was right about the house. In daylight, the surroundings were much more salubrious that they had appeared last night in the dark. Rough sailors and the abject poor did not dwell here. Tradesmen, clerks, and merchant seamen, even of the officer class, might. There were similar areas in every port and close to every dock he had ever visited.

The building itself was a two-story cottage squashed between taller neighbors. There was a window on either side of the front door, which opened straight off the street. The upper floor had three windows.

Solomon rapped the well-polished knocker.

"I wonder if *he's* the man who has already sailed," Constance murmured.

But it seemed not. Solomon was just about to peer in the window when the door opened.

A fit, weather-beaten man stood there, looking curiously but not irritably from Solomon to Constance. It was hard to guess his age, for his white hair made him look older than his face. He could have been anywhere between forty and sixty.

"Yes?" he said.

"Mr. Samuels?" Solomon said, touching the brim of his hat.

The clear eyes never left his. If there was a shade of concern in the man's expression, it did not appear to be personal. "No, I think you must have the wrong house. My name is Clarke. I don't think I know a Samuels on this street."

"The one we are seeking is a ship's carpenter, recently aboard the *Queen of the Sea*, which docked at the beginning of the week."

"Well, I am a carpenter—if you're looking for one?"

"Not just at the moment," Solomon said. "It is Mr. Samuels in particular we would like to speak to."

Clarke did not ask why. But then, he wouldn't, if Samuels was a stranger to him. "I'm afraid I can't help you."

"You have the complexion of a seafaring man," Constance said with a smile. Her hair and her bonnet were straight and respectable once more. "That must be the source of the confusion."

"I do work outdoors often. Just back from a long job in Berkshire, building an elaborate summer house for someone with more imagination than sense."

"We're sorry to interrupt you," Solomon said. "It was Miss Lloyd who told me you lived here." It wasn't *precisely* a lie.

"Miss Lloyd? But she knows my name is not Samuels." He smiled, not without amusement, even fondness. "She can be very forgetful and vague, bless her."

"Then she visits you often?"

"Oh, not me. My sister. We grew up on the Lloyds' country estate and she still looks in on Hetty, especially when I'm away from home. My sister does not keep terribly well."

Which did rather explain Miss Lloyd's charity claim. It seemed they had solved one minor mystery by finding the wrong carpenter.

⊰⊱

RETURNING TO THE office for luncheon, Constance was not surprised to discover Janey entertaining Lenny Knox as they munched through a plate of sandwiches.

"Well met, Lenny," Solomon greeted him. "You're just the man we were looking for."

"I am?" Lenny had sprung up from the stool in Janey's cubbyhole. "I just dropped in to see if you had any work for me. Miss Janey thought I could help her…"

"Oh yes, of course," Solomon said. He picked up the plate, offered it to Constance, then took two sandwiches himself. "First, though, we want your professional opinion about a wooden chest in Mayfair."

Janey glared daggers at Solomon, who didn't even notice. Constance kicked her foot in warning, and she sniffed.

Lenny had once been a bit of a firebrand radical, organizing resistance to unlivable wages and unreasonable rents for tiny spaces in dangerous buildings. Because of the latter, he had recently lost his wife and child. Because of the former, he had lost his job. He was in the process of beginning again on his own, both in his trade and his life, but it would take time for the fire to return. Constance, who liked him, didn't doubt that it would, but Janey was hoping for too much, too quickly, and Constance didn't want her hurt.

Right now, it was his skills as a carpenter she and Solomon needed, Accordingly, after luncheon, they whisked him off to the

Lloyds' residence, where they asked for Mr. Lloyd.

"Is this the culprit?" Lloyd asked eagerly as he strode into the small reception room where Garrick had left them. He looked Lenny up and down contemptuously.

Lenny, in his workingman's clothes with the lines of suffering on his face, gazed back without shame or much interest.

"No," Solomon said. "This is Mr. Knox, an excellent carpenter of our acquaintance. Knox, Mr. Lloyd."

Of course, Lloyd ignored the introduction. Lenny nodded curtly, as though to an equal, though Lloyd didn't even notice.

Solomon continued. "We want his opinion of the chest in your strong room."

Lloyd's face was blank. "Why?"

"To give us a clue as to who built it. The chances of any man on your expedition just happening to possess a chest exactly like the one you dug up are not high. Someone must have made a copy deliberately, and it might be helpful to know whether or not that copyist was an amateur or a tradesman."

Lloyd turned away. "Wait here," he said. "Garrick will fetch you."

Obviously, Lenny was not to be granted the privilege of seeing how to open the strong room door. Constance exchanged glances with Solomon.

At least they were not kept waiting for long before Garrick, clearly resenting the mundane task, summoned them to follow him upstairs, where Lloyd awaited them by the open strong room door. The ring of keys weighed down his coat pocket.

Constance stood back and Lenny walked into the strong room, ignoring everything but the chest. He examined every plank minutely, from inside and out. Then he heaved it on to its side and inspected the bottom. He poked around the joins and rubbed at the heads of few nails, even prying one up with a tool in his pocket to inspect it more closely before reinserting it and knocking it back in.

He half turned to look up at the others. "Looks like a craftsman's work to me, except the wood don't match. None of it. It was made from scraps of different trees and different ages. One bit *here* looks to me like new wood, just dirtied up a bit to match the rest of it. I'd say *this* piece and *these* two had spent a long time in seawater—part of a ship or a boat, maybe. *That* nail is new, just with its head dirtied. The rest seem to be old nails dug out of somewhere else and reused, rusted or not."

He rose to his feet, his fearless gaze moving between the three watchers. "Does that help?"

"Ask my investigators," Lloyd said vaguely. He appeared to be deep in thought.

"I rather suspect it does," Constance said. "It looks as if this chest was put together in a deliberate copy, as we suspected, and by a carpenter who knew what he was doing. Your ship's carpenter, perhaps. I believe his name was Samuels."

Lloyd's face spasmed. Beneath his sun-bronzed skin, he seemed to have paled. "He would not have dared!"

"Did you know him well?" Solomon asked.

Lloyd waved a hand. "Of course not. He was just one of the crew. A sad old man who'd made nothing of his life."

"And yet he probably stole your treasure," Solomon said. "Or at least contributed to the theft. How well do you know Captain Tybalt? Do you trust him?"

"Implicitly. He has never let me down."

"Have you ever let *him* down?" Constance asked.

Lloyd flared his nostrils. "The man is always paid his worth. We have always had a successful partnership. Why else would he keep accepting my commissions?"

"Why indeed?" Solomon murmured. "Thank you, Mr. Lloyd—I believe we have seen enough for now. Oh, that sad old carpenter, Samuels? You don't happen to know where he lives when he's ashore, do you?"

"Of course not," Lloyd said with distaste. "Ask Tybalt. He knows them all."

In which case, Tybalt had lied to them.

JEMIMAH, WHO WAS supposed to be supervising the studies of her younger sister for the afternoon, was quite happy to let Rachel run off and spy on Papa's investigators. Jemimah had seen them arrive with a workingman in tow and mentioned the fact to Rachel, who had immediately dashed off about her own investigations.

Very little happened in this house without Rachel's knowledge, and she was always willing to share—which proved useful when she needed to know if Ben Devine had called. Not that he had. Papa's return appeared to have cooled his ardor, which Jemimah took as a personal insult.

When he called next, she would definitely be very cool toward him. No more assignations in the garden for him! She might grant him one dance at Mrs. Grafton's party next week, but she would be very offhand about it and talk mostly about other admirers—while looking so beautiful that he would ache for her to be as warm as she had been toward him before. She wondered where Mrs. Silver bought her gowns.

Perhaps she would pop down and ask—just when the investigators were leaving, of course.

She refocused on the needlework in front of her, spotting innumerable misaligned and clumsily large stitches. Mama would not be pleased. For a little time, she wondered whether or not she cared, then gave a resigned sigh and unpicked what she had already done.

She had almost redone it when Rachel whisked back into the room.

"They're looking at the chest. Again."

"Why? If it's not the original treasure chest?"

Rachel shrugged. "Maybe they're looking for false bottoms and hidden compartments? Though Sydney says there was too much to be hidden in such a place. *They* suspect it's a good copy, made by someone who knows carpentry."

"Well, that lets all of *us* off the hook. Though we'd have to have been quick anyway, to knock it up during the night. Even if there were a point, which I can't see."

"No, they know it wasn't made here. They think it was made on board the ship, and switched there with the treasure. Remember?"

"Well, neither Papa nor Sydney know anything about carpentry!"

"They could have paid someone."

"Why on earth would they do that?"

"Actually, I can't think of a reason, unless it was some complicated ruse to save the treasure from thieves and it went awry."

Jemimah stared at her sister, frowning. "It's possible, I suppose. Papa would never admit it. Sydney might. Why don't we ask him?"

"Or we could ask Ben."

"Ben? What has he to say about anything?"

"He can do carpentry. He told me once. His father made him learn practical things so he didn't grow up useless, like real gentlemen."

Jemimah opened her mouth and, finding herself speechless, closed it again. At last, she said, "Ben was not on the ship."

"But he has connections among shipowners and sailors. And he might have managed to swap the chests somehow on the quay. Or perhaps Papa did that to fool the thieves and Ben took advantage by breaking into the strong room that night."

"You are thinking," Jemimah said slowly, "that Ben…"

"…sucked up to you to get his hands on the keys and find out exactly when the treasure would be here, so he could steal it."

"And marry me on the strength of the proceeds?" Jemimah said in disbelief. "Where *did* you acquire such an imagination?"

"Oh, just observations," Rachel said modestly. She laughed. "Don't look so worried, Jem—I don't believe it either."

And yet it would, Jemimah thought bleakly, explain Ben's

recent absence. He didn't need her anymore.

She got up suddenly and threw down her work. Seizing Rachel by the arm, she pointed her at the schoolroom desk. "Finish copying that or Mama will find you out. Find both of us out!"

Rachel sat with a perfectly understandable sigh of boredom. Honestly, what was the poor child expected to learn by copying out endless passages of worthy drivel?

"Perhaps we should go on an outing tomorrow," Jemimah said impulsively.

"Mama won't let us go alone."

"Well, if she doesn't, and she won't come herself, we can always take Aunt Aud. Though she will twitter."

"I don't mind her twittering. She's funny with it."

Actually, she was, Jemimah remembered, as she ran downstairs to catch Mrs. Silver.

Mr. Grey and the workingman were hovering, waiting patiently for Constance to button her coat.

"Oh, Mrs. Silver," Jemimah said brightly. "I wonder if I might have a word? Good afternoon, Mr. Grey." She spared him a curtsey, because he was a handsome man even if he was quite old, but kept her attention on Mrs. Silver.

The lady's brows rose slightly, but she turned to the others, saying, "Go on without me. I'll make my own way back to the office." She smiled at Jemimah. "What can I do for you, Miss Lloyd?"

Jemimah led her quickly into the small reception room, where no one would be at this time of the day, and shut the door. And then, although she had meant to inquire about dressmakers, she told her about Ben instead.

CONSTANCE, WHO HAD been looking forward all day, with a rather delightful frisson of anticipation, to dining at Solomon's house, was now desperate to speak to him. Jenks, the same discreet, lugubrious servant she had encountered the only other time she had been here, welcomed her with a bow and a small smile. He took her coat and hat, then led her up to Solomon's large drawing room, which appeared to be also his dining room and his study.

It was, she reflected, a comfortable place for a lonely man who had no intention of entertaining. But it was not a home. There were few personal touches, save an oil painting of a ship above the fireplace, and one of lush, sunny countryside on another. She wondered if it were Jamaica. There were no portraits or mementos of any other kind. The intimate round table was set for two.

Solomon himself, elegant in evening dress, turned from the sideboard and came to meet her. The last time she had been here, he had been rather endearingly flummoxed, though he had quickly veiled every expression. Now there was open pleasure in his melting, dark eyes, and her heart gave one of its foolish little flutters.

He took her hand and kissed it, then leaned down and kissed not her cheek but her lips. "I have been looking forward to that all day."

Her stomach tied itself it knots. There was no doubt this time that she was the one who had lost her bearings, and he the one in control. This was a glimpse into the successful Solomon of the business world, the man who had decided what he wanted and was delighted to be going after it. Against all the odds, he wanted *her*. And not as the tarnished trophy most other men saw. It was terrifying. It was wonderful.

Tongue-tied, she accepted the glass of sherry he had poured out, and rather desperately reached for what she had been so eager to tell him.

"Ben Devine is competent at woodwork," she blurted. "I'm not sure what it means, if anything, because I still don't see how he could have copied the chest in time, even if he had been at the docks to see it unloaded. Nor can I see the point, yet, but I thought it was interesting."

"It *is* interesting," he allowed. "And his father does have shipping connections."

He led her to the group of comfortable chairs by the fire, indicating she should sit on the small sofa, where, to her pleasure and disturbance, he joined her, not quite touching. She sipped her sherry—excellent, of course—and hoped her fingers were not trembling. This was ridiculous.

"But we think now the chests were switched while still aboard ship," she said, "so I'm not sure that this helps us—just muddies the waters even further. Unless there is a connection between either him or his father to Captain Tybalt or Samuels the ship's carpenter."

"I couldn't find one in my inquiries this afternoon."

"The other interesting thing about Ben," she continued, "is that he has stopped calling on Jemimah Lloyd. She is afraid he was merely using her to get close to the treasure. Which could now be in his possession."

Solomon nodded thoughtfully. "Perhaps we should look into any other changes in his behavior. And whether or not he has plans to leave the country."

"I gather his father is in the north, where Ben is avoiding joining him. I thought it was Jemimah that kept him in London, but perhaps it isn't."

"Did you get the impression that Jemimah might have been in league with him? Stolen the keys at least, if not the treasure itself?"

She shook her head. "If Jemimah did it, either alone or with Ben or Sydney or both, what is the point of the fake chest? I even wondered if Lloyd himself had ordered the fake chest because the original was falling apart, and an aged chest full of treasure looks so much more impressive for all his family and friends and intimate gentlemen's club lectures. But I can't see why he would not have told us."

"We already know he is selective and often misleading in

what he tells us and everyone else around him. I don't recall ever dealing with anyone quite so…slippery." He raised the glass and drank. "I have learned rather more about Captain Tybalt, too. I did wonder why he always seemed to be available, often at short notice, for Lloyd's expeditions. Lloyd's pay is hardly generous, and not enough to live on with often years between voyages. Nor are his crew the top of the trees."

Constance set down her glass. "And?" she said eagerly.

"There was a tragedy when he sailed for onetime partners of mine. He was shipwrecked, losing several men and all his cargo. These things can happen at sea all too often, but in this case, there were accusations of drunkenness and incompetence on the part of the captain. Also, that he had swindled from previous cargoes."

"Not quite the clean potato," Constance murmured. "Do you think he and Samuels were in it together? Created the fake chest to give themselves time to flee the country?"

"It's the likeliest solution I've come up with. It would explain Tybalt's reluctance to give us Samuels's real address."

Constance caught her breath. "Samuels has already left the country with the treasure, and Tybalt will follow at leisure…"

"Possibly. On the other hand, it's human nature, sadly, to kick a man when he's down. Tybalt could have made mistakes in his past and paid for them with the loss of his reputation and much of his livelihood. It's more than possible he never stole in his life. Either way, we need to speak to him again. And to Ben Devine."

Constance nodded and picked up her glass again. "We don't seem to be getting any closer, do we? Every minor discovery just jerks us from suspect to suspect without any real evidence against any of them. Meanwhile, the treasure could be sailing further and further away from us. Literally. This could be our first failure, Solomon."

"Oh, we're not defeated yet. Not by a long chalk."

The manservant appeared. "May I serve dinner, sir?"

"You may," Solomon replied, rising and offering his hand to Constance.

Discussing the case had settled her nerves, and as they dined, the beguiling comfort of his presence spread over her once more. No one else had ever brought her this strange combination of excitement and ease, where she could converse and banter and yet be so intimately aware of his physical presence.

"My compliments to the cook," she said as Jenks cleared away their sweet course. "That was a truly delicious meal."

Jenks bowed. "Thank you, ma'am. I shall pass your kind words to the cook. She will be gratified."

"She probably will," Constance said when he had departed, and they sat once more on the sofa with the remains of their wine. "You don't notice what you eat, do you?"

"Not always," Solomon replied. "Unless it's bad—I notice that in the end. Usually. And I notice with you. Everything tastes better."

She was not unmoved, but said lightly, "A compliment, Solomon? Come, come."

He did not respond with the banter she expected. "If I don't give them, it isn't because I don't feel them. I just can't find the right words."

On impulse, she took his hand and held it to her cheek. "That's the best compliment of them all." Without warning, her throat tightened and her eyes filled. "Oh Solomon," she whispered, "how did we get to this place? How can we even be considering…"

"Love," he said softly, gripping her fingers. "I thought we had agreed on that."

His kiss was firm, allowing no reluctance, and yet the tenderness caused a tear to trickle out. He kissed that too.

"You don't know," she said brokenly. "You don't know who I am, what I have done."

"I know who you are now. I'm not sure I care what you have done in the past."

"But the past made us both. And mine…affects our future. I think you have harbored illusions about me. First that I was this hardheaded, scheming siren of a whore constantly enriching myself via men. Then that I am some kind of chaste saint, bent only on charity. Neither of those are me."

His voice remained steady. "I may be besotted, but I am not so shallow as to believe either of those portraits."

"I am not pure. How could I be? I wasn't taken advantage of. I did it for money the first time, to buy something trivial I can't even remember now. It was horrible. It was always horrible through the few I endured at the beginning. But I discovered men would pay dearly. Plus, I stole from them. I let them walk into danger. I picked pockets. I did everything imaginable to make money and get out."

"And you did," he said.

He didn't want to hear it, but he was listening. So unplanned confessions spilled out, the things she had refused to remember and the few things she had been proud of. Or, at least, some of them. When she stopped talking, he was still holding her hand in a tight grip.

There were shadows in his dark, unfathomable eyes, but she could find no disgust there, only pity and tenderness that were almost equally unbearable.

"You see the point, Solomon?" she said anxiously. "I don't know what you expect of me, but I am not the pure wife you deserve. Nor am I the skilled lover men dream of. I will lie in your bed because I love you, not because I am capable of giving or receiving the pleasures of fantasy. I am only a shrewd businesswoman with a sordid past and a kind-ish heart."

"Stop, Constance," he said gently. "There was never any *only* about you. We all do what we have to in order to survive." He brought up his free hand and touched her cheek, her lips. "I guessed most of this, you know, or something very similar, once I truly began to see you. Your strength, your will, is part of whom I love. As for the skills you speak of—they are not what I want or expect. I want only what you give freely. Love, passion, companionship."

Now it was she who gripped too tightly. "And if there is no passion?"

"Oh, there is," he whispered, and kissed her mouth as if he would never leave it. The only man who had ever stirred her like this…

"Do I love you because you make me feel like this?" she murmured against his lips. "Or do I feel like this because I love you?"

"Does it matter?" he asked, and claimed her lips once more, holding her head, caressing her nape.

"No," she whispered, and surrender was sweet. *God, I love this man. I would do anything to make him happy…*

Though his caresses were bolder and her willingness, her eagerness, must have been all too apparent, he drew back, leaving her panting and bewildered. His own breathing was ragged.

"This is what I want," he said, his voice harsh with suppressed lust, which was curiously thrilling. "All of you."

"I am yours."

He uttered a sound that was half laughter and half groan. "Sweetheart, don't say that to me now. This is hard enough. But we will do this properly."

It struck her, finally, that she had the power to change his mind. To seduce him beyond the point of no return. And for the first time in her life, she wanted to. He must have seen it in her eyes, for flames flared suddenly through the clouds of desire in his eyes.

He swallowed. More humbly, he said, "If that is what we both want."

Constance, who was so befuddled that she no longer knew what she wanted, began to laugh, and he grinned back and helped her re-pin her hair and straighten her clothes.

After all, the carriage would call for her in less than half an hour.

CHAPTER TWELVE

SYDNEY FLUNG HIS overcoat over his arm and picked up his silk hat from the bed. Looking forward to his evening, he was whistling to himself, and when the knock sounded at his door, he cheerily called, "Come in!"

His mother entered. "Oh, you're going out," she said. She did not sound disapproving, though she did, annoyingly, close the door as though she intended to stay.

"I'm meeting Ben Devine," he said. "I don't want to keep him waiting."

"Of course not. Are you meeting him to keep him away from Jemimah? Or because you still have anything in common?"

"Dash it, Mama, he's a friend. Why should it have anything to do with Jemimah?"

"I thought you might want to please your father."

"Why on earth would I want to do that?"

"Because you have a guilty conscience?"

Sydney scowled. He began to tap his hat against his thigh. "What are you accusing me of, Mama?"

"Nothing. I am merely *asking* if you are responsible for the switching of the treasure."

He gazed at her, amused and yet not a little uneasy. If she had spoken her suspicion to his father... "Why would I do anything so crass? I was to get a quarter share of the treasure. The word is, that would amount to far more than I'd get selling the whole lot to some greasy fence."

"Then you *did* think about it," she pounced.

"Contrary to popular opinion, I do think occasionally. Sometimes, I even daydream. Does my father, having insisted I accompany him on the damned treasure hunt—which was utterly laughable right up until the moment we found it—actually accuse me of stealing from him now?"

"Of course not! But I am your mother, and I well know the mischief in you, Sydney Lloyd. And I know your temper, which is not so unlike your father's. I know you must have irked each other over the months of forced proximity on the voyage."

He stopped tapping the hat and plonked it on his head instead, as a signal that the conversation was over. "Mama, you are barking quite up the wrong tree."

"I hope so. You can still fix things if I'm not, but it has to be quick. One thing more."

He paused, his hand already on the door. "Yes, Mama?" he said with exaggerated patience.

"Did you know any of the crew on the *Queen of the Sea*? Had you seen any of them before?"

It was not a question he had expected. His erratic curiosity surged, along with a fleck of the mischief she had just accused him of.

"No. But I believe Papa did."

He didn't like that look of fear in her eyes. He had seen it before, usually in the company of Papa, or in conversations *about* Papa. So he did what he always did. He ran away from it.

"I have to dash, Mama," he said, sparing her a swift kiss on the cheek before he swept out of the room. "Goodnight!"

WHEN CONSTANCE ARRIVED back at her establishment, the regular evening party was in full swing. She entered by the front door, made sure with the large footmen on duty that all was well, and gave them her outerwear to dispose of before entering the main salon.

She was hailed from all over the room, by the women and by the regular clients who took their ease there, sipping wine, nibbling from the delicacies on the buffet table, and flirting. She could see at a glance who had retired to privacy, and that all was as it should be.

She began to mingle, pausing to talk to all the guests, particularly the influential and the wealthy on whom the rest of her work depended. She had long ago developed the professional hostess face she showed the world, and she knew how to sparkle, how to lift a party and endow it with life and enjoyment. Tonight, she had no need to pretend. She was sparkling inside with Solomon's love and understanding.

Stephen, the young footman bearing a tray of wine, touched her elbow and she stepped aside, inclining her head to hear his murmur.

"Bit of trouble in the hall, ma'am. Lord Rawleigh has brought a couple of friends who refuse to pay till they've—er...sampled the wares."

"How very rude," Constance said. "Thank you, Stephen. Excuse me," she added to the group beside her, and flitted through the throng to the hall to calm whatever situation had developed.

Two of her long-standing footmen—or guards—looked particularly stony-faced as they stood blocking the way of three young gentlemen. One was Lord Rawleigh, looking rather sheepish.

"Not the rules of the game, old fellows," he was saying to his companions as she approached. "Happy to lend you the blunt."

"That's not the point," said a voice that was only too familiar. Feeling slightly sick, she took in the identities of her difficult guests, just as they looked round and saw her.

Sydney Lloyd and Ben Devine.

For an instant, the scene stood still. She felt totally exposed as her two worlds collided. She had lost the case for Solomon. She had probably lost Silver and Grey for them both.

The young men's mouths had fallen open.

Lord Rawleigh hurried into speech. "Mrs. Silver! So sorry to be the cause of trouble. These gentlemen are my guests, and I am happy to make their contribution to the club."

Constance pulled herself together. She had more important responsibilities right now, and allowing clearly drunk and contemptuous men into her establishment to "sample the wares" was against everything she had fought for.

"My lord, with your recommendation, of course your friends may apply in the usual way. They may then return when sober and I might reconsider. Good evening, gentlemen."

Rawleigh, who was amiable and had never given her cause for concern, looked crestfallen. His companions still seemed too flabbergasted to object. As the footmen stepped forward, they all stepped back. The porter opened the front door and the three would-be guests stalked out into the cold.

"You'll pay for this!" Sydney raged from the step. He even shook his fist from a safe distance.

"Probably," Constance murmured ruefully, and returned to the salon.

JOSHUA CLARKE WAS uneasy about his visitors this afternoon, and very glad it was time to go.

Everything was packed and ready. Almost.

Leaving his battered valise in his bedroom for the time being, he went downstairs with only a candle against the darkness, took the plate from his tiny larder, and sat down at the table to eat his final meal in the house he had called home for more than a decade.

Yet he was not sad to be going. Instead, he enjoyed the relative silence of the night, time alone to say a quiet goodbye to his old life, and welcome the new with soaring excitement and, if he were honest, not a little triumph.

He who laughs last...

Solitary footsteps sounded in the street outside his shuttered window. Through the cracks, he even saw the figure block the light from the streetlamp for an instance. Then the footsteps halted.

Clarke's heart lurched. Staring at the open door of his kitchen, he laid down his fork and kept the knife in his hand as he rose. He was being foolish, of course. Someone had stopped to tie their shoelace, or light a pipe, or just to have a rest. Any moment now, he would hear the footsteps continuing on their way and fading into the distance.

He didn't.

Instead, he heard the sound of a key in the door, inserted surreptitiously and swiftly turned. His shoulders sagged with relief and he walked eagerly into the hall. The lamplight gleamed through the window above the front door, shining on the last face he expected to see.

"You!" he uttered in disbelief.

Pain exploded in his chest.

He who laughed last truly would laugh the longest.

I LOVE THIS man. I would do anything to make him happy...

Her thought from the previous evening stayed with Constance through the night and was still there in the early morning. It burned more strongly even than the rejected visit of Sydney Lloyd and Ben Devine to her establishment.

Assuredly, Jemimah should not marry Ben, not for many years at least, though Constance suspected she was coming to that view on her own. Not that a sheltered girl like Jemimah would know anything about such establishments as this... No, the main outcome of last night's disaster was the likelihood of Silver and Grey being dismissed from the Lloyd case. She should warn Solomon first thing...

Solomon. One of the subjects they had not discussed last night was David. She knew very little of the boy's disappearance, only that Solomon had been looking for him for twenty years. And that there had been a report of a boy around the right age being forced onto a ship in Kingston.

If Johnny the sailor was indeed David Grey, what on earth had happened to him, and why would he not jump at the chance to be reunited with his twin?

Because there had been some quarrel between them? Perhaps David believed Solomon was somehow responsible for whatever had happened. There was even the uncomfortable possibility that he was. Children did and said things from temper without always understanding the consequences. Which could have led to a lifetime of trying to put it right.

Or Johnny might not be David at all.

Since she had first got to know Solomon, she had acknowledged a desire to make him happy, to take away his loneliness and somehow give him joy. And surely the best way to do that was to give him David. He needed to know one way or the other, be rid of the uncertainty that ate at him. At the very least, he needed to be rid of the possibility that the brother he had sought for so long and missed so terribly had rejected him.

So she rose at once, early as it was and despite her lateness to bed the previous night—she never seemed to need a great deal of sleep. She wore her simple "working" dress.

Before it was even light, she was outside Jackson's tenement building. Already the place was busy with people heading to or from places of work. Women with bundles of laundry or mops and buckets, men with seamen's kits on their shoulders or tools in wooden boxes and canvas bags. A few vagrants popped up, shivering in doorways and scratching themselves. Already the costermongers were there, selling hot and probably disgusting tea, thin sandwiches, and yesterday's pies.

Once, she had been used to entering such ominous doorways with dark stairwells, the stink of all manners of filth in her nostrils. She had entered this one only yesterday. But she had grown soft. Climbing the stairs in daylight with the protection of Solomon and Captain Tybalt was quite different from doing so alone in the gloom of dawn. Now, her flesh crawled and she felt far too exposed.

A large man running down with a sack on his shoulder barged past, swearing at her for getting in his way. And suddenly Constance remembered how she'd survived. She swore back at him, and felt much better when an old woman cackled from an unseen doorway.

Constance stopped, peering into the gloom. "Morning, missus," she said cheerfully. "Looking for a sailor called Jackson. He does live here, don't he?"

"Now and again. Next landing, second door, but he's out."

This suited Constance, but she just said, "Maybe he's come back. Thanks, missus!"

There wasn't even a lock on the door. She lifted her hand and knocked lightly, then louder. No one answered, and when she held her ear close to the door, she still heard nothing. It was too good an opportunity to resist.

She was aware, as she pushed open the door and called softly, "Hello, anyone home?" that Solomon would lambast her for endangering herself. Curiously, this made her bolder, as though the very thought of him protected her.

The room did not smell pleasant. A small family of mice, feasting on some crumbs on the floor, regarded her somewhat insolently without fleeing. Clearly, they were used to living here untroubled. There were four cots in the room, none of them occupied—fortunately—and only one of them had the blanket pulled up. Odd bits of rough clothing were scattered across a couple of the other beds. On the rickety table in the center of the room stood part of a loaf, a couple of dirty mugs, and a half-finished wooden figure of a ship with a knife beside it.

Leaving the door slightly ajar, she moved closer to the table and withdrew a crumpled piece of paper from beneath one of the mugs. On one side was an official, printed form of some kind, in a foreign language she couldn't read. On the other, a pencil sketch of a face she instantly recognized as Jackson.

The door of the room swung open and Solomon walked in.

Solomon, wearing rough seamen's clothes, at least a day's stubble on his chin, and his hair miraculously grown by several inches since last night.

Her heart lurched. *David.*

It could only be David, Solomon's twin.

He stopped at sight of her. "Who are you?"

His voice was enough like Solomon's to give her gooseflesh. But the accent was wrong.

"My name is Constance Silver," she said, since he seemed only mildly surprised by her presence. He certainly didn't object to it.

"Jackson and Squibbs won't be back till tonight," he told her.

"That's fine. It was you I came to see."

His eyebrows flew up. "Me? I don't know you."

"I know your brother."

He scowled. "I don't have a brother."

Oh, Solomon, what happened between you? "He sent you his card, via Jackson."

Thrusting his hand in his pocket, he pulled out a familiar Silver and Grey card. So Jackson *had* given it to him. "You are Silver. What do you want with me?"

"I want you to go and see Mr. Grey."

"Does he have a ship?"

"I believe he has several. Just go and talk to him."

His gaze dropped to the sketch in her hand, but he said, "Why do you call him my brother?"

"You'll know when you see him. He looks just like you."

His eyes flew back to hers, alarmed and searching. Then he smiled, a cynical, sardonic kind of amusement. "Really." It wasn't a question of any kind. "I'll think about it. Was there something else?"

"Yes, as it happens." She set the sketch of Jackson back down on the table. "Do you know who drew this?"

"I did. Why?"

"It's very good. You have talent."

He shrugged. "It passes the time on long voyages."

"Do you have others?"

She could see he was about to deny it. Then something kept him from saying the words. He was a stranger in a strange land, a man without a home. Like Solomon, who had a mere house and a very similar, chronic loneliness behind his eyes.

Without a word, he walked to the made bed, lifted the mattress, and withdrew several other pieces of crumpled paper, some torn scraps, some full sheets, printed or written on one side. He held them out to her and she moved to take them from him. He watched her steadily as she glanced through them with growing excitement.

One was of a girl, pretty and laughing. The next was Captain Tybalt, staring into the distance. Barnabas Lloyd glared at her, his arrogance visible, somehow, in every line. Then came a couple of strangers to her, although their faces were interesting and they obviously fascinated the artist. She glanced at the last, and her breath caught.

"Clarke," she said. Clarke with a beard. But certainly the man whose sister Audrey Lloyd visited. The man who was not...

"Samuels," the sailor corrected her. "Our carpenter on the *Queen of the Sea*."

This changed everything! It had to.

"Thank you," she said breathlessly, already dashing to the door. "Don't forget to call on Mr. Grey! He truly wants to see you."

BEFORE SHE HURRIED on to Clarke's house, she took the time to tear a page out of her notebook and scribble, *Samuels is Clarke. Sydney saw me at establishment last night—be prepared. C.* She folded it and wrote Solomon's name and the address of the office, just to be on the safe side. Then she cornered an urchin and asked if he knew how to find the address. When he nodded eagerly, she gave him a sixpence and told him he'd get another when he delivered it.

The lad sped off, highly delighted, and Constance, equally elated for different reasons, dashed on toward Clarke's house. This was surely the connection they needed. Why should Clarke have used a false name on the ship, grown a beard that he had subsequently shaved off, unless he was up to something nefarious? Because Lloyd might recognize his real name? Or even his beardless face? He was the carpenter, likeliest candidate to have made the swapped chest currently in Lloyd's strong room, though exactly how the switch was made remained unclear to her.

Was she about to find the treasure itself? Not that Clarke-Samuels was likely to simply hand it over. Probably she would need to keep him talking until Solomon got here, hopefully with another strong man. Perhaps she should send for her own footmen...?

She could just observe the premises until then. It would be wiser and safer, although it went against the grain. Then again, if she bumbled in there, even if she got out again safely, she would not be able to arrest the man, only warn him they were onto him. He would flee with the treasure and they would be back to the beginning again.

Reluctantly, she came to the conclusion that she must merely observe. Unless he went out, in which case, she was prepared to either call on the sister or simply break in.

Her decision made, she had to rethink everything. For when she knocked on the familiar blue door, it creaked and moved under her hand. It was open already. She glanced at the windows, which were still shuttered, although it was light now. Unease crept over her.

She pushed the door again and stuck her head in. "Hello?"

Silence greeted her. She pushed again, meeting resistance, but finally stepped into the little hallway, which had a door on either side and a steep, narrow staircase leading to the floor above.

It was a moment before she saw what had impeded the door. The still figure of Clarke the carpenter lying on the floor. There was blood around his chest and on the floor, and his eyes were open.

In horror and pity, Constance threw herself to her knees and reached for his hand, seeking a pulse. His flesh was cold and lifeless. He had been dead for hours.

Behind her, the door slammed. Before she could even jerk around, something crashed into her head. There was blinding pain, and then the world went black.

SOLOMON, THRILLED BY his growing closeness to Constance, entered the office with all the eagerness of an infatuated schoolboy.

"Good morning, Janey," he said cheerfully as the girl appeared while he was removing his overcoat. "Is Mrs. Silver here yet?"

"Morning, sir, and no, not yet, but she shouldn't be long. I know she was up early."

Janey presented him with tea in his office and a new letter of inquiry. Before he could sit down to read it, the knocker sounded on the front door. Maybe Constance had forgotten her keys…

And maybe it was David.

He tried to remain calm, though his heart thundered so loudly, Janey should have heard it before she even entered the room.

"Mr. Sydney Lloyd, sir," she said so firmly that he knew the young man had set her back up and she had only just prevented him from the impropriety of barging in unannounced. Very few people, he imagined, got the better of Janey. "Shall I show him in?"

"Yes, and tell Mrs. Silver when she arrives."

"Of course, sir." She curtseyed, which was more than she usually did, and left, saying grandly, "Mr. Grey will see you now."

She had barely finished speaking before Sydney brushed past her like a gust of wind, striding into the room.

"Two things, Mr. Grey!" he announced, and for the first time, Solomon saw Sydney's arrogant father in his expression. The man was angry and worried and yet very, very superior.

"Please, sit down and tell me," Solomon said civilly, rising to his feet. "Tea?"

"No, I don't want any damned tea!"

Sydney threw himself into one of the armchairs next to Solomon's, so Solomon sat down again and reached for his cup. "I'm sure there is good reason for your…haste."

If Sydney recognized the rebuke for discourtesy, he gave no sign of it. Instead, he glared aggressively. "Your so-called partner is a damned whore, and I'd like to know what you mean by foisting such a vile creature on my mother and—"

Solomon had knocked over his cup and sprung to his feet without realizing. The rare red mist was down over his eyes as he hauled Sydney to his feet by his waistcoat and raised one purposeful fist. Only the sudden fright in the youth's eyes held that fist in check.

"If you want to live," he said, hearing the danger in his own soft voice, "you will keep your nasty little mouth shut. On your way out."

Sydney's face flamed. He tugged violently, failing to free himself until Solomon let him go so suddenly that he fell back into his chair.

"I can't go," Sydney said in sudden panic. "I am here on behalf of my father."

"What?"

"Aunt Aud… My aunt has disappeared from the house. Her bed has not been slept in and most of her clothes are missing, along with personal items such as…" He trailed off.

"Understand," Solomon said slowly, "that I will do nothing for your father or have anything to do with your family if I hear one word against the lady who will be my wife."

Sydney swallowed. A weak flare of defiance sparked in his eyes and died. When Solomon neither moved nor spoke, merely regarded him with infinite contempt, he finally really realized he was expected to answer.

"I understand," he said hoarsely, and tugged at his collar.

"Then begone. I will be at your father's house directly."

"The carriage is—"

"I have no intention of sharing a carriage with such an ill-conditioned pup."

The door opened again and Janey came back in bearing a scrap of folded paper. "An urchin brought this, says the lady promised him sixpence. I gave him a shilling. It's from Mrs. Silver."

Solomon took the note while Sydney sidled out of his chair and toward the door, which Janey held for him.

"I did see her there," he said defiantly.

Solomon didn't answer. He was too busy scanning Constance's note. His blood ran cold. Because he knew she had gone alone to Clarke's. And if Clarke was Samuels, then he was surely also the thief. With nothing to lose if he were discovered.

CHAPTER THIRTEEN

CONSTANCE STRUGGLED UP through the mists toward consciousness. Her ears were singing and her head was pounding. She couldn't think why, or where she was. She was not in her own bed. In fact, she seemed to be lying on her front, which she never did, and what felt like someone's arm was beneath her.

Every nerve in her body screamed with fear and fury, and she must have jerked in instinctive response to get away, for excruciating pain sliced through her head. She let out a groan because she couldn't help it.

"Constance!" came a blessedly familiar voice from very far away.

Solomon… She tried to speak, but no sound came out. She had to move, she had to run, run to *him*, but she seemed to be in one of those nightmares full of shadows and threat where she was trapped, and… If only the infernal pounding of her head would stop. Or was that noise outside her head? A particularly loud one seemed to prove that.

An exclamation, a footfall. Someone touched her shoulder and she cried out.

"Oh, Constance, my dear…"

Solomon. The brokenness of his voice moved her to weak tears. But he was lifting her, turning her, his arms so very strong and safe and wonderful… With a gasp and a huge effort, she flung out her own arms and clung to his neck.

Everything flooded back to her. Johnny, who was surely David, his sketches, Samuels the carpenter, who was Clarke, and his dead body on the floor.

Dear God, had she fallen on him when she was struck?

She tightened her grip on Solomon, who was holding her against his chest, his hand at the back of her head, murmuring incomprehensible, soothing words.

Just his voice was enough. She had always loved his voice.

"Clarke is dead. Someone hit me." It was her voice, just weak and husky.

"I know, my darling, I know. Hold on."

He rose with unusual awkwardness, taking her with him, and for a moment dizziness overwhelmed her. He set her down gently in an old, upholstered chair in a small parlor.

"The wound has stopped bleeding," he murmured. "I'll see to it in a moment. First, I'd better send for the local constable."

She didn't ask if he would come back. She knew he would. And, in fact, he was only gone a minute or two, for the street outside was busy at this time of the morning and no doubt his battering at the door had already attracted the neighbors' attention.

When he came back, he had a bowl of clean water and a cloth in his hands, and he walked with brisk, soothing efficiency.

"One of the neighbors has run to fetch a policeman. What happened?"

"I went back to Jackson's room," she said, trying not to wince as he touched the wound in her head.

"Why?" he asked.

She stopped herself just in time from blurting out the truth. She didn't want him to know yet that David—if he really was David—had denied having a brother. And she certainly didn't want him to believe that if David came to see him, it was only because she had persuaded him.

"I just thought something was wrong there… Anyway, don't get cross because the door was open and no one was there. I found sketches there of the crew of the *Queen*, and Clarke was one of them. I knew then he had to be Samuels, so I sent you word… Did you get the message?"

"I did. Janey overpaid the boy who brought it."

"Does no harm to have willing helpers and messengers scattered across the city." She swallowed. "The door here was open, too, though something was impeding it and I couldn't get in at first. It was Clarke's feet. I knelt beside him to see if he was still alive—he was cold; I knew he was dead—and then someone moved behind me, and before I could turn, he hit me." She shuddered. "I fell on him, didn't I?"

"Just on his arm. He didn't mind."

In spite of everything, a snort of laughter surged up. It might have been hysterical, but something lightened in Solomon's intensely focused eyes.

"Who hit you?" he asked after a moment.

She shook her head, then wished she hadn't. "I don't know. I didn't see."

"You said *he* hit me."

"I'm making an assumption. I feel better about being bested by the stronger sex."

"So where did *he* come from?" Solomon asked. "What was behind you?"

"The front door."

"Then he wasn't in the house already. Do we have *two* attackers, then? Someone who shot poor Clarke and scarpered, leaving the door open? And then another man who hit you and then departed, carefully locking the door behind him?"

"Bizarre," she admitted, frowning, grasping at impressions and memories. "There were feathers in the hall."

"Well, it wasn't an armed bird who shot him. I think we need to let a doctor see this. It might need stitches."

It said a great deal about her weakness that she did not object either to the doctor or, after the constable had taken their names and addresses, being taken home and carried into her own establishment via the mews.

SOLOMON HAD NEVER been so terrified as when he had seen her lying there on the floor of Clarke's house, the back of her head soaked with blood, already matting her hair. Her hat had been knocked askew and tumbled off, probably, when she fell forward. Only that one vocal groan had given him hope, until he felt her breathing. His heart had almost broken when she reached for him like a child seeking comfort.

His anger at her recklessness had vanished into that mess of fear and pity and love. And sheer relief when she began to sound more like herself. Still, head wounds could be nasty. His own father had died of one, falling from his horse. He too had seemed to recover, and then died that night. Leaving Solomon truly alone in the world.

He still remembered that odd, rootless emptiness, different from the gradual loss of David, and yet just as all-encompassing. He had had to work hard to overcome that fear, to make his own decisions and spread his wings.

Constance was too young, too vital, and much too precious to be allowed to die. And so he carried her inside, to the vocal anxiety of her household. One of the women, Sarah, led him upstairs to Constance's bedchamber, with Constance nattering reassuringly all the time.

"I'm fine. I just had a bit of an accident, and Solomon is making a huge fuss. I'm perfectly capable of walking, Solomon—do put me down."

"You be quiet, ma'am, and let the gentleman carry you up," one of the other women said sternly. "Joseph's gone to fetch the doctor, and you are going to your bed."

"I most certainly am not!"

"You most certainly are," Solomon said firmly, laying her

down. "I'll wait through here while your friends help you undress. Absolutely no corset," he added by way of instruction.

"Why, Solomon!" Constance mocked. "What do *you* know about a lady's corsets?"

"You'd be surprised by what I know," he said, walking into what appeared to be her private sitting room.

Pacing while he waited, he distracted himself by gazing around her boudoir. Two armchairs and a comfortable chaise longue. A neat, businesslike desk with lamp and writing materials. A bookcase with a wide variety of volumes, from novels to philosophy and travel and various scientific treatises. A constant surprise, was Constance Silver.

The decoration of the room was tasteful, uncluttered, and yet feminine. Soothing, cool blues and warm creams. An atmospheric landscape in oil hung over the fireplace. A watercolor still life on another. A couple of statuettes stood on the mantelpiece, a vase of hothouse flowers on a small table, another on her desk.

The women emerged. "Well, we got her into bed," Sarah said. "We're relying on you to keep her there, at least until the doctor has been."

"I will," he promised, already in a hurry to reassure himself of Constance's wellbeing.

She was propped up on a sea of pillows, wearing a wispy lace nightgown of the type he remembered only too well from the Maules' house, when they had pretended to be married. And now they really would be, if only he could keep her safe long enough.

As though she read his mind, she said, "It has happened before and we have discussed it before." She held out her hand to him. "It is the life we chose, Solomon."

He took her hand and sat on the side of the bed before he kissed her fingers. "I know. I just wish you had waited for me."

"So do I—now. I only meant to watch the house until you came, but the door was open and I knew something was wrong. I couldn't *not* go in. If only we had been earlier, we might have saved him."

"I don't think so," Solomon said. "Not unless we had gone last night, and I confess it never entered my head that Clarke and Samuels were the same man."

"Has Lloyd dismissed us?" Constance asked ruefully.

"No, but I had a visit from Sydney, in self-righteous indignation that you were in a brothel."

"Well, so was he until I threw him out. He and Ben Devine appeared in the train of an amiable young lord who is a regular visitor. They, however, were drunk and insulting. But I knew it would rebound on Silver and Grey. I'm sorry, Sol."

"There's no need to be. Lloyd actually sent Sydney to fetch us because Miss Audrey Lloyd has apparently vanished."

"Miss Lloyd who visited Clarke's invalid sister," Constance said slowly. "And that's odd, too. Why didn't the sister hear the commotion? If Clarke was shot, there must have been a devilish explosion…"

"She wasn't in the house," Solomon said. "While you and the neighbors were talking to the constable, I nipped upstairs to look for her. To be honest, I was afraid I'd find her dead like Clarke himself—unless she was the one who shot him. But if he really has a sister, there is no sign of her ever having lived in that house. The second bedroom was almost entirely empty, apart from an old seaman's chest and a few tools."

"Then Miss Lloyd lied to us… That sweet, vague lady who lives for her charities. And now she has disappeared."

"Interesting, isn't it? Also interesting is that there was an open valise on the bed, with clothing and personal items strewn about the bed and the floor."

"As though he had packed his valise to leave," Constance said, "and someone else emptied it out, searching for something. For the treasure?"

"If so, they may have found it. Although I doubt from the descriptions and the photographs that he would have been able to pack it all into that valise, even without the clothes."

"Then what the devil has he done with it? Who would have

killed him? His accomplice on the ship? Tybalt? He lied to us, after all, about Samuels's address."

Solomon smiled grimly. "A lot of people have been lying to us."

They both thought about that for a few moments, then Constance said uneasily, "What if whoever shot Clarke has harmed Audrey too?"

"I can't think why," Solomon said, although the idea had occurred to him too. "The connection is inexplicable."

Constance sighed. "Everything in this case seems to be. Did you learn anything about her disappearance? When did anyone last see her? What has she taken with her?"

"She took most of her clothes, apparently, and some personal items. I don't know any other details yet."

Constance's eyes widened. "You haven't been to the Lloyds' house yet?"

"No, I came straight after you."

"Well, off you go now."

His lips twitched at her imperiousness. "When the doctor has seen you."

"By then, Sydney might have filled his ears with poison against us," she said urgently.

"Oh, I think that moment has passed, don't you? He was never going to tell his parents, or he would have to admit where and how he found out. Whatever Lloyd's own habits, he is not the kind of man to turn a blind eye to his offspring's. And confession might also end completely Ben Devine's chances with Jemimah. Sydney might retain some sibling loyalty, or regard for his friendship with Ben."

She looked doubtful, then thoughtful. Finally, she said, "I don't like this, Solomon. That my other profession is a liability to Silver and Grey. Any prospective client who walks through our doors could know me."

"Well, we are not hiding," Solomon pointed out. "It is our names on the door and on our cards. Investigation is not normally regarded as a particularly respectable profession. I don't see that clients would care."

She regarded him fixedly, not without fascination. "Seriously?"

He smiled. "Seriously. I have a plan." There came the sounds of people crossing the outer room, so he released her hand and stood up. "Which I shall tell you about later."

Sarah, who had led him with his beloved burden to Constance's bedroom, came in again with a brisk young man with a medical bag.

"And you are?" the doctor said, his voice wintry.

"Grey. Mrs. Silver's betrothed."

That appeared to take the wind out of the doctor's protective sails, for he merely grunted and turned immediately to his patient. "It's stopped bleeding and looks clean enough, but it had better be stitched. First, though, look at my finger—follow it with your eyes."

He proceeded to ask a lot of other odd questions, while he turned her face to the light and peered into her eyes, lifting the lids to see more.

"Concussion can be a nasty thing. You must rest for at least twenty-four hours—and I mean *bed* rest, Mrs. Silver. I also want someone to be with you during all of that time. If you notice any change," he flung at Solomon and Sarah, "send for me at once. Now, I'm afraid this is going to hurt..."

⇥⇉⇥⋘⋘

IT WAS AFTER midday before Solomon finally left Constance and walked round to the Lloyds' house. He could still feel her suffering as if it were his own, even though she had been brave and stoic. The doctor had given her a mild draft, he said, to ease the pain, and when she finally slept, Solomon reluctantly left her in the care of her devoted handmaidens—a maid and a prostitute and a girl called Libby whom she was teaching to read.

Arriving at the Lloyds' residence, he was shown immediately into the master's study.

"I sent for you hours ago!" Lloyd said, springing from his chair at his desk. "Is something more urgent than the disappearance of my poor, gentle sister? Does my employ mean nothing to you?"

"It means a great deal, sir. In fact, I was detained by an assault on my partner, Mrs. Silver, while she was about your inquiries."

"Eh?" Lloyd frowned and sat back down, waving irritably to the chair on the near side of the desk. "What happened? Is she well? Who did it?"

"She was struck on the head," Solomon said, seating himself. "In the house of one Mr. Joshua Clarke, whom I believe you know."

"Clarke? It's a common enough name, but I can't think of him offhand. What makes you think I know him?"

"He was the ship's carpenter aboard the *Queen of the Sea*."

"Was he?" Lloyd's eyebrows flew up. "You suspect him of the theft of my treasure?"

"Yes, I do."

"Well, have him arrested, man! I'll go straight to the police station myself!" As if suddenly remembering the matter of his sister, he coughed. "Audrey would want the man caught and the treasure returned. If only nothing ill has happened to her. You haven't told me how Mrs. Silver is."

"She needed stitches to her head and the doctor is still concerned for her. Wounds of that nature are dangerous."

"Terrible business. We'll charge Clarke with that too."

"I'm afraid we won't," Solomon said. "Clarke is dead."

Lloyd blinked rapidly. "Dead? How?"

"Shot through the heart, by the look of it. The police surgeon will no doubt discover more details."

"Good Lord," Lloyd said faintly. "What on earth does this mean?"

"For you? That our chief suspect in the treasure theft has died without explaining how it was achieved, or what he did with the treasure. Perhaps the police will find it when they search the place for clues."

"The police?" he said quickly. "The police are involved?"

"Of course. A man was murdered. Mrs. Silver could easily have been."

"I just thought you would handle the matter, but I suppose… Do you think this Clarke might have attacked Mrs. Silver? And then someone else shot him for the treasure?"

"It's possible. He might have had an accomplice aboard the ship who got greedy. How well do you know Captain Tybalt?"

"Known him for years. Good fellow. Never let me down."

"So you said. He must be expensive to hire."

Lloyd shrugged. "Not too bad. I'd rather have a man I can trust."

"Then you trust Tybalt not to have stolen the treasure?"

"Of course! He's a gentleman. Sort of."

"What of the rest of the crew?"

"They're Tybalt's business. I had nothing to do with them."

"Nothing?" Solomon said, raising his eyebrows. "Sir, you spent weeks—months—amongst those people. You must have noticed *something* about them. Their names, their friendships, their fitness."

"Not really. Though we had to leave one fellow at Madagascar. Left him aboard another ship with a doctor on board."

"Think about it," Solomon urged. "You must have heard the captain giving orders from time to time, the men complaining or cracking jokes, talking to each other. Names must have been used."

"I suppose so. Some of them had funny names. Like Squibbs."

"And the men who carried your baggage, including the chest, off the ship in London?"

"Johnny," he said after a moment or two. "And Squibbs. And Samuels, who tied up the chest. Not sure he carried anything, but he might have."

"Did you trust them?"

"Certainly, while I was watching them!"

"You left your bags below for these men to bring up on deck, while you and your son and the captain were up there, waving to your family, even entertaining them, I believe."

"You think the chests were swapped during that time? I don't see how, but I suppose you must be right. How does Clarke come into it, then?"

"Were there not people called Clarke among the tenants of your estate?"

"Possibly," he said, mystified. "Never had much to do with the estates. Got a steward in who knows the land. Not my forte."

"Your sister was the one who knew the tenants?"

Lloyd sighed. "Charity, always charity with Audrey. She did a great deal of it here in London, too. My fear is, Grey, that some charity case has turned against her, robbed her, hurt her in some way…"

"It seems unlikely," Solomon said dryly. "She took most of her things with her, did she not? What else did she have to run away from?"

Lloyd drew himself up. "Nothing in this house."

Solomon switched tack. "When did you last see your sister?"

"At dinner. She's always at dinner."

"You did not see her after that? Did you not join the ladies in the drawing room?"

"Yes…" He frowned. "Come to think of it, I'm not sure Audrey was there then. We must ask the other ladies."

"And the servants, if you don't mind. And your son and your younger daughter, too."

Lloyd shifted restlessly. "I suppose we need her to be found."

Which was an odd way of putting it. But then, Lloyd regarded everything from the angle of how it affected him. He did seem genuinely put out about his sister's disappearance, and he had certainly sent Sydney to fetch him as soon as he knew.

"How did you learn that Miss Lloyd was missing and not just gone out about her charitable missions?" Solomon asked.

"Jemimah told me. She'd gone up to see her aunt—with Rachel, I think—and thought the room seemed too tidy. The bed was not slept in and the maids had not yet made it up."

"Does Miss Lloyd have a personal maid?" Solomon asked.

"Oh no. She has access to my wife's woman, of course, whenever she needs her."

"Then I'll begin with Garrick," Solomon said, rising to his feet.

"What would the butler know about it?" Lloyd demanded, clearly frustrated that Solomon was not out tearing London apart in a frenzy to find his sister.

"Oh, butlers know most things," Solomon said, and went out.

CHAPTER FOURTEEN

G ARRICK, ODDLY ENOUGH, seemed almost human when Solomon encountered him in the hall. He made no effort to walk away or even to look down his nose. He even walked to meet Solomon, saying bluntly, "Can you find her, sir?"

"I hope so," Solomon returned. He glanced around at the housemaid bustling by and added, "Come in here a moment, will you?" He walked into the small reception room close to the front door, and Garrick followed without objection, even closing the door at Solomon's silent command.

"When did she leave the house, Garrick?"

"I don't know," the butler said with what seemed to be genuine misery. "I didn't see her go."

"Were any of the doors unlocked when you came down this morning?"

"Oh dear, you don't think she went off in the middle of the night, do you?" Alarm stood out in his face. "Poor lady's got no idea about the nasty world out there—anything could have happened to her!"

Solomon regarded him more closely. "Why do you say that?"

"Well, she's the kindest of ladies, sir, wouldn't hurt a fly, give you anything she could from a kind word to a sixpence for medicine when you got a cold. Knitted winter scarves for all the maids, she did. But she's vague, sir, forgets stuff, and never had to find out there's villains in the world who'd rob her blind or knock her down for her handkerchief."

"I understand she does a lot of good works, through the church and various charities. Do you really think she could go among the poorest in society, into areas that most of us would hesitate to venture, without coming across *life*?"

Garrick closed his mouth, ruminating on this novel point of view. "I never thought of it like that," he said at last. "I just know she's not valued in this house as she should be." He glanced somewhat fearfully toward the door as though he expected his employers to charge in and dismiss him for effrontery or disloyalty.

"What makes you think so?" Solomon asked.

"They don't pay any attention to her. Oh, they feed her— except when they have guests to dinner, then she gets a tray in her room. She doesn't go calling with them; she doesn't go to parties or join Mrs. Lloyd's entertainments."

And she didn't go to the opera with them. "Why is that, do you suppose?"

Garrick shrugged, his upper lip curling very slightly. Probably, he didn't even notice it happening. "She makes the house look untidy, gives away the fact that they neglect her. She was brought up with a maid to help her dress and do her hair, and now the staff is so cut back here, the housemaid's got no time to see to her."

"What of the younger members of the household?"

"Children follow the lead of their parents," Garrick said darkly. "Though Miss Rachel still goes up to her often enough. She likes children, Miss Lloyd does. Such a pity she never had any of her own."

Solomon returned to the original question. "*Were* any of the doors unlocked this morning?"

Garrick shook his head. "No, that's one blessing."

"Is it? Her bed hadn't been slept in, I understand, so she must have left the house before you bolted the doors for the night. When did you last see her?"

"When dinner was served. Oh, God..."

"Not after dinner?"

"No, I don't... Wait, I did notice her go upstairs when the other ladies went to the drawing room. That wasn't unusual. Sometimes she came back down again with her book or her work basket."

"Did she last night?"

"I didn't see her if she did."

"Did the upstairs maids see her at all, either last night or this morning?"

"No, sir," Garrick said unhappily. "But that's not unusual either. She just goes about her own business and no one notices."

If she was so very kind to the servants, they might well notice... "I may want to speak to the other servants later, but I'd better see the rest of the family, if they're in."

"The ladies are in the drawing room, sir. Shall I announce you?"

"Yes, if you please," Solomon replied, trying not to blink at this unprecedented courtesy. Garrick really was worried. "Um, and where would I find Miss Rachel? In the schoolroom?"

Garrick regarded him. "If I drop a word, I daresay she might run into you."

Mrs. Lloyd and her elder daughter were seated in the drawing room, both with needlework on their laps, although neither appeared to be attending to it.

"Oh, Mr. Grey!" Jemimah exclaimed, springing up so that her embroidery frame slid to the floor. "Have you found my aunt?"

"Not yet," Solomon said, bowing to both ladies. "But I understand it was you, Miss Jemimah, who first realized she was missing from home."

"It seems so, yes. Rachel and I went to her room—"

"Rachel should have been in the schoolroom," Mrs. Lloyd interrupted, frowning.

"Oh, she is bored, Mama! You cannot expect her to sit there day after day with no company, no teacher, and the tedious task of copying out long, dreary passages from supposedly improving books that don't improve anything at all except one's interest in something—anything!—else."

"Jemimah!" exclaimed her mother, clearly shocked, and slightly embarrassed.

"I promised Rachel we would go on an outing, only I knew you would kick up a fuss if we went alone, so—"

"Kick up a fuss?" Mrs. Lloyd repeated, apparently more stunned than angered by the language.

"Exactly. So we went to Aunt Aud to see if she would come with us. We thought she might enjoy it, too. After all, the poor old thing never does anything but charity—which is very worthy, of course," she added hastily, "only I can't help thinking it would be very dull *all* the time."

"And your aunt was not in her room," Solomon said, bringing her musings back to the matter in hand.

"No. We thought we had missed her until Rachel noticed that the bed was still turned down from last night, and looked quite unslept in. Plus, the place was *tidy*, and Aunt is never tidy. Her dressing gown was gone from the back of her door, and when we looked in her wardrobe, most of her clothes had gone too. So had her old carpetbag that she used to take when she accompanied the poor children to the seaside for an overnight stay. She did enjoy that."

"You believe she has gone to the seaside?" Solomon asked.

"Hardly," Mrs. Lloyd said disparagingly. "Not without telling us. She had not asked my husband or me for the money to travel."

"Then she did not have means of her own?"

"No. We make her an allowance of course, though it has to be small, for otherwise she would waste *pounds* on her wretched charities—which, as far as I can see, give far too much to the thieves and loafers who should be doing a decent day's work to keep themselves and their families."

Solomon let that one go. "When she went to the seaside with her poor children, where did she go?"

"I don't actually know," Mrs. Lloyd said in surprise.

Jemimah looked humbler, if not ashamed. "Neither do I. Isn't that shocking?"

"Did Miss Lloyd join you in the drawing room after dinner?" Solomon asked.

"Yes," Mrs. Lloyd replied.

"No," Jemimah said at the same time. She glanced at her mother. "That is, I don't think so. I didn't particularly notice because I have a great deal on my mind just now."

"My sister-in-law is so quiet, one doesn't always notice her," Mrs. Lloyd added.

"So, you didn't actually notice whether she joined you last night or not?" Solomon pressed.

"I assumed she had," Mrs. Lloyd said. "She generally does."

"But the last time you actually *recall* seeing her was at dinner? She *was* at dinner?"

"Yes!" Jemimah said, triumphantly, apparently unaware of his sarcasm. "For she dropped her fork with a terrible clatter and we had to distract Papa before he—er…got angry," she muttered, avoiding her mother's gaze.

"But you did not see her after that? No one went to say goodnight to her?"

"We respect her privacy," Mrs. Lloyd said stiffly. "If she is in her bedchamber, that is clearly what she desires."

"Then you and Miss Lloyd are not in the habit of visiting each other's bedchambers?"

"No," Mrs. Lloyd said haughtily. "Ours was not that kind of relationship."

"And yet you must have known each other for more than twenty years. How many of those has she spent in your house?"

"All of them. My husband decided to let our country estate, so she could not stay there. When we have gone back there between lets for a month or so, she comes with us, of course."

"I see… Well, thank you for your time. I shall just go and have another word with your servants, if you don't mind." He paused, his hand on the doorknob, and glanced back. "One more thing. Have either of you met a Mr. Joshua Clarke?"

"No," Mrs. Lloyd replied after the briefest pause.

Jemimah frowned. "Isn't he Papa's solicitor?"

"No, that's Clark*son*," her mother said impatiently.

"Oh. So it is. Sorry, Mr. Grey. Please find the old thing. We miss her."

Solomon rather doubted that, although of course they were used to her, and there was a genuine if mild affection in Jemimah's voice, at least. It looked to him very much as if Audrey Lloyd had left the house of her own volition, avoiding family and servants. And he wasn't altogether sure he blamed her.

Had the worm turned? Had she somehow found out that the treasure was in Clarke's possession and *shot* him for it?

He couldn't truly imagine the vague, charitable, kind woman doing anything so violent. And yet she had lied to him about Clarke's sister. Had she discovered that Clarke was Samuels the carpenter from the *Queen of the Sea* and guessed that he was the thief? Knowing she would get no share of the treasure from her brother, had she decided to take it and flee to a new life? Perhaps she had merely meant to threaten, and Clarke had attacked her and the gun had gone off.

Where the devil had she got a gun?

"Good afternoon, Mr. Grey," said a voice from above.

He realized he had been walking along the landing toward the flight of stairs that led upward to the bedrooms, not down to the kitchen as he'd originally intended. Rached gazed down at him from a stair halfway up. She looked rather more serious than when he'd seen her before.

"Good afternoon," he replied. "I believe you are just the person I wish to see. Can you take me to your aunt's room?"

She turned and climbed the stairs two at a time. So did Solomon.

"When did *you* last see your aunt?" he asked casually.

"At teatime yesterday. *My* teatime. She was on her way to

change for dinner, although I'm not quite sure why she bothers, for her gowns all look the same. I wanted to buy her a new one with my share of the treasure money—a lovely bright blue to match her eyes."

Now he thought of it, Miss Lloyd really did have rather bright blue eyes, despite their continually vague expression. Or was it a mask rather than an expression?

"That was a kind thought," he said. "Were you all to be given a share of the treasure, then?"

"So I understood. Sydney says he only ever meant to keep it himself, though, even the quarter Sydney was promised for helping to find it. *Our* shares were to be in better food, new clothes, a governess, and even freedom from the bailiffs."

Solomon blinked. "Did you mind?"

"Only about Aunt's dress, because I knew Mama would forget."

"You are an observant creature, aren't you?" he said as Rachel opened the door at the end of the narrowing passage, next to the servants' stairs. He followed her into a room that he suspected was smaller than hers. "I don't suppose you noticed anyone leaving the house yesterday evening?"

"No, I didn't. Well, apart from Harry the footman, who's courting the upstairs maid two doors down." She took a deep breath. "I think she left yesterday evening, immediately after dinner when Papa was in his study and Mama and Jemimah were in the drawing room. The servants would have been clearing up after dinner, and it would have been easy for her to escape unnoticed."

Having cast his eyes around the meager, tidy room that yet had an air of emptiness, he returned his gaze to Rachel. "Why that time in particular? Why not any time up until Garrick locked the outside doors?"

"I went up to see her before I went to bed. I sometimes do. And last night I wanted to ask her to come with Jemimah and me on our expedition. She didn't answer when I knocked or when I called, so I glanced in and the room was in darkness. I thought she'd already gone to sleep, so I left again." She dashed her hand angrily against her eyes. "We might have found her if I'd only thought, and told someone, and—"

"Did you tell your father of it this morning?"

"Yes, but he didn't listen. He never does."

"Do you want to search the room with me?" he offered on impulse.

"If you like, though we already did. There's only a shawl with holes, a disintegrating chemise, and a particularly repellent gown."

"She took all her jewelry?"

"I don't think she had any. She never wore it if she did. She probably gave it to charity. She was a bit of an angel in her own way, wasn't she?"

Did angels shoot people for stolen treasure? "She does sound rather saintly. Do you happen to know if she possesses a gun of any kind? A little pistol, perhaps? Does she know how to shoot?"

Rachel stared at him. "I have no idea. I never heard about it if she could shoot, and I certainly never saw her with a pistol. I suppose she would be safer if she was armed."

"I suppose she would," Solomon said noncommittally.

He had wanted Rachel here instinctively, to stop himself feeling so much of a sneak, poking into a woman's private possessions. But it was as if the room had been wiped clean, as if Audrey Lloyd had never been there. Wherever she was and whatever she had done, she seemed to have planned it meticulously.

"Did she have no personal possessions?" he asked with odd frustration.

"She had the little wood carvings that were pretty. A dolphin, a mermaid that we thought looked awfully like her." Rachel cast a sweeping glance around the room, as though she might have missed them before. "They've gone too. They wouldn't have taken up much space."

As a last resort, Solomon hefted up the mattress. Then he looked under the bed.

Sighing, he sat on it. "I believe your aunt took poor children to the seaside sometimes."

"She did. Quite often, so that all the children could get a chance. I asked to go once because it sounded great fun, but Mama would not let me."

"Where did she take them?" he asked.

"I'm not sure. I want to say Folkestone, but actually, I don't know why. Someone else may have mentioned it."

The railway went to Folkestone from Tower Bridge. Or was it Waterloo? Either way, the trains connected with the ferry to Boulogne. It was the most convenient way to get from London to France. "I shall look into that. Thank you. Rachel…you once mentioned to me in passing that in her youth, your aunt had been disappointed in love. Who with?"

"I don't know," Rachel said with regret. "She only referred to it obliquely, and when I asked my parents, they denied knowing what I was talking about."

"Perhaps they didn't."

"No, I expect he wasn't good enough for Papa. He preferred the *appearance* of a spinster sister to a mésalliance."

Because that way he could blame Audrey for the failure? Solomon suspected that was what Rachel thought, though she was too loyal—just—to say it.

"Have you ever met Captain Tybalt?"

"Papa's sea captain? What on earth makes you ask that?"

"A shade too innocent," he observed dryly. "I imagine you have contrived to make the acquaintance of all your parents' friends. And your siblings'."

"Well, I did speak to him once or twice. I was curious—the captain being the person most in control of Papa's safety during his expeditions."

"What did you think of him?"

She considered. "Too polite. I didn't *dis*like him, but he never smiled as though he meant it. To be fair, though, many people are not amused to be accosted by a nosy child, especially people who cone on business."

"Then he was never a dinner or a party guest?"

"Oh, no. To Papa, he was staff."

"Do you think your aunt might have known him?"

Her eyes widened. "I never considered it, but I suppose she might have. She is involved with a seamen's charity, and Captain Tybalt… I have this idea that Papa knew him in the country."

"On the estate? So if your father knew him, so might your aunt?"

"It's more than possible. Have I said something helpful?"

"Very helpful," he assured her, standing. "One more question about your observations, Miss Rachel. What do you think of Ben Devine?"

"Oh, we've known him forever," she said dismissively. "He's too used to following Sydney around, but otherwise I don't mind him." She frowned. "I wouldn't marry him, though."

"I wouldn't let your sister do so either, if I were you. Not for a few years, at least."

"Wild oats," Rachel said with a vague yet wise nod. "Where are you off to now? Can I help?"

"Do you know where Sydney is?"

"We can see if he's in his room."

CHAPTER FIFTEEN

S OLOMON HAD NO objection to invading Sydney's privacy. Part of him really wanted to knock the cub down, hurt him for what he had said about Constance. But then, it was not so different from what the rest of the world said, only the world would never say it to him, not with impunity. Besides which, he was aware that some of his unusually short temper was down to David. Whether or not this Johnny was David—and he was beginning to think not—he would have to come to terms eventually with the reality that he would never find him. The idea that David might not *want* to find him was almost as unbearable as imagining what had happened to him all those years ago.

None of that was Sydney's fault, and Solomon was not known as a cool head for nothing. So he was perfectly in control of his temper when Rachel knocked on Sydney's door.

"Sydney, are you in there?"

The door was wrenched open to reveal a scowling Sydney, who looked as if he'd been catching up on very necessary sleep. "Go away!"

"I can't," Rachel said without any pretense of apology. "I brought Mr. Grey."

By then, Sydney had already seen Solomon. His color fluctuated and a wide array of expressions sped across his face, making them impossible to read.

He tried for the high moral ground. "Mr. Grey. I'm sure my

father is delighted you could spare us the time."

"Are you?" Solomon said coolly. "I'm sure you will be equally delighted to hear that Mrs. Silver, while sustaining severe injury in your father's service, is likely to make a full recovery."

He said it to gain a reaction, to judge Sydney's complicity in the attack, which had surely to be connected to the theft of the treasure.

But Sydney rubbed his forehead in a bafflement that looked genuine. "Mrs. Silver was attacked? How? By whom? Is it related to my aunt's disappearance?"

"Almost certainly. May I ask you a few questions about your aunt?"

Sydney held the door wide. "I can hardly say no, can I? Go away, troublesome child." He grasped Rachel by the arm and whisked her outside the door. She barely had time to cast Solomon a look that said quite clearly, *You see what I have to put up with?* before her brother closed the door with finality.

As Solomon had guessed, Sydney's bedchamber was much larger and more comfortable than Audrey's.

"Do you happen to know if your aunt had—or ever had—any admirers?" he asked, refocusing his attention on the young man, who threw himself into an armchair in an attitude he clearly meant to be insolent. Solomon remained standing.

"Suitors, do you mean?" Sydney said with some amusement. "It's hard to imagine, but maybe she did when she was young."

"She is not so very old," Solomon pointed out. "What age is she? Thirty-five, thirty-eight or so?"

"I suppose. Something like that."

"Was she acquainted with Captain Tybalt?"

Sydney raised his eyebrows. "I can't think of any reason she would be."

"But to the best of your knowledge," Solomon said patiently, "*was* she?"

"No. Though she did come on board with Mama, just before we disembarked. I don't think either of them spoke to Tybalt."

"Did you know him? Before you set sail, I mean."

"Well, my father introduced him when we were planning the expedition."

"You didn't meet him before then? At your family's country home, perhaps?"

Sydney scratched his head. "No, but then, I've hardly ever been there. Mostly, we let it. You should talk to my father."

"I will. Rachel seems to think your father forbade Miss Lloyd to marry a man he considered unsuitable. Do you know anything about that?"

"Lord, no, but he's a terrible snob, my father. I could easily imagine it, though Rachel *is* a child with a large imagination." Sydney glanced up suddenly. "Good Lord, you don't think Aunt Aud's suitor was Tybalt, do you?"

"Is there any reason it couldn't be?"

"Yes," Sydney said. "My father still speaks to him. If you haven't noticed, he's not a forgiving man."

"What if the price of your father's continuing to employ him was that he stay away from Miss Lloyd?"

Sydney closed his mouth. "I did hear there was some trouble in Tybalt's past. So maybe he was desperate for the work. Seemed a good fellow to me, though. Some difficult sailing, too, I don't mind telling you."

"Did Joshua Clarke seem like a good fellow, too?"

Sydney looked bewildered. "Who is Joshua Clarke?"

"You might know him as Samuels. Ship's carpenter aboard the *Queen of the Sea*."

"Was he? Didn't you mention him before?"

"He helped move your trunks and bags and the treasure chest out of your cabin and your father's, before everything was carried up onto the deck for your leaving the ship."

Sydney's face cleared. "I remember him now. He didn't do much of the carrying, though. Left that to the younger men, the one with the funny name and the fellow we picked up in Madagascar."

"Johnny," Solomon said, still watching him.

"Yes? I believe you're right. They loaded it all onto the carriage for us, too."

"Think back, if you please. When you had packed and closed your trunks, did they *all* sit in the gangway with the treasure chest?"

"They were all there, with my father's baggage, when I went up on deck. Except the treasure chest. The carpenter fellow was helping Papa tie the chest shut, since the clasp had broken."

"Were Captain Tybalt's bags there, too?"

"I don't *think* so."

"Very well. When you went up on deck, did you leave Johnny and Squibbs with the bags?"

"Yes, I think… No, wait, they went up ahead of me, hauling one of my father's trunks between them. Not the treasure chest. And my father came up himself a moment or two later."

Leaving Samuels alone with the treasure… Solomon's skin prickled with a sense of resolution tantalizingly close. "Did Johnny go straight back down for the next trunk?"

"No, Tybalt shouted him over to the other end of the deck about something or other."

Was that deliberate? Were Tybalt and Samuels in this together? Was it Tybalt's revenge for being denied Audrey Lloyd as his wife? Had Audrey eloped with Tybalt? And had Tybalt killed Samuels-Clarke to avoid having to give him any of the treasure? And to leave no witnesses behind…

Were Tybalt and Audrey together in Paris now, selling bits and pieces of treasure to finance the rest of their journey to wherever they wished to go?

He could *almost* see it. Almost. He could well imagine Audrey's desire for freedom from this house, where she was neglected and confined as an embarrassing spinster aunt. But he needed Constance's insight.

And he needed to know *how* the treasure had got from its original chest into the replica made by Samuels-Clarke during the return voyage. The man might have had time to move the treasure itself—at a pinch—but surely someone would have noticed the fake chest being lugged down there? There seemed to have been nowhere it could have been hidden.

"So when did Johnny and Squibbs bring up the other baggage?" Solomon asked.

"Oh, not long after."

"In what order?"

"Lord, I don't remember," Sydney snapped. "I wasn't really paying attention—more concerned with getting off the damned ship where I'd been rotting for the better part of a year!"

"How many trunks did you have on board?"

"Just one, and a bag or two."

"I don't suppose," Solomon said without much hope, "that you have the trunk and bags here in this room?"

"I do, as a matter of fact. We seem to have less servants every time I turn around. Discovering the treasure was meant to change all that."

Clearly it had never entered Sydney's head that he could remove the items himself and put them in the attic or wherever such things were stored in this house. But he rose without fuss, went to the far side of his bed, and pulled a large trunk into the middle of the room. He opened it without being asked and spread his hands like a stage conjurer displaying the emptiness of his vessel. Inside were only a couple of empty, soft leather bags.

"How full was it?" Solomon asked, with the inkling of a possibility nudging his mind.

"About half, I suppose. My father wouldn't let me take much, in case we found *masses* of treasure to bring home. I thought he was delusional at the time, and in fact, I came back with less than I'd started with. I threw out a coat and several shirts that were damaged beyond repair."

"And the bags?" Solomon asked.

"Empty," Sydney said wryly. "Again, my father insisted I take them."

Was Sydney deliberately—or accidentally—pushing suspicion onto his father? Implying Lloyd himself had planned to hide the treasure elsewhere in the luggage?

"And they were equally empty when you unpacked here?"

"I can only assume so," Sydney said. "The servants unpacked everything."

"Your father had two trunks, according to the seamen I spoke to."

Sydney's smile was cynical. "A mark of status. Though, of course, his trunks were slightly smaller than mine. Tell me, how is any of this helping my aunt?"

"I'll tell you when I know. Thank you for your time."

QUESTIONING THE LLOYDS' servants confirmed Solomon's belief that Miss Lloyd had left the house almost immediately after dinner. Before he tried to untangle his thoughts and theories, preferably with Constance, if she was up to such discussions, he dropped into the study once more.

Lloyd scowled at him. "Good God, are you still here? You should be out *there*, finding my poor sister!" He flung one arm toward the window, indicating, presumably, the rest of the world.

"I shall be, in just a few minutes. I have been collecting clues as to where she went."

"She did not leave voluntarily, sir!" Lloyd exclaimed, clearly affronted by the very idea.

"There is no evidence of visitors or of any struggle," Solomon pointed out. "In fact, she seems to have planned her exit quite carefully to give herself maximum time before her disappearance was noticed. It was probably her bad luck that your daughters chose that morning to go to her room early. Otherwise, it might have been this evening before anyone commented on her absence."

Lloyd opened his mouth to deny any such claim, then bit it back and said only, "In which case, she must have been coerced in some other way."

"Or misled, perhaps. To find her, I need to know something of her past. Particularly when you lived in the country. I think Samuels, who was then known as Clarke, came from your estate."

"Good God man, it's possible, but how can I be expected to keep track of such people?"

"Then you truly didn't recognize Samuels aboard the *Queen*?"

"Of course I didn't!"

"What about Captain Tybalt?"

"Of course I knew Tybalt—he's captained my ship many times."

"Did he aspire to your sister's hand in marriage?"

Again, irascible denial glared out of his eyes. Then the anger died abruptly and they widened. "Good God. You think Tybalt is responsible for this outrage? *And* the theft?"

"Both are possibilities I need to look into at the very least. If Tybalt was denied the wife he wanted, he had a grudge against you."

"We had an agreement," Lloyd said roughly. "He would stay away from Audrey and I would continue to employ him. Without me, he could not support himself, let alone a wife. No one else would give him a ship. He lost one, you know—his fault. No one else would employ him."

"But you were prepared to risk it?"

"I took a chance the first time," Lloyd admitted. "But in fact he's damned good, and though he has some difficulty getting crew, those that do sail with him respect him. If it wasn't so, I'd certainly never have risked taking my son".

"So you are Tybalt's only means of support?"

"Probably. I send him small commissions from others from time to time, in between my own voyages."

"How did he meet your sister?"

"At first? Some assembly ball in Portsmouth twenty years ago, when she was a girl. Naturally, she didn't look at him, though I could see *he* was smitten. I expect you find that odd, but she was damned pretty in her day."

"And you had better plans for her."

"I did," Lloyd said ruefully. "Though none of them came to anything. I expect that's why, when they met again here at this house, she actually considered him."

"Did he ask for her hand?"

Lloyd nodded. "That's when we made our agreement."

"What did Miss Lloyd think of that?"

"She never knew. Just that I rejected him. She understood he could never be accepted by the family—a disgraced merchant seaman, for goodness' sake! But she was so desperate not to remain a spinster that she would have taken him. Not against my wishes, of course."

"Of course," Solomon said expressionlessly, though he suspected her desperation was more to get out of this house than to attain the status of a wife.

Lloyd was staring at him. "You think she's gone to Tybalt!"

"It is a possibility, no more. I am going to his house now."

"I'm coming with you," Lloyd said grimly, springing to his feet.

"No," Solomon said. "That would not be helpful at this stage. You could spoil any hope of ever getting your treasure back." It was the only threat he could think of that might keep Lloyd away from Tybalt in the short term. "I shall report as soon as I have evidence." Hopefully with Miss Lloyd in tow.

FIRST, THOUGH, SOLOMON took a hackney to Tybalt's house. The light was fading, as it did so early in winter, and there was a cold drizzle in the air. At first, no one answered his knock, until he kept up a continuous barrage that caused heads to poke angrily out of neighboring windows, roundly cursing him.

The front door flew open and a large woman with her hair tied up in a scarf glared at him, her raw-boned hands clenched into fists. "What d'you want, making that racket? He ain't here!"

His stomach dove. "Where is Captain Tybalt? Has he gone back to sea?" *Please, no, not yet…*

"What's it to you?"

"I owe him something," Solomon said cunningly.

"Tough. He don't tell me where he's going." She would have shut the door in his face if he hadn't been ready for the move. He caught the edge of the door in one hand and inserted his boot to prevent it closing.

The woman looked slightly stunned.

"And you are?" he demanded.

"I'm just the bloody cleaning woman!"

Why would he need the cleaning woman if he had gone to sea? "When will he be back?"

"He didn't say."

"Then when did he leave?"

"Couple of hours ago, maybe," she answered with reluctance. "If you've got something for him, I'll take it in."

Solomon held her gaze. "I'll give it to the lady."

The woman looked genuinely confused. "What lady? There's no lady here."

Reluctantly, Solomon believed her.

He touched his hat, removed his foot from the danger of violence, and told the waiting hackney to take him back to Grosvenor Square and Constance.

CAPTAIN TYBALT, HAVING alighted from the train at Folkestone Harbor, left the station against two tides of people, one swarming in the direction of the Boulogne ferry, and the other who had just got off the ship to return by railway to London and all points beyond.

After a moment's hesitation, he turned away from the town. He knew her well enough to try the beach first. It was pebbly rather than sandy, but still a pretty place from which to look out to sea as the sun went down. Even in the drizzle that seemed to have followed him from London.

It took him some time, and it wasn't the pleasantest of strolls, with the wind off the sea freezing the moisture on his face and hurting his ears. How come he never noticed such discomforts at sea, when they were so miserable on land? The relentless drizzle formed a semitransparent mist in front of his eyes.

Since the weather had driven most people indoors, he followed the one speck he could make out in the distance until it resolved into the unmistakable, endearingly untidy shape of Audrey Lloyd. She wore a surprisingly bright shawl over her old bonnet to keep off the rain. Or as the symbol of the brave new life she had chosen.

He wished she had chosen it—he wished they both had—seven years ago.

She seemed to become aware of his footsteps on the shifting pebbles, for she halted and turned quickly to face him, almost losing her footing.

He reached out to catch her arm and she stumbled back from instinct, before he steadied her. She peered through her rain-misted spectacles, looking surprised in that vague yet unafraid way of hers that was quite unique.

"Captain Tybalt," she said with a smile.

He raised his hat. "Miss Lloyd. May I join you? And may I further suggest we turn around and seek some shelter?"

"Yes," she said willingly enough, accepting his proffered arm.

"They know you've gone," Tybalt said. "Your nieces found you out this morning."

"Did they?" she said wistfully, then smiled again. "Don't

worry, I'm not going back."

He had never seen her eyes so determined. Nor were they vague in the slightest. There had always been more to Audrey than the obvious, and the world—including Tybalt—had been unbelievably foolish not to realize it.

"I'm glad you've come," she said. "I have been so worried."

CHAPTER SIXTEEN

C ONSTANCE, HAVING SLEPT for a couple of hours, still had a horribly sore head, inside and out. But she was restless about being in bed while Solomon was on the case, and her friends would not lot her get up, even into the chair. She tried arguing and pleading and ordering, but she had taught them too well and none of them gave in.

"Can't you see this inaction is making me feverish?" she said at last.

"No it ain't," said Fran, feeling her forehead to be on the safe side. "Just relax. He'll be here soon enough."

How dare she think I'm so desperate to see him? She glared at poor Fran, but the trouble was, the girl was right. She *was* desperate to see Solomon, and not just to find out what was going on. She also worried for him. The murder of Joshua Clarke and the attack on her in his house had turned the case into one of acute danger and violence.

Eventually, Fran consented to bring her the small writing desk, but when Constance tried to write anything down, her head hurt and her eyes would not focus. She shoved it away in more fright than anger. It seemed she was more hurt than she thought.

Then why does Solomon not come?

At around half past six, Janey whisked into the room.

"'Ere! What the bloody hell you been up to? What you sodding done to yourself?"

She looked so terrified that Constance didn't even tell her off for swearing. The girl only lapsed now at moments of extreme stress.

"Hurt my head," Constance said carelessly.

"Someone hurt it for her," Fran said dryly, "but she'll be fine, Dr. Donaldson said, if she just stays in bed for a day."

"And I'm counting the wretched hours," Constance said with a grumpiness that seemed to relieve Janey of the worst of her fears.

"You here for a bit, Janey?" Fran asked.

"Yes, I'll stay with her," Janey said with a warning glare at Constance, presumably in case she argued.

"Then I'll go and get meself some nosh before the punters turn up."

"Did you see Mr. Grey?" Constance asked Janey as soon as Fran had closed the door.

"Nah. I locked up the office. But he sent a note to say you were fine but recovering in bed from an accident. The girls is dead worried about you. Scared us all to death, you have."

"Sorry," Constance said meekly. "How is the case of Bibby's locket?"

Janey glowered some more, lowering herself onto the bed. "Good and bad. Found the cove what nicked it—well, he found it on the ground and kept it. I said it was Bibby who'd lost it, and he said she can't have it back 'cause he's giving it to his wife for her birthday! There's worse scum than thieves out there, I'll tell you that much."

"Sadly, there are," Constance agreed. "Who is this man?"

Janey grimaced. "Customer of another girl further down the street. Young fella, thinks he's better than us, drops by every once in a while, apparently."

"Why don't you take Bibby and this other girl round to his house, bump into him and his wife on their way to church? I expect he'll give it back quick enough just be rid of you."

Janey seemed much struck by this suggestion. "I thought we was supposed to be honest."

"It's not dishonest to walk in the man's vicinity. What he reads into it is his own affair."

"So it is," Janey agreed, grinning.

They ate a companionable meal together while the guests began to arrive in the house. He wouldn't come, now. Constance knew that, and she hated the longing within her, the emptiness of disappointment. Love came with vulnerabilities she had never imagined. Only, after his tenderness in finding her in Clarke's house and bringing her home, she had thought he would come back today…

Angry with herself for being so pathetic, she told herself he knew she was safe here among her friends and protectors. It was the case she needed to hear about, nothing more.

Eventually, Bibby appeared in the doorway, grinned to see Janey there too, and said, "It's my turn to sit with you, ma'am, only Mr. Grey is here. Should he wait?"

Constance threw back the bedclothes, more from instinct that any real intention to get out of bed. Janey caught them and pulled them back up, glaring.

"Send him in, Bibby," Constance said, with a reasonable effort at calm. Inside, she was astonished. Had he really walked through the front door among all their usual gentlemen? Or snuck through the kitchen and up the back stairs with Bibby, the way Constance herself entered when she didn't want to be seen by customers?

Janey stood up as he walked in. He still wore his overcoat and carried his hat. Back stairs, then. To her anxious eyes, he looked cold, and air of excitement cut through the concern in his eyes.

"Watch her, sir, she's getting restive," Janey said. "Ring if you need us. And she's not to be alone until the morning. Bibby."

He didn't ask Janey for a health update, though he did spare her a searching glance before his attention returned to Constance.

He walked across the room and sat where Janey had been. He took her hand. Warmth flooded her. He *had* come.

"How are you?" he asked, examining her bandage and then

her face.

"Better, I think, as long as no one touches my head." The door closed behind the other woman, so she added, "You can kiss me if you like."

He smiled. "With no hands," he said, spreading them wide as he bent and kissed her mouth.

"Your lips are warm," she said huskily. "But the rest of you is cold and tired. Why don't you come up beside me and be comfortable?"

As though he had been waiting for the invitation, he kicked off his shoes and leaned against the pillows beside her, his long legs stretched out in front of him. Then he took her hand again.

A man on her bed, even if not quite in it. A man's hat and coat cluttering her feminine room. Unprecedented. And rather wonderful, considering it was *this* man. Intimate…

"Did you come up the back stairs from the area door?"

"No. I came in the front, all ready to waste a great deal of time persuading your extraordinarily large footmen to admit me, but they merely sent for the girl who brought me up the main stairs without a quibble. Did you warn them to expect me?"

"Actually, no. I didn't think you would come at this time. I suppose word has got around. It seems you are approved, since you brought me home this morning."

"Not because I am your husband-to-be?"

Husband. Good grief, I shall have a husband. "I wonder if this has ever happened in my family before?" she murmured.

"It certainly happened in mine. We have a history of odd marriages."

She knew his mother had been a Maroon, the descendant of an escaped slave, who had married his plantation-owning father. "What was she like, your mother?"

He leaned his head back against the pillows, close to hers but not touching. She wondered if he would answer.

"Warm," he said at last. "Fierce." He smiled. "And funny."

"Was she happy?" Constance asked.

"Yes, I think so. Most of the time. She was happy by nature, and against the odds, she did love my father. But it was not always easy for either of them. There was prejudice, ill feeling. Some of my father's acquaintances regarded her as a slave. Some of hers regarded him as a monster, and her as a traitor of some kind. It used to worry him that if he died first there would be no one to protect her. There was often trouble between the Maroons and the white people... But in the end, she went first and my father never married again."

"Was there prejudice against you too?"

"Some," he said with a shrug. "Not so much."

"And here? In London?"

"Here in London, not everyone notices or cares. I could be from anywhere. I am not above exploiting that for business reasons, though I never hide my origins."

"Why should you?" she said stoutly.

He turned his head against the pillow and met her gaze. "Why should you?"

"You've met my mama," she said lightly.

"I like your mama. She gave me you."

She searched his eyes. He was telling her not to be ashamed of who she was, because *he* was not. They were both oddities in their own ways. And somehow, they had found each other. And fitted.

She must have still been weak from her head injury, for her throat tightened with foolish tears. She swallowed them back as best she could.

"What of the case?" she asked rather desperately. "What have you been doing all day? Have you found Miss Lloyd?"

"No, but I have found some rather interesting connections. Between Audrey Lloyd and Captain Tybalt, and between Tybalt and Samuels, also called Clarke. I have also discovered the hackney driver who picked Audrey up in Oxford Street last night and took her to the railway station. I think she's in Folkestone."

Constance sat up straight and winced. "Folkestone? Why

Folkestone?"

"Because Tybalt is there with the treasure. So are regular packets to France. And she was at the railway station just in time to catch the ten o'clock boat train."

"Then what are you doing here?" she demanded, nudging him as though pushing him off the bed. "She could already be in France!"

"I'm tired," he said calmly, and she smiled, because she knew it was a lie. He was here with her because he wanted, maybe even needed, to be.

"Tell me," she instructed him, and he gave her an account of his interviews with Lloyd, Garrick, Rachel, and Sydney, his failure to find Tybalt at home, and the conclusions he had drawn.

"So Tybalt stole the treasure," she said with excitement, "motivated by resentment against Lloyd and love of Audrey. He used Samuels to make a replica chest, which he hid in his own cabin until he managed to switch it with the real one just before everyone disembarked. Oh! What did he fill the fake one with to make it seem so heavy?"

"Who knows? Probably the rubbish still piled beside it in the strong room. Stones he'd collected from various beaches on their travels, wood and rusting tools, general rubbish from the ship. I think a lot of the weight probably came from the thickness of the wood itself. Sydney would never have carried the original chest, so he had nothing to compare the replica with when he carried it upstairs from the drawing room. It's more surprising the seamen didn't notice the discrepancy when they unloaded it from the ship. But they were probably concentrating more on getting to the Crown and Anchor."

"Tybalt was last to leave the ship," Constance mused. "So he had as much time as he wanted to unload the treasure and dispose of the original chest. And *he* shot Samuels so he could never give away how he had performed the trick." She frowned. "But then, why did Clarke change his name to Samuels on board the ship?"

"I suspect because Lloyd might have recognized his name as one of a previous tenant's—not realizing that the Lloyds never notice the names of people they consider beneath them. He even grew a beard for the role."

Constance nodded. "Then it was Tybalt who hit me, too? Why did he hang around so long? Clarke must have been dead for hours to be that cold—though, to be sure, he was in a draft from the partially open door. Had Clarke kept the treasure for him? Did he suspect Clarke was about to abscond with it?"

"It's possible, though I can't see him trusting the man with that much temptation in his house for several days. Perhaps he was looking for and removing any connection between himself and Clarke. He certainly made a mess looking for something."

"Presumably, he found it and is now at least on his way to France with his lady love and the means to support her and himself in some style." She frowned because it wasn't quite right. "Whatever her affection for Tybalt—or even her perfectly understandable desperation to get out of that house—I can't see Audrey countenancing the murder of anyone, let alone a man she knew."

"No, I doubt he'll tell her that part."

"And why did she lie about Clarke's nonexistent sister?" Her frown cleared. "Aha! She and Tybalt met in Clarke's house, to throw her controlling brother or anyone else off the scent. Poor Miss Tybalt... Solomon, we have to stop her marrying him! For her sake as well as ours. A wife cannot testify against her husband, can she? And without her, we have no evidence of Tybalt's motive."

"Actually, at this point, we have no evidence at all," Solomon pointed out, "only speculation."

"Then we need to go to Folkestone tomorrow—and on to France if necessary."

Solomon's eyebrows flew up. "You have a passport?"

She scowled. "No, actually. I have difficulties with official paperwork. But I can go as far as Folkestone."

"We shall see," he said smoothly. "In the morning."

It was not an outright refusal, and she loved him for that. Even while she knew that she would go anyway, with his escort or without. Providing she felt well enough not to disgrace herself. She wondered if she could rebind the dressing on her head, so that the bandage was hidden by her hat. Just as she had done the last time a murderer had hit her over the head.

"Solomon? Do you think he'll do away with her, too?"

He shook his head. "I would say she is the one person who is safe with him. He could have fled to France days ago if he was not waiting for. He didn't need her to steal the treasure."

"On the face of it, she is an unlikely Helen of Troy figure," Constance mused.

"I imagine love is never very explicable, let alone convenient. Though I'm finding it very convenient right now." He kissed her fingers and spread them on his warm, muscular thigh, his large hand over hers.

Her skin prickled. So did the pit of her stomach. And it was not remotely unpleasant.

She closed her eyes. *I like being with you, Solomon Grey.* She didn't think she said the words aloud, but she might have, for she felt his lips on her forehead and smiled without opening her eyes.

Then she snapped them open. "When are you leaving? If I fall asleep, will you wake me?"

"I'm not leaving. I shall stay with you here."

That was worth a smile too, though she was too sleepy and much, much too comfortable to know if her lips obeyed.

SHE WOKE AT some point during the night to find his head still on the pillow beside her, his face toward her, his breath sweet on her skin. His arm was draped over her, with all the covers still between them. He lay on top of the bed, with his coat and a blanket draped over himself.

She wondered at his determination to treat her with such propriety. Some might have called it priggish, in the circumstances, but she didn't think he was priggish at all. He was no stranger to women. With her, he was different. And he wanted to be different to her, nothing like the other men who had used her years ago, and who now paid to use her willing friends.

Very lightly, she touched his face with her fingertips, then burrowed under his blanket and coat to place her arm around his warm body. At once, he shifted closer without waking and gave a small grunt of annoyance at all the covers between them. But it was not enough to wake him. His arms tightened around her, as though he were trying to gather her closer, and then relaxed.

Every night, she thought in wonder. She would have this closeness—*more* closeness—every night, once they were married. It was a delightful knowledge to hold as she drifted back off to sleep.

SOLOMON WOKE EARLY, as he always did. It was sweet to feel her arm around his shoulder, and they seemed to be pressed as closely together as they could get with all the blankets between them. Desire was not his friend. He knew she would be happy if he got properly into bed with her, and God knew he would probably have given in to the temptation had she not received such an injury yesterday.

Instead, he lay as he was, listening to the rhythm of her breathing. He had dreamed last night that her fingers caressed her cheek… Perhaps they had. It was not light yet, so he could not make out her features. Nor did he wish to disturb her rest with the clumsiness of his touch, let alone his desire. So he lay still at her side, just feeling her presence. This remarkable woman, so improbably chaste and pure of heart. He had never found compassion like Constance's before, all the more important for being exercised in secret behind the brash exterior of the hardheaded courtesan.

He lay watching her until the night lightened into dawn and he began to see her features. She was uniquely beautiful, alluring in her fine nightgown with her hair spilling decadently across her forehead and breast. And she was his.

Protectiveness surged and had to be calmed, for she did not want that controlling kind of protection, and she did not deserve it. They could only protect each other.

Her long lashes fluttered. She saw him watching her and smiled. He had to kiss her. How long that might have gone on, he never discovered, for a knock sounded at the door.

Reluctantly, he threw off his blanket and climbed into his rumpled coat as he crossed the bedroom and opened the door.

It was Janey, bearing a tray of coffee and an expression of anxiety. "How is she?"

"She slept well," he managed. "For the rest, we shall see in a little while."

"I've brought coffee. Do you want breakfast together, or do you have to get home?"

Solomon ran his hand over the rough stubble of his jaw and eyed the limpness of his crushed coat with displeasure. "I do need to go home, don't I?"

"You could," Constance said, "have breakfast first."

"I believe I will," he said, glad he had given her the choice and happier yet to stay. "I want to see how you are."

"I'll open the office as usual," Janey offered, setting down the coffee pot, and leaving them to it with a pleased expression.

"She's an old romantic at heart," Constance said.

So am I, God help me.

TWO HOURS LATER, properly washed, shaved, and dressed, he was back with his comfortable, well-sprung traveling carriage. He had left Constance being examined by the doctor, and having her dressing changed. The doctor's instructions would determine whether or not she journeyed with Solomon, but he had already decided that the carriage, where he could control the speed and the number of stops, would be smoother for her than the train.

As she had pointed out in no uncertain terms, if they found Miss Lloyd in Folkestone, Constance would be a considerable asset in persuading the lady to return to her imperfect family. She would have lots to say about the possibilities for a woman's independent life without involving a man.

Not for the first time, it struck him what Constance was giving up to marry him. She currently had no fetters except the law, and *that* she was managing to get around by means of her own. Once she married him, he was legally and financially her master. The world would no doubt see it as a wealthy man ensnared by a courtesan. He knew better, and the level of her trust in him was humbling.

When the liveried footman admitted him, she was already in the entrance hall, elegantly dressed for an expedition, her bandage hidden beneath a wide-brimmed hat tied with ribbons.

"The doctor says I am quite well enough to travel," she said by way of greeting.

"Not quite, he didn't," said Sarah, materializing behind her. She appeared to be Constance's lieutenant. "What he *did* say was that a short, gentle outing with a little fresh air might be beneficial, but she's still to rest."

"Well, what else would I be doing in a carriage?" Constance asked tartly.

Solomon met Sarah's gaze, and she gave the tiniest shrug. He bowed to the inevitable, offering Constance his arm, and was rewarded with a blinding smile that took his breath away.

"I'M SURE WE would be quicker by railway," Constance said anxiously. She had removed her hat and drawn the loose hood of her warm traveling cloak over her hair instead.

"Not if we had to alight at every station because your head was so painful from all the rattling. Besides, the carriage will be handy if we have to find their lodgings in Folkestone."

"And if we find they have already gone to France?"

"Then you must take the carriage back to London—the coachman will have his instructions—while I go on to France and try to find them there."

She lapsed into silence.

He said, "We should set about adding you to my passport when we are married. Then we can go abroad on a wedding journey or whenever else we choose."

"Really? You mean we could for no reason? Just for fun?"

He knew a twinge of pity for the girl who had never known leisure time and holidays. For all her talk of happiness and friendship, they were snatched moments in the midst of work and responsibility. Even when she took her household on little jaunts into the country, they were never for more than a day. They all had their days off. Constance never did. If she was not looking after the establishment or its denizens in some way, she was investigating with him. The very idea of Constance focused only on happiness, on her own pleasure, was intoxicating.

"I look forward to it," he said intensely, and to his secret delight, she blushed.

CHAPTER SEVENTEEN

IN TALKING TO ticket collectors at Folkestone Harbour, Constance and Solomon discovered no trace of anyone like Audrey Lloyd, either alone or with a man of Tybalt's description, going forward to the Boulogne ferry.

"It doesn't mean they're not in France," Solomon said discontentedly when they had returned to the carriage. "It just means no one noticed them. But I suppose before we comb France, we should first seek them out in the innumerable hotels and short-term lodging houses in the town."

Constance thought about that. "Audrey is actually quite memorable in her own way. I suspect it's only among her family that she merges into the background where they put her. The servants think well of her. Tybalt seems to have remained loyal to her for most of his adult life. Your hackney driver remembered her well enough. And so do you, judging by the descriptions of her you gave at the harbor."

"Perhaps you are right. And so we shall find her more easily."

This did not, however, prove to be the case. With Constance masquerading as Miss Lloyd's niece, and Solomon, occasionally, as her man of business who needed to speak to her urgently, they scoured the hotels and lodging houses. Their lack of success was disheartening until, toward the end of an exhausting afternoon, Solomon called a halt and insisted on taking Constance to a hotel for the night.

Constance, whose head had indeed begun to pound again, did

not argue.

"We can begin again early tomorrow morning," she said optimistically. "Shall we be Mr. and Mrs. Smith?"

Solomon did not answer, and for a moment she thought he had missed her provocative joke, for he was staring broodingly out of the carriage window. Then he suddenly straightened in his seat and thumped on the carriage roof. The coachman slowed the hired horses to a halt.

Solomon already had the door open. "It's Tybalt," he said, and flew down the road the way they had just come, slowing only to pass pedestrians without jostling them.

Constance kicked down the step and followed at a more leisurely pace. Solomon had not caught up with Captain Tybalt. In fact, he was following him from a few yards' distance, until the captain turned into a gateway right next door to the small lodging house they had just left. This one bore no sign of any purpose other than a home.

Constance, headache forgotten, hurried to catch up. Ahead of her, Solomon sped through the gate and laid a hand on Tybalt's shoulder. Tybalt spun around, jerking into the defensive posture of a man who had experienced many dangers on the world's docksides over the years.

Constance's stomach heaved with fear, but Solomon, despite the poise that told her he was ready for attack, did not react. He merely stood still, gazing down at Tybalt, who dropped his hands.

She had seen this happen before. It was as though he quelled would-be opponents with the sheer force of his presence. Not that it always worked, of course, and she was somewhat surprised that it did now, considering Tybalt had already coolly stolen from his employer, killed his partner in crime, and whacked Constance over the head.

"Mr. Grey." Tybalt sounded both surprised and bewildered. "What on earth are you doing here?"

"Looking for you," Solomon replied. "And Miss Lloyd."

Tybalt's gaze flickered to Constance, who waited now at the

gate a few paces behind Solomon. "Then let us repair next door to my own lodgings. I am only visiting here."

Tybalt even took a pace toward the gate, but Solomon did not budge, still blocking his exit.

"Let us all call on Miss Lloyd together," he suggested.

Tybalt searched Solomon's face, as though he could thus dig out his thoughts. "Why should you imagine Miss Lloyd is here?"

"Because you are," Constance said. A door opened across the road. Someone else was talking in the street. "Shall we go inside before we are observed by too many gossips?"

Tybalt glanced from her to Solomon, determination and decisiveness in his hard eyes. "She is not going back to her brother's house."

"I see no reason why she should," Constance said.

"Don't lie," Tybalt snapped. "You work for Barnabas Lloyd."

"So do you," Solomon pointed out.

"Not right now, I don't. My obligation to him ended when I left his ship a week ago."

"With his treasure," Solomon said.

Tybalt's eyes widened. "I did not take his damned—"

He was interrupted by the front door flying open.

Audrey Lloyd stood there in her untidy, ill-matched garb of dull colors, except for a brave, bright red and blue shawl worn over her coat. Behind her spectacles, she blinked rapidly at the delegation before her.

Tybalt jerked around to face her. "You had better go back inside," he barked.

She sighed. "We had better *all* go inside. I am prepared to postpone my walk."

As she turned away, Tybalt glared at Solomon and then Constance. "I won't have her upset," he growled. "Understand?"

"Perfectly," Constance said, sailing past him into the house.

Audrey led them to a small parlor at the back of the house. "Everyone else is having tea in the dining room, so this room is usually quiet at this time of day…"

The furniture consisted of a small sofa, several comfortable old armchairs, a low table, and a bookcase containing a variety of literature, from worthy tomes to cheaply bound novels and magazines.

Audrey sat on the sofa. If she expected Captain Tybalt to join her there, she was disappointed, for Constance, quite deliberately, took the place instead. Despite the woman's calmness, she was tense, her eyes shadowed from more than one sleepless night.

She was worried, as she had not been by the loss of her brother's treasure. Had she found out what a dangerous man she was tying herself to?

"Why are you here?" Audrey asked bluntly, as Solomon closed the door and leaned negligently against it.

"*I* came to escort you on your walk," Tybalt said.

"And you, Mrs. Silver? Mr. Grey? Did Barnabas send you?"

"He asked us to find you," Solomon said, and she glanced up at him quickly.

"Does he know I'm here?"

"Not yet," Constance said. "We need to know why you left first."

Audrey blinked and smiled. "I am of age, dear," she said wry-ly.

"Then no one drove you out or compelled you to come here?" Constance asked.

"Oh, dear me, no."

Quite suddenly, gazing at her, Constance thought it would not be quite so easy to compel Audrey Lloyd as she had imagined. There was a firmness about the set of her mouth, a stubbornness that was not obvious on first acquaintance.

"The thing is," Solomon said gently, "it is likely the police will be looking for you now."

"The police?" she said, startled. "Why, what do they think I have done?"

"Your visits to Mr. Clarke's sister must have been noted by someone," Constance pointed out. "Particularly since he didn't have one. It gives you a questionable connection to the murdered man."

A frown formed between her brows. "What murdered man?" she asked in what appeared to be genuine bafflement.

Solomon straightened, watching Tybalt as Constance observed Audrey. "There have been some developments in the case since you left home, ma'am. Did Captain Tybalt not tell you that Mr. Clarke was murdered?"

The lady's lips parted. She stared at him, then suddenly jumped to her feet, wringing her hands together so tightly that her knuckles were white. "Don't lie to me! Don't say such things! Oh God, *please* be lying to me!"

Even as Constance rose and caught the older woman's hand in instinctive desire to comfort, she began to think they had got everything horribly wrong.

"Who *is* this Clarke?" Tybalt demanded. He too had risen, and his frustration looked as genuine as his concern for Audrey.

"Samuels," Solomon said. "Your ship's carpenter. The one who made the duplicate chest that enabled you to steal Mr. Lloyd's treasure."

"What? I didn't take his damned… Audrey—Miss Lloyd, please don't distress yourself. Please sit down."

But Audrey seemed incapable of it. She was grasping Constance's hand so hard that it hurt, her eyes so full of anguish that it was impossible to doubt her.

"Joshua is *not* dead," Audrey whispered. "Tell me you made it up. Joshua is not dead."

"I'm sorry," Constance said helplessly. Tears were spilling unnoticed down Audrey's cheeks. "We didn't know it would upset you like this." Was the woman weeping for Clarke—whom she called Joshua—or because she suspected Tybalt of his murder?

"Did you shoot him when you took the treasure from him?" Solomon asked Tybalt.

"Dash it, I didn't even know he was dead!" Tybalt exclaimed.

"Where and when was he shot?"

"In his own home. There was no sign of the treasure, but his bag was packed—before someone flung the contents all over the room."

Audrey let out a low moan and would have collapsed had Constance not put her arm around her.

Tybalt was staring at Audrey. "*He* was the one? Samuels?"

"*What* one?" Solomon demanded, but Tybalt's attention was all on Audrey, pity and hopeless love softening his harsh face. "Captain!"

Tybalt spared him a glance. "What?" he asked without interest, returning his gaze to Audrey, now being coaxed back onto the sofa by Constance. He took a flask from his pocket, unstoppered it, and thrust it into Audrey's hand. "Drink," he said gently. "Just a spot. We have to decide what is best to do."

When he urged her hand upward, she drank obediently like a child, just one swallow. She didn't choke on its fire, but it did seem to shock her back into awareness.

"To do?" she said. "I don't care now. No wonder he didn't come…"

"You were waiting for Mr. Clarke," Constance said cautiously. "Not Captain Tybalt?"

"Then what, sir, brought *you* here?" Solomon demanded.

"I have friends in Lloyd's house who sent me word that Miss Lloyd had disappeared," the captain said.

"Garrick," Solomon guessed.

Tybalt did not deny it. "I guessed she would have come here. It's where she brought her orphans and poor children to enjoy the seaside. Her one escape from that house."

Like Constance, Solomon was clearly trying to revise their theory, taking Audrey's very odd romance with the mere carpenter into account. "You are telling us, captain, that Samuels stole the treasure without your help?"

"Of course he did," Audrey said unexpectedly. "It was my idea, but Joshua carried it out perfectly."

"*Your* idea," Constance repeated, exchanging glances with Solomon. "How did that come about?"

"I never begrudged my brother anything," Audrey told her. "I was content to give him my inheritance from my parents, along with that from my godmother and my aunt. He spent it all on his expeditions, of course, which are terribly important to him. And he has found some remarkable items. So when old Silas Cauley gave him the treasure map, I really believed the treasure was there and that Barnabas would find it. I knew Cauley, you see, through my sailors' charity. So did Joshua."

"So you came up with the idea to steal it?" Constance said gently. "Because Barnabus had taken your inheritance from you?" And with it, any chance of an independent life in a home of her own.

But Audrey's watery eyes widened. "Oh no. Well, Joshua might have. I'm afraid I only did it for revenge, because of what he did."

"Which was what?" Solomon asked, coming to sit down at last.

"He evicted the Clarkes from the land they had held for generations. Just because Joshua and I wanted to marry. Joshua had almost finished his apprenticeship, but Barnabas ended that too. Joshua went to sea for a few years to make some money, which he saved to begin his own carpentry business—or at least, that which he didn't give to his struggling family. He is very good, you know." She closed her eyes. "Was…"

"Did he make you the sculptures Rachel said were gone from your room?" Solomon asked.

She nodded. "Each time he came home, he made me one. But inevitably, we lost track of each other. I didn't know where he was until I ran into him a couple of years ago at a sailors' charity." She smiled. "We were no longer young, but it was just as it had used to be when I was seventeen. Better, because we understood so much more. We were going to get married, despite Barnabas's objections. Joshua had enough money by then to keep us both in that comfortable little house. But I knew…"

She trailed off, her eyes bleak again.

"Knew what?" Constance prompted her.

"That Barnabas would never leave us alone. He would find a way not just to cover up such a mésalliance, but to end it. He would find us, and destroy Joshua all over again. Then he—Barnabas—started talking about old Cauley's buried treasure. He decided to take Sydney with him—to make a man of him, apparently—and I knew how to do it when I saw the size of Sydney's trunk. I knew Joshua would easily be able to copy whatever vessel the treasure was found in—Cauley claimed it was wooden—and find some way to hide the real chest inside Sydney's large trunk during crucial times."

"Of course, you had been aboard the *Queen of the Sea*," Solomon said quickly. "So you knew the layout of the ship, and where the crew's quarters were in relation to the captain's and the passengers'?"

"Of course. Barnabas showed the ship off to us years ago when he first acquired it. Naturally, I had to leave the minutiae, the precise timings, to Joshua, since I couldn't predict such things with any accuracy. But I knew he would find a way, with or without using Sydney's trunk. We had a few alternative plans for different situations…

"It was easy enough for Joshua to join the crew of the *Queen*—they needed a carpenter because of the ship's state of repair. Joshua went aboard with plenty new wood, replaced the rotten pieces, and kept the old wood to make a replica chest if necessary."

"He took a risk that Lloyd wouldn't recognize him," Tybalt interjected.

"It didn't matter," Audrey said. "He grew a beard to throw him off the scent, as it were, but even if he did spot him, Barnabas would never have acknowledged him. If he noticed him at all, he would merely pat himself on the back for having kept me away from a man who had clearly never made anything of his life. In

Barnabas's view."

There seemed to be nothing anyone could say to that. Constance and Solomon exchanged another glance. Audrey seemed about to lapse back into her silent world of misery, but Captain Tybalt would not allow it.

"So how the devil *was* the theft accomplished?" he demanded. "How did he do it?"

Audrey blinked a few times, as though dredging her memory. "He made the replica chest during the voyage, roughing it up and dirtying it further in places, to make it as similar as possible to the original."

"But he never noticed the carved initials beneath the fastening plate," Constance said.

"No, until he helped Barnabas tie it closed for disembarking, he had only ever seen the chest open, with the initials covered by the plate, so he missed that until it was too late. But then, so did everyone else until you two saw it on the photograph…"

"Go on," Constance urged.

Audrey shrugged, half weary, half impatient. "Joshua picked his moment carefully that last morning, while Barnabas and Sydney were breakfasting with Captain Tybalt. Sydney was already packed, so Joshua hid the copy of the treasure chest beneath Sydney's bunk. Then he went back to his duties. There was a small chance Sydney would notice the chest beneath his bed, but Joshua didn't think it likely."

"What about the customs men who came aboard?" Solomon asked. "I understood they were very thorough."

Audrey shrugged again. "All they would have found was a rotting old chest and assumed it was just for throwing out, especially as Joshua had filled it with bits of rubbish from his workshop on board—broken tools and bits of wood, a few rocks from the island beach. When the customs officers had left the ship, Joshua was left briefly alone with all the trunks while other sailors took up the first one."

"Johnny," Constance murmured. "And Squibbs."

"Joshua then whisked the treasure chest into Sydney's trunk—or at least *heaved* it somehow. I believe it was pretty heavy, but then, Joshua was a very strong man. He brought out the fake chest from Sydney's room, and so this was the one that was taken up on deck and placed so carefully under Barnabas's jealous eyes.

"Joshua made sure he was the one to haul Sydney's trunk up. No one was paying much attention by then, because they were all so eager to get home, and I confess I played my own small part in distracting my family with particular silliness…

"So Joshua dragged Sydney's trunk to the back of the baggage line, until he was sure no one was watching. Then, more surreptitiously, he moved it to a place further out of sight, behind the wheelhouse or whatever it is called, while everyone else was on the other side of the ship waiting to disembark. He removed the treasure chest from Sydney's trunk, then returned Sydney's to its place at the back of the queue.

"Captain Tybalt had already completed his inspection of the crew's quarters, so he had no reason to do more than collect his own baggage from the deck and leave the ship when everyone else had disembarked—little knowing," she added apologetically to Tybalt, "that Joshua was still there, lurking in the crew's quarters with the treasure chest until everyone had gone. He had plenty of time to amble alone onto the deck with his rotting old chest and haul it home."

"No one noticed that Samuels was still there," Tybalt said, frowning. "*I* didn't, though I watched the men all go off in ones and twos…"

"People take Joshua for granted." Audrey stopped and swallowed. "Took," she corrected herself in a wavering voice. "But you see, it can be a strength—as you and your partner have just discovered, Mrs. Silver. Neither of you suspected me for a moment. And you only saw your way to Joshua because I had the misfortune to leave his house that day just as Mr. Grey was passing. Even then, he almost walked by me."

"My mind was certainly elsewhere," Solomon admitted. "We had pieced together much of this from bits and pieces, but you are right, we never truly suspected you. Only Captain Tybalt."

"Well, I too have a grudge against Lloyd," Tybalt admitted. "He took advantage of my fall from grace to underpay me and my crew. In fact, I wouldn't be surprised if he didn't revive the rumors against me whenever he could, just to keep my fee low. And because he never forgave me either for aspiring to his sister's hand."

"I thought he might agree to you," Audrey said in a flat, dispassionate sort of voice. "But then, I suppose he couldn't, since he had already destroyed whatever gentlemanly credentials he considered you had in the first place."

Constance looked from her to Tybalt. "According to Mr. Lloyd, you two first met at an assembly ball a long time ago."

"We did," Audrey said, "back in Portsmouth when I was young. But I turned him down then because of Joshua. It was always Joshua, you see. Until, seven years or so ago, Captain Tybalt and I met again—when Barnabas was showing us all over his ship, in fact. My life was bleak at the time, and I had lost touch with Joshua. Captain Tybalt took me to funny little tea shops and made me laugh. When he asked me to marry him this time, I said yes."

"She thought she could thus escape that house," Tybalt said ruefully. "She told me at the time her heart was still with her lost first love."

"You showed me a kindness I had forgotten," Audrey said sadly, "and I was grateful for that. I thought we could have been content together…until Barnabas refused. And then I met Joshua again…"

"And you embarked together on a piece of very clever piracy," Solomon observed.

"Was it piracy? Old Cauley had found the treasure first, or perhaps he stole it. Its true ownership is certainly moot. At any rate, Joshua and I could have traveled the world and lived very comfortably off the sale of all that gold plate and jewelry."

"Where is the treasure?" Solomon asked. It was, after all, what they had been engaged to discover.

Audrey slumped again. "I expect Barnabas has it back. He'll have taken it when he shot my Joshua."

❦

CHAPTER EIGHTEEN

SOLOMON GAZED AT Audrey. She sounded so certain, so dispassionate. But then, she was numb with old pain and new grief.

"Then he knew where Clarke lived all the time?" he said. "Did he know you went there to meet him?" If so, why was Lloyd not more suspicious when Clarke appeared among the crew of the *Queen* under a different name?

"I hadn't thought so, but obviously he did," Audrey said. "None of us is quite so clever as we imagine, it seems…"

Was it possible? Or was she simply projecting old anger onto the new crime? Solomon exchanged another glance with Constance. Oh yes, they both thought it possible. Lloyd, of all concerned, saw himself as above…

"So what is your next step?" Tybalt asked him, with a hint of aggression. "Are you going to the police with this? Or straight to Lloyd?"

"We need proof to go to the police. We shall go back to London, and I strongly suggest you and Miss Lloyd accompany us."

"She is not going back to her brother's house," Tybalt warned.

"That is Miss Lloyd's decision," Constance said flatly.

If necessary, Solomon knew, she would take Audrey to her own establishment. His mind rather boggled at the idea, though in her present state, at least, Audrey was unlikely to object or even notice that many of her companions were whores and courtesans.

In the end, both Audrey and Captain Tybalt accompanied them back to London. Neither brought any luggage.

"You don't expect her to go into Clarke's house, do you?" Tybalt said uneasily. "She can just tell you where the treasure was hidden, and you can see if it's still there."

"I want to go in," Audrey said. "I need to. The house is mine now, in any case."

Everyone looked at her in surprise.

"There is a will," she said without much interest. "Joshua made it before he sailed with the *Queen*. Accidents happen at sea, after all, and he didn't want me left with nothing, should anything happen to him."

"Do you know where his will is?" Tybalt asked. "Will the police have found it?"

"It is lodged with a solicitor. I know which one. It doesn't matter, really. I can't stay there without him." She spoke in a detached yet certain voice, as though even in her numbing grief, in the collapse of all her hopes and happiness, some things were still written in stone.

She could sell the house and live where she pleased. With a few items from the treasure...

Audrey had a point. Whatever the legal ownership of the treasure, the moral case was dubious. Silver and Grey's moral duty was not attractive either. But if Lloyd had murdered Joshua Clarke, he should pay for it—and his heir would own the treasure. Presumably Sydney. Would the son be more generous than the father, more understanding of his family's happiness?

Part of Solomon itched to go straight to Lloyd, now, to discover if he truly had retrieved the treasure from Clarke, and if he would admit it... Mostly, he worried about Constance, who was not fit for all this travel. For speed, they should have taken the train back to London, but Constance held out for the carriage to give Audrey some privacy in her grief.

Solomon and Tybalt sat opposite them, both worrying, he

expected. But at least the carriage was comfortable, the changes of horses quick and painless, even in the dark, and he was glad to see Constance sleep for a good part of the journey. Audrey closed her eyes too, some of the time, but all too often, he noticed them open and staring.

They should not be confronting Lloyd after a sleepless night… Constance must go straight home to bed while he dealt with Clarke's house, and with Lloyd…

But, of course, Constance had other ideas. She woke with the noise of the London streets, which were always busy, even so early in the morning before it was light. As she sat up straighter and fixed the angle of her cloak hood, Audrey opened her eyes too and began rummaging in a large reticule. Her fingers re-emerged clutching a key.

"What if there is still a policeman there?" Constance said.

"Then he can run and fetch his superiors," Solomon replied.

But, in fact, although the door was locked, no policeman had been left on duty to guard it. All four of the travelers alighted from the carriage, and Solomon instructed his poor coachman to wait. The groom, with whom he had shared the driving duties, was asleep upright on the box beside him.

Audrey opened Clarke's door with her key, as she must have done many times before. Her hand shook slightly, but not enough to slow her down.

It was dark inside, shutters and curtains all closed against any nosy members of the public. Solomon, who had brought a lantern from the carriage, held it high to let them all see around the modest house. Stray feathers remained scattered about, as though a bird had flapped around the hall at one point and no one had swept them out. Ominous stains still marked the hall floor, where Solomon had discovered Clarke's body. And the semiconscious, helpless Constance…

His stomach rebelled with the echo of that moment, and he quickly shifted the lantern's direction.

Audrey walked straight into the parlor, Tybalt at her heels.

Constance lit a couple of candles from the lantern, which served to provide a bit more light.

"We need to move this sideboard," Audrey said.

It was not a particularly large piece of furniture, and even full of what looked like Clarke's mother's best china, it was easy for Solomon and Tybalt to carry into the middle of the room.

Audrey stood staring at the floor. "How like Barnabas to miss what was right under his nose. But then, he never hid things as a child, you know. It wouldn't have been fun for him unless everyone knew where his hiding place was and something else—preferably fear—kept them from looking."

"Like the treasure chest," Constance said. "On the night you came home."

"His is not a likeable nature, is it?" Audrey said. "Once I thought all men were like that. But they aren't."

She knelt down on the dusty wooden floor and, using the key in her hand, pried up a loose floorboard. Tybalt took it from her, while she lifted up the one next to it. Solomon shined his lantern closer while Constance pressed in to his side. Four bundles, wrapped in oilcloth, lay in the cavities.

Without a word, Audrey reached in and, using both hands, lifted each of the bundles out, placing them on the floor beside her. Then, leaning further in, she reached beneath the still intact boards and drew out two larger, flatter parcels.

"Gold plates," she said, lifting them one at a time. "I think that is all, but you can check if you like. Open them."

With some awe, Constance and Tybalt knelt and unwrapped the parcels. The lantern light glinted on gold, on tarnished silver and jewels that glittered like fire. Huge, solid-gold plates, ornate candlesticks, necklaces, chains, exquisite figurines in gold, antique coins, and unset precious stones.

"Joshua would have meant to put in in bags at the last moment," Audrey said. "Barnabas didn't even give him time to bring them downstairs. If he shot Joshua in the hall, he didn't wait to ask him first where he had put the treasure. It wouldn't enter his head that Joshua would have had the gumption to hide it."

"Why did no one hear the shot?" Solomon asked. "Why did no one respond?"

"Feathers," Constance said suddenly. "There were feathers in the hall when I found the body. They're still there. Mr. Clarke was shot through a pillow, or a cushion. Perhaps two. The noise would still have been heard, but it would have been muffled, less startling or concerning."

Solomon regarded her with fascination. How did she know these things?

She met his gaze. "We had a client once who killed people for money."

He didn't know whether or not to believe her. She might have been warning him—yet again—of the unsavory nature of her past. Or winding him up. Worrying and yet curiously exciting that there were still parts of her he did not know and perhaps never would…

Tybalt sat back on his heels. "You really mean to give all of this to Barnabas Lloyd?"

"He employed us to find it," Solomon said. "And according to the law, it is his."

"Is it?" Tybalt asked. "Only because he found it and dug it up. Did we not just do the same?"

"Not entirely," Solomon said dryly. "Miss Lloyd stole it from her brother."

"Properly speaking, Clarke stole it. There is no proof, beyond her own grief-stricken words, that she was involved at all."

"Except that she clearly knew exactly where to find it," Constance pointed out. "What exactly is it you are trying to persuade us to do?"

"Let her choose a few pieces to keep," Tybalt said. "He owes her that for years of misery. But he never needs to know."

"I would know," Audrey said. "It's not the same anymore. I won't draw the rest of you into my theft. Mine and Joshua's." She touched a ring of diamonds and sapphires, and let her fingers trail back over the coins beside it. "We should just have gone the night he came home. If we had, Joshua would still be alive…"

"Perhaps Lloyd would always have found you," Tybalt said. "Wherever you went."

Audrey stood up. "Would anyone like a cup of tea?" she asked.

"Actually, I'm parched," Constance said. "Let me help you."

Solomon's lips twitched, but he saw the sense of it. They needed to make plans. And Constance needed a rest.

Tybalt went out and came back with milk and fresh bread. They all sat around Clarke's parlor table, drinking his tea and eating fresh bread and Audrey's home-made jam from the cupboard.

Which was how Inspector Harris of Scotland Yard found them when he walked into the room shortly afterward and groaned.

"I heard you two had involved yourself in this business." He glared at Constance. "Haven't you had enough?"

"Lord, no," she said affably. "How are you, inspector? Sergeant Flynn. Do I need to introduce you to Miss Lloyd and Captain Tybalt?"

"We're very glad to see you," Solomon said. "Because we have found the treasure and, we think, the murderer of Mr. Clarke. Perhaps you would care to join us in breakfast?"

"I would not," Harris said bitterly. "But I have the nasty feeling I'm going to need all my strength to deal with the next couple of hours."

FORTUNATELY, THE POLICEMEN had brought their own rickety carriage, so although they all traveled in caravan, they had room to pick up Ben Devine on the way.

"Why him?" Constance asked in clear surprise.

"Why not?" Solomon replied. "I feel everyone concerned should be in at the—er...final act."

Constance was no fool. She continued to hold his gaze until his lips quirked without permission.

"And because I am not yet entirely convinced," he admitted. "If Barnabas murdered Clarke, why wait until now to do it?"

"Because we had just told him Clarke was Samuels and he guessed the man had stolen his treasure?" Constance suggested. "Or because he guessed Miss Lloyd was involved with him once more? Or the combination was too much for him."

Audrey said, "He is the sort of man who believes he is different from the rest of us who must follow the law or be punished. Barnabas is above all that."

"But he is not violent, is he?" Solomon said. "He has subtler means of getting his own way, of bullying. You may well be right that something simply snapped inside him. Everyone has a breaking point, after all. I'm just not convinced quite yet that this was his."

"It's never easy to suspect a client," said Constance, who had fought for a long time against suspecting their last employer. "And we certainly need to talk to him. To *all* of them, I suppose."

To his visible outrage, Ben Devine was more or less forced to travel with the policemen. Constance smiled out of the window at him.

Although it was full daylight by the time they drew up to the Lloyds' Mayfair house, it was still ridiculously early for a morning call.

Garrick admitted them with some consternation, for there were far too many of them to stuff into the usual small salon near the front door. Then Audrey stepped out from behind Captain Tybalt and said, "Don't worry, Garrick. I'll take everyone up to the drawing room. You had best tell Mr. and Mrs. Lloyd that their presence is requested."

"Also Mr. Sydney," Solomon said, "and the young ladies."

"Ladies?" Garrick repeated in clear dismay. "You want Miss

Rachel there too?"

"If possible. She is the most observant of the household, I have found."

"Yes, but—"

"Don't worry, Garrick, I shall look after her," Audrey said.

"Very good, miss." He bowed. "And may I say how very good it is to see you back home?"

Audrey looked more dismayed than charmed by this accolade, though she nodded polite acknowledgment and led the way upstairs to the drawing room. Here, even before everyone had sat down, they were joined by Barnabas Lloyd himself, who strode in like a whirlwind, his gaze sweeping around until it landed on Audrey, who alone did not rise from the sofa. Beside her, Tybalt stood, though with more intent to guard, Solomon felt, than submit.

"Audrey, thank God!" Lloyd exclaimed, starting toward her with his arms held wide. "Have you any idea how worried we were? What on earth were you thinking about to disappear like that without a word?"

"You mean behave like you?" Audrey said, her voice level and dispassionate.

He closed his mouth, apparently stunned by her answer, or perhaps only by the fact that she chose to give one rather than apologize. His arms dropped back to his sides. Then, as though seeing the captain for the first time, he blinked.

"Tybalt? What are you doing here at this hour? Is all well with the ship?"

"I assume so, although I have no knowledge of it. I merely accompany Miss Lloyd."

An ugly look sprang into Lloyd's eyes and quickly vanished again, possibly because he had already noticed the policemen, to say nothing of Devine, Solomon, and Constance. Still, it was enough to make Solomon think again.

He had begun to doubt Lloyd as the murderer, but the man was certainly capable of uncontrollable temper. He had torn the house apart on first discovering the loss of his treasure, scaring everyone from family to kitchen maid.

"You have learned something new?" Lloyd flung at Solomon.

"A great deal," Solomon returned, "though I think we should wait for the rest of your family before we discuss it."

"Where did you find my sister?" Lloyd demanded. "With this—"

"We found her alone in a respectably run boarding house," Solomon said curtly. "Beyond that, you may, of course, ask Miss Lloyd for clarification."

Lloyd did not ask at that moment, possibly because all three of his children had entered the room, conferring and arguing together.

"Aunt Aud!" Rachel exclaimed, rushing over to her aunt, who this time did not repel the embrace. In fact, a tear stood out in her eye and she hastily wiped it away. Jemimah went to her other side and touched her shoulder. Sydney grinned and saluted her from where he stood next to his father.

Then he noticed Constance and definitely flushed, though whether with shame or outrage was hard to gauge. He glanced at Devine, raising his eyebrows. Devine merely shrugged.

"Can we get on with this?" Lloyd said impatiently. "I have appointments this morning."

"We still await Mrs. Lloyd," Solomon pointed out.

"What on earth can she have to say about any of this?" Lloyd demanded.

It came to Solomon only then how little they knew about Christine Lloyd, who appeared such the devoted wife, delivering up her dowry to her husband's adventures, waving him off and welcoming him home with wifely happiness. Only she probably enjoyed herself more when he was away. She held dinner parties, called on friends, took her daughter into Society. Solomon suspected it was a much more relaxed household when its master was absent. Had this submissive worm had enough, like Audrey, and turned?

Did she know about her sister-in-law's renewed liaison with Joshua Clarke? Had she been the one to guess who had stolen the treasure and gone looking on her own?

"Audrey, go and hurry her up," Lloyd snapped. "She'll be all morning otherwise. She probably doesn't realize you are even home."

"I'm not," Audrey said. "I suggest you go yourself for greatest effect. Otherwise, there are servants to convey messages."

Lloyd looked at her as though she had grown horns. Constance wore an expression of approval. The silence was tense.

Perhaps it was fortunate that Christine Lloyd sailed through the door at that point, saying, "Barnabas, what is all this about? Is Audrey…?" She caught sight of her sister-in-law and her eyebrows flew up. "I see you are. What on earth were you about? Do we not have enough to worry about?"

"Are you worried?" Had Audrey's voice been less vague, she might have sounded surprised. As it was, she merely seemed to puzzle Christine, as she was already puzzling Lloyd.

"Sit down, my dear, sit down," Lloyd said impatiently, as his wife began acknowledging her odd variety of visitors, who had all, apart from Audrey, stood up at her entrance. There followed something of a flurry as she chose her chair and everyone else sat down again too.

"Well?" she said.

Inspector Harris rose with one of the bags into which they had piled the treasure at Clarke's house. Sergeant Flynn had brought another two, and Solomon the last. They set them all on the table near the center of the room, and Lloyd's eyes widened with both hope and shock.

"You found it!" he exclaimed. "My treasure?"

He strode up to the table, almost ripping open the straps of the nearest bag and forcing it wide open. His breath caught and he began to smile.

"Thank God." He dragged his gaze from the glittering contents of the bag and met Solomon's watchful eyes. "Did *you* find it? Or the police?"

"Strictly speaking, Miss Lloyd found it, in my presence and that of Mrs. Silver and Captain Tybalt. Since it is connected to a murder, we have handed it over to Inspector Harris here."

"Murder?" Lloyd said quickly. "You mean the carpenter's murder? Then he *did* take it! I must say, I never thought he had it in him."

"But then, you underestimate many people," Audrey said. "He took it from under your nose, and we hid it together beneath the floorboards of his front parlor. You couldn't even find it after you shot him and ransacked his house."

"What?"

Lloyd clearly acted most of his life—the perfect and generous head of his family, the joker, the great adventurer and explorer. But Solomon could almost swear the bafflement in his eyes was genuine.

Lloyd's gaze flickered from his sister to Solomon, then to the policemen who still stood by the treasure on the table. "You think *I* killed Clarke?"

"Did you?" Solomon asked steadily.

"Of course I didn't!" The words all but exploded out of Lloyd. "What would I want with such a nobody, a failure at everything he tried, from carpentry to seamanship to fortune hunting for a bride!"

"You're wrong." Triumph blazed out of Audrey's eyes, startling in its contrast to the dull numbness of grief that was all she had displayed up until now. "Joshua Clarke had a thriving business that made him a very decent living. He and I would have lived happily on that, but I chose to punish you for what you did to him and his family, to *us*, for all these years apart. He signed on to the crew of the *Queen of the Sea*, and you didn't even notice!"

"Of course I noticed," Lloyd said. "I chose to ignore him. The coward didn't even use his own name."

"But he still stole your precious treasure from under your nose."

"How?" Sydney demanded, leaning forward. "How exactly did he do that?"

Solomon explained it succinctly and without emotion.

"Clever," Sydney said admiringly. "I wondered why my best shirt had thread pulls and crumbs of dirt on it."

"*Clever?*" his mother repeated, staring at him. "Is that all you can say when your aunt tried to take everything from us? Your aunt who took our kindness and hospitality all these years—"

"We weren't *that* kind to her," Rachel interrupted. "We showed no interest in any of her charities. We used her as an extra servant—not even a housekeeper—and never took her on any of our outings. In fact, we made her dine in her own room whenever we had guests."

Mrs. Lloyd's eyes flashed venom. Color swept up her neck and into her face.

"What rot," Lloyd said. "You are a mere child. You understand nothing of relationships and economies—"

"The child understands more than you," Tybalt interrupted. "You spent your sister's inheritance and dowry so that she had no choice but to live here and feed your distorted view of yourself as benevolent brother. While you alternately made use of her and humiliated her, refusing to let her marry in case people remembered that she had once had a dowry."

Lloyd curled his lip. "I wondered how long it would take you to cast that up. Of course I would not allow my sister to marry a disgraced seaman—"

"An honorable sea captain," Audrey interrupted. "He was cleared of fault in the inquiry into his shipwreck, but the world chose to forget that—prompted by you, no doubt."

"No doubt," Lloyd said viciously. "And believe me, he will get no further commissions from me."

"I would not accept any," Tybalt said at once. "But you owe a few people some wages, so you had better start dividing up that treasure."

"Good point," Sydney said with a grin. He held out his palms.

"Hand over the loot, Papa."

"A moment," Inspector Harris interrupted, and everyone blinked at him as though they had forgotten his existence. "The treasure is evidence, supplying a possible motive for the murder of Mr. Joshua Clarke, also known as Samuels on board your vessel."

Lloyd scowled. "Be sensible, man. Whoever murdered him for the treasure must have known it was there. No one of my family knew—except my treacherous sister, apparently. If we had known, why would we have employed Mr. Grey to find it for us?"

"Then you are casting the blame onto your gentle sister?" Tybalt said in disbelief.

"Of course not," Lloyd said irritably, although Solomon thought that was exactly what he was doing. "I am professing my own innocence and that of the rest of my family. I didn't like Clarke—everyone knows why—but a thief will have enemies of his own criminal class."

"Like you, Barnabas?" Audrey said.

"Don't be silly, Aunt Aud," Sydney said. "My father isn't perfect, but he's never stolen anything in his life."

"Don't be naïve, Sydney," Audrey retorted. "He stole the livelihood of the Clarkes, his own loyal tenants. He stole the reputation of Captain Tybalt. He took my money—and your mother's—and never repaid a penny he'd promised from any of his so-called successful expeditions. *You* may inherit whatever he has left, but I doubt either Jemimah or Rachel is provided for."

"Aunt Aud, you can't—truly you can't—hurl accusations of thievery at him when you just stole the entire treasure that would save our family!"

Audrey laughed, a surprisingly pleasant sound of genuine amusement, though there might have been pain behind it. "Would it? Or would it have paid a few of the most clamoring debts and financed the next pointless expedition?"

Sydney gazed at her, speechless.

It was his mother who said angrily, "And that is meant to excuse *your* theft, Audrey? Sydney is right—you stole from all of us! Just to run away with a poor carpenter? At your age? You were always a fool. Now you will be a laughingstock if this ever gets out."

Jemimah had stepped back from her aunt, her eyes confused and unhappy, but Rachel stayed where she was.

"You're all *telling* her what she was going to do with the treasure," she said. "*You* tell us, Aunt."

"Travel abroad," Audrey said sadly. "Find somewhere quiet and beautiful to settle down and be happy where your father would never look for us… We would never have needed all that." She waved one oddly disparaging hand at the bags full of treasure. "I was going to invest about three-quarters of it for you"—she lifted her gaze to her sister-in-law's—"for you and the children, Christine. This time, so hemmed in with legalities and secrecy that Barnabas would not have been able to touch it."

Some sort of communication passed between the two women then. Solomon doubted they had ever been friends, but they had lived together for a long time and they understood each other.

Mrs. Lloyd's eyes fell first. "I'm sorry," she muttered.

Sorry for what? Solomon's skin, his very brain, seemed to be prickling. What was she sorry for? For misjudging Audrey? For her lack of kindness? Or for shooting Joshua Clarke to get her own hands on the treasure?

She could never have moved that sideboard alone. Had she still been looking when, early the next morning, Constance had blundered in and found Clarke's body?

It could fit. But Constance was ahead of him.

"You told your husband," she said to Mrs. Lloyd. "You knew about Audrey's affair of the heart and you told your husband where Clarke lived."

CHAPTER NINETEEN

MRS. LLOYD JUMPED up, whirling away from gawping eyes so quickly that her skirts swayed like waves at sea. "I told him," she whispered. "I told him I took your key to Clarke's house from you."

The silence was appalled.

Audrey said, "I had another. I had two cut because I am so forgetful."

Everyone stared with varying degrees of incomprehension from Audrey's calm figure to Christine's back.

Except Ben Devine, who rose to his feet. "I really don't see why I have been brought here to intrude on what is clearly a family matter, so with your permission, I shall take my leave."

"No," said Solomon. "You were brought here to eliminate certain possibilities. Just about everyone here had a motive to steal the treasure back from Clarke, and shoot him either in punishment for the theft or for daring to raise his eyes to Miss Lloyd. The only question is who knew Clarke lived in that house, and who could have been there around midnight on the night he died."

"Miss Lloyd knew," Constance said. "And apparently Mrs. Lloyd knew. Mr. Lloyd knew because his wife told him. Captain Tybalt did not know."

"Neither did the children," Audrey said quickly. "Christine would never have told them such a shameful thing."

Mrs. Lloyd turned very slowly back to face the room, but her gaze avoided everyone.

"Very well," Solomon said, though his brain still seemed to be running ahead like a series of photographs, examining and discarding images as he went. "Then let us consider who was out and about and who has an alibi for the time concerned. Mr. Lloyd, where were you at midnight last night?"

Lloyd's gaze locked with his wife's. Something was being conveyed, communicated...

But he turned quite suddenly on Solomon, his nostrils flaring with contempt. "You cannot seriously ask me that and expect an answer! You work for me!"

"Not anymore," Solomon said mildly. "We were engaged to find your treasure—which we did—and then your sister, which we also did. Our agreement never extended to covering murder."

"Your wife has just told us that you knew where Clarke lived," Constance added. "So where were you last night around midnight?"

"In bed!"

"In my bed," Mrs. Lloyd said hoarsely.

"Oh, for the love of..." Rachel began, bouncing to her feet. "Does no one tell the truth in this house, ever? He was *not* in your room! I and half the servants heard him snoring his head off in his own room!"

"And are *you* telling the truth?" Solomon asked. "Or covering for your parents?"

"Neither of them went out that night. I was awake and watching from my window. Papa came home before eleven and then went to bed. Mama did not go out at all."

"Who did, Rachel?" Solomon asked quietly.

"We know Sydney did," Constance said. "As did Mr. Devine."

"Mr. Devine came to see *me*!" Jemimah piped up with defiance.

Lloyd started angrily toward Devine and was yanked back by Syndey's unexpectedly strong hand on his shoulder.

"Not helping," Sydney said.

"Not at midnight, he didn't," Constant said firmly. "We know exactly where he was then and in what kind of state, so don't muddy the waters with yet more lies."

"You can't speak to her like that!" Devine exclaimed furiously before he swung around on Lloyd. "And as for you, sir, it's time you knew exactly who it is you are employing!" He pointed dramatically at Constance. "That woman is no more than a common prostitute with a brothel only three streets away from here."

Sydney cast his eyes to heaven, muttering, "Imbecile." Everyone else was staring at Constance in horror. Only Constance herself appeared to be quite unmoved, although Solomon knew otherwise.

Her smile was too bright, her eyes too hard in their glitter. "Oh, there is nothing common about me, sir. I own that establishment."

Devine almost choked.

"Mrs. Silver," Solomon said, deliberately attracting all attention to himself, "is the owner of the largest charitable institution in London catering for fallen and abused women. As you would know had you been granted entry and not turned away at the door for the kind of drunken abuse her establishment mitigates against. To more important matters."

Everyone was still staring at him, but it was the wonder in Constance's eyes that almost broke his heart. Just because he had stood up for her. Just because he had told the truth of the way things were, not as they were perceived. Perhaps he erred a *little* on the side of charity, but not by much. The women were protected from men like Sydney and Devine. There was more that he could do, but that was for later.

"What?" Sydney asked sulkily. He must have known he was in for a massive dressing-down from his father—providing Lloyd was not arrested for murder.

"You, Devine, and your other friend left that establishment just before midnight," Solomon said. "Where did you go?"

Sydney scratched his head. "Dashed if I can remember, old man. Ben?"

Devine frowned. "White's? Might have been White's. Actually, it *was*! Rawleigh's idea. You were against it, though, and you were quite right because I only lost."

Sydney nodded wisely.

Solomon's heart beat like a drum. "Did you lose, too, Sydney?"

"Must have." Sydney smiled ruefully, pulling out the linings of his pockets to show their emptiness.

"Not at White's, you didn't," Devine said. "You must have gone to some other hell, because there was only Rawleigh and me at White's. I'm sure that's why I lost... What?" He stopped, swallowing nervously as he glanced from Sydney's fixed smile to Solomon and Harris.

Got you, Solomon thought.

"No," Rachel said. "Whatever you're thinking, Sydney came home at midnight. I saw him. He left Ben and came home."

Of course he did. He needed his pistol and the cushions to muffle its report. "And then he left again, didn't he?" Solomon said gently. "With a bag or a roll under his arm?"

The scared look in Rachel's eyes, the awful understanding that would forever ruin her innocence, tugged at his heart. He was sorry, but he could not go back.

"Inspector, I think you might like to search Mr. Sydney Lloyd's rooms for the murder weapon."

"No! I will not have it!" Barnabas Lloyd exploded. "I forbid you! My son never touched that man. *I* killed Clarke, because of Audrey and the treasure. My wife told me where he lived and I went there and I shot him."

"But it wasn't you she told, was it?" Constance said. "It wasn't you to whom she gave the key she had taken from Audrey. That's why you looked so surprised when she said it and why you're taking the blame now. Because it was *Sydney* she told, and Sydney is the one person you will protect. The apple, as they say, never falls far from the tree. He thought it was his right to kill Clarke for the treasure."

"Only you couldn't find it, could you?" Solomon said to Sydney. "And I expect you took fright, with all that blood. So you ran until you talked yourself into going back. Fortunately, your father sent you to me that morning, because of your aunt's disappearance, so you were able to nip back to Clarke's house on the way—only to discover Constance there. So you hit her and came to me. No wonder her name was almost the first thing you said to me. She was on your mind more than your aunt. You thought you might have committed murder twice."

Sydney smiled, walking toward him. "Only a jumped-up carpenter and a whore," he said deliberately. "Or so I thought."

He moved quite suddenly, snatching Solomon by one arm, and Solomon felt the cold, sickening metal at his throat. The barrel of a pistol.

"You see," Sydney said apologetically, "the murder weapon is *not* in my room."

"*CHRISTINE WOULD NEVER have told them such a shameful thing.*"

For some reason, Audrey's words in defense of her brother's children kept echoing around Constance's mind. Not because the words were necessarily wrong, but because the intonation was.

Audrey was not sure. She was trying to convince herself because she had got used to thinking of her brother as the author of all her ills. He had become a convenient villain for her, and rightly so in many things, but not necessarily in all.

Sydney, whom none of them could read or understand, the darling of both his parents, who had exchanged such a long, intense look—Christine silently begging, and Barnabas just as wordlessly agreeing, to take the blame for their son.

Solomon must have been thinking along parallel lines, briefly distracted by his need to defend Constance. Though there was no need in her eyes, it felt curiously sweet and warming, because he understood.

And yet that softness had made them slow at just the wrong moment. As Sydney had edged toward the table with the treasure, right by Solomon and the policemen, she realized suddenly that the culprit was about to run—with at least some of the treasure. She even jumped to her feet, but then he held a pistol to Solomon's neck and anguish seemed to shriek in her ears.

For a horrible moment, she thought she would faint. Certainly, her head pounded like a drum in a marching band. But she could not allow it.

As if from very far away, Sydney said, "You see, the murder weapon is *not* in my room."

His smugness barely registered with her. Her every instinct was to hurl herself bodily between Sydney and Solomon, but the gun was already pressing into his neck, right over the artery. Any sudden movement, any twitch of Sydney's finger, and Solomon would die.

The hugeness of that threatened to overwhelm her. She had never felt so helpless in her life. But she would never go back to the belief that nothing good ever happened. Solomon had already happened. Love had already happened.

She moved slowly, creeping nearer, staying outside Sydney's line of vision. But Sydney was paying no attention to her, to any of the women, in fact. It was his father and Devine he was watching. The policemen he must have trusted to do nothing that would risk Solomon's life.

Solomon himself appeared quite unconcerned, though at least he was not foolish enough to make any sudden movements that might hasten his own demise.

Help, when it came, was from an unexpected quarter.

Rachel took a step toward him. "What are you doing, Sydney? You can't shoot Mr. Grey."

"My poor, deluded child, I might as well be hanged for a sheep as for a lamb, and I am more than capable of shooting Mr. Grey."

"But Sydney, I *like* him."

A frown crossed Sydney's brow, as though he were puzzled by the concept. Certainly, it distracted him, but Constance was not yet near enough to take advantage. Besides, the gun never wavered.

"Sorry, pip-squeak," Sydney said with what sounded like genuine regret. "You like people too easily and you have no discrimination. I don't want to kill him, though I will, and I do hope you like me better than him." He let go of Solomon's arm and, still watching his father, reached for the bags on the table with his free hand. He gathered up the handles of two.

"You missed one," Solomon said conversationally.

"What?" Sydney asked, just as Solomon's elbow crashed backward into his chest.

Oh God! Oh God, help him! Even as Constance launched herself forward, the business end of the pistol had slid off Solomon's skin while Sydney doubled over with a howl of pain.

Solomon spun around, seizing Sydney's wrist, but the younger man fought back, re-finding his grip on the weapon and dropping the bags in order to punch viciously at Solomon.

"Sydney, stop that this instant!" Lloyd commanded, and a weird gurgling issued from Sydney's throat. Incredibly enough, he seemed to be laughing.

"Sorry, Papa," he panted, maneuvering the pistol to aim it once more at Solomon's body. Constance leapt, shoving up his arm.

She didn't see what happened next, but she heard the report of the pistol just as she threw herself at Solomon to protect him.

She felt no pain. In the small, disastrous silence, her world did not darken.

Mrs. Lloyd cried out, a low of grief as old as the world. Behind Constance, there was much scuffling. She thought Sergeant

Flynn threw his coat to the floor. Over Sydney?

Solomon's arms were around her, and hers were around him, hard.

"It's not me, Constance," he murmured. "He turned the pistol on himself."

God knew there was tragedy in that. It would haunt her all her life.

But it was so much better than the alternative.

"Don't you ever," she said, "do anything as foolish as that again. Or I'll shoot you myself."

She felt his smile in her hair. "I do love you, Constance."

IT WAS NOT even midday by the time Constance and Solomon were able to leave the house. Captain Tybalt had left shortly before, expressing sorrow to the bereaved family. Subdued, he had nonetheless pressed Audrey's hand by way of farewell, as though reminding her that she was not alone.

Audrey, of course, remained with her brother and his family, who were stunned by their loss. She seemed bewildered rather than numb.

"Why?" she murmured, when no one but Constance was listening. "Why did he do such a thing? He was never cruel like Barnabas, never bad natured. How could he *kill*? Joshua, himself… Destroying his family. How did he reach that place and no one saw?"

"No one saw that you were at the end of your tether, either," Constance pointed out. "We all withdraw behind the faces we show the world. To some extent."

"But Sydney is not—was not—evil. I *know* he was not."

"He had been brought up with his father's example of rather monstrous self-belief. Whatever he wanted was right."

She nodded slowly. "I did that too, didn't I? I wanted to hurt

Barnabas, even if I would have mitigated it for the others if I could… And now they are in pieces. I can't leave them like that. Unless they cannot bear the sight of me."

"They will need you. But Miss Lloyd?"

"Yes?"

Constance took her hand, drawing her surprised attention back. "Don't lose yourself again. Your Joshua might be gone, but your life is not over. You can still find another place to live it. If you wish. You have friends."

A spark lit Audrey's eyes, perhaps only curiosity. "You are a very strange and very kind young woman. Brave, I think. I ran away. The next time, I shall walk. For now, there are the children…at least until the funeral is over."

Rachel, shivering, came and sat very close to her aunt. Jemimah, horror still in her eyes, had her arm around her mother, while Lloyd was saying an awkward farewell to Ben Devine and the policemen.

"We should go too," Constance said. "Goodbye, Miss Lloyd." She tucked a Silver and Grey card into Audrey's hand. "Don't forget where we are."

She was still shaking with reaction to Solomon's near brush with death as she took his arm and murmured the correct words of sympathy to the family. To her surprise, Lloyd chose to show them out.

The shock of what had happened stood out in his face, the loss he was only beginning to comprehend. And yet somehow Constance was not surprised when he said abruptly, "I trust I might count on your discretion? As to what happened here today."

"Of course," Solomon said. "But you will find it difficult to hide. Obviously, there can be no charges against your son now, but a shot was fired here and speculation is inevitable."

"Inspector Harris has already promised me he will be as discreet as he can be. I am acquainted with some of his superiors."

Of course he was.

"Discretion is part of our business," Constance said. "But I believe you would limit talk if you divided your treasure as your sister intended. You have more to deal with now than the next adventure."

He stared at her. "You mean I should reward her for stealing from me?"

"Is that really all she has ever done for you?"

His eyes fell. "No," he admitted, reaching for the front door. "Goodbye, Mrs. Silver. Mr. Grey. You will receive my final banker's draft for your services in the morning."

They walked out of the house with a shared sense of release—that they could walk away from someone else's grief, that it was not their own.

"Do you think we really will receive his draft?" Solomon said cynically.

"Maybe. Though we might have to wait until he sells the wretched treasure." She stopped, gazing at Solomon's carriage, which awaited them in the street. "I can walk from here."

"No," Solomon said, guiding her with firm gentleness toward the carriage. "You are in desperate need of rest. I shall see you safely into bed at last."

She fluttered her eyelashes in a decent attempt at self-mockery. "Why, Mr. Grey, you will make me blush."

"I hope to. One day." He handed her inside and sat beside her.

The tired horses moved forward at a walk. Constance, gazing out of the window, felt Solomon's nearness like a gift she had almost lost. The hugeness of that overwhelmed her. She could not keep the tears quite at bay until she was alone, yet still when he took her hand in the silence, she clung to it.

He didn't ask, but she knew she had to answer.

"We have been here before, endangered, frightened for each other... This life we lead, this life we have chosen, will only get harder. The more I know you, the more I love you, the more dreadful every moment like *that* becomes."

He knew what she meant. After all, he had found her uncon-scious person by Clarke's corpse only two mornings ago. His fingers tightened around hers.

"Can we bear it, Solomon?" she whispered.

"Can you?"

"I don't know." Right now, she felt she could not. Her throat ached, and still she trembled. "What alternative do we have?"

"We can do something else. Or nothing else. Silver and Grey is not our living. We have the luxury of closing it down if we wish."

"It was meant to be our fun. Today was not fun."

"The fun was never about the tragedies behind the crimes, or about the dangers we risk to ourselves."

"What *was* it about, Sol? Remind me."

She felt rather than saw his shrug. "Puzzling out the truth. The excitement of finding the patterns, of bringing justice. And if I am strictly honest, I believe I *do* enjoy the risks."

"I enjoy them too," she admitted, glancing around to him at last. "I just don't enjoy yours."

"Nor I yours," he said, brushing his thumb across her cheek to wipe the fallen tear. "Shall we end Silver and Grey Inquiries? And concentrate instead on love?"

His dark eyes were serious and intent on hers. The idea of his focus being entirely on her, on love, was breathtaking. Slowly, she lowered her head until it rested on his shoulder, and thought about it.

"Can we do both?" she asked.

"If we do it together, I believe we can do anything."

"Then let's do both," she said, and he smiled and kissed her lips. And that was right too.

CHAPTER TWENTY

THE END OF a case was always difficult. Often, it had left them physically as well as mentally and emotionally bruised. This one was no different. And yet Solomon was glad Constance did not want to end their inquiry business. It had become part of who they were. But she was right that risking each other would only become harder. Talking about it had made it easier to face, but it would never be easy to experience.

By the time he left her in the care of her maids, with instructions that she was to go to bed and rest until at least the end of the afternoon, the white look had gone from her face and she no longer trembled. Her smile still dazzled him, and her kiss was sweet.

I would do anything for you. To keep you. To protect you. To make you happy...

The thought stayed with him as he got the carriage to drop him at the Silver and Grey office. He would make his own way home.

Janey was waiting for him, charging up the hall to meet him. "There you are! I got the necklace!"

His head was so full of Constance that it took him a moment to grasp her meaning. "Bibby's necklace? Constance said you'd tracked it down but the character who found it wouldn't give it back."

Janey grinned. "I went to his house to see him, just as Mrs. S. advised. He coughed it up double quick to be rid of me. Now you're back, *please* can I run round to the house to give it to Bibby? Oh, and how's herself?"

"Sleeping, I hope. So don't wake her. Go on. I'll stay here for the afternoon, since I have a few things to do."

"Oh. Yes, you do, there's a client in the waiting room. Shall I send him in?"

Sometimes, the girl had her priorities wrong. He frowned at her. "Yes."

Unmoved by his displeasure, she grinned as he strode into his office. "Funnily enough, he looks quite like you," she said cheekily.

It was enough to make him pause, his fingers on the door handle.

David.

He had thrust the pain associated with his brother to the back of his mind over the last couple of days. He was so used to doing so by now that it hadn't even been difficult. Only the unease had remained like the background hiss of a gas lamp. Was Johnny David? And if so, why was he avoiding Solomon? Because of that childish quarrel Solomon could no longer explain?

His heart thundered as he hung up his coat and hat and turned to face the door. Had his visitor come to explain, to make things right? Or at least tell him what was wrong? Was this greatest mystery of his life about to be solved at last, for good or ill?

Or had Johnny come to tell him there was no connection but some random similarity in appearance?

As soon as the man walked through the door, Solomon knew.

Recognition stabbed him.

Wishful thinking. He might have been looking in a mirror as far as the man's features went. Johnny was tall and lean, his limbs muscular from years at sea. But his hair was longer, wilder. There was a scar across one side of his face, probably from a knife fight, and another across his knuckles where they grasped a seaman's kit bag. He was roughly dressed, and his eyes were hard. Not with hate, just with life.

For a moment they looked at each other.

Mechanically, Solomon stretched out his hand, indicating the comfortable chair. Johnny sat, though he looked anything but comfortable. He placed a familiar card on the low table.

"Mr. Grey?" Johnny said.

Solomon quirked his lip, inclining his head. "Mr. Grey."

Johnny blinked. "I doubt it. Look, mister, I don't know who you are. Some people got doubles, looks like we do, but the truth is I don't know who you are."

"I'm Solomon Grey and I believe I am your twin brother. I don't think you can have forgotten that."

Johnny smiled. It was a very odd smile, containing genuine amusement as well as cynicism and something that might have been shame.

"That's where you're wrong, Mr. Grey. I have forgotten everything I ever knew before my illness."

"Illness?" Solomon repeated stupidly. "When?"

Johnny shrugged. "Nine or ten years ago. Something like that. I woke up in a hospital in Marseilles. Didn't know my own name, where I was born, how old I was, nothing. Funny thing was, I spoke English, though I understood French. They told me I'd come off a ship and assumed I was a seaman. Seemed they were right. Ships were familiar."

"And you can read," Solomon said, gesturing to the card.

Johnny's lips quirked in a smile eerily like Solomon's. "Don't make me a gentleman like you, though."

"But you allow the possibility."

"Oh, I allow any possibility. So what is my story, then? Who am I?"

A lump had formed in Solomon's throat, so constricting he could barely get the words out. "David Grey. I believe you were born in Jamaica in the same hour as me. Our father was William Grey, an English plantation owner. Our mother was Lillian, a Maroon."

"Oh. I see."

"I doubt it. They were married. We inherited the estate be-tween us, only you were lost. You vanished during the slave revolt of 1832."

"That's a lot of time I don't remember."

As it had more than once before, a horrible fear came to the fore. "Were you a slave? Did they enslave you?"

Johnny shrugged, as if it didn't matter. "One good thing about no memory. If I was, I don't recall it. I get paid like anyone else. Though there's certain ports I still avoid."

I have everything. You have nothing. But there was only wariness in Johnny's hard eyes, no recognition, no envy. This was one solution to the mystery of David's disappearance that Solomon had never thought of, never imagined. And he had no idea how to deal with it.

Solomon swallowed. "I believe you are my brother, whom I have missed."

Their eyes, so alike and yet so full of differing experiences, met again. "I'm sorry," Johnny said. "If I ever missed you, I've forgotten. I came because she told me off and I was curious. I wanted to see if you would make me remember."

In despair, Solomon didn't even ask. He could see there was no recognition, no memory of their shared childhood adventures, fun, and quarrels...

"Is she your woman? Your wife?" Johnny asked.

Solomon should have known Constance would go to Johnny when he lacked... What? Courage? He'd been too full of pain at rejection. And now there was the pain of being forgotten.

"She will be my wife. I never forgot you."

"I'm not him," Johnny said quickly. "Even if I was born him, which I doubt, I'm someone else now."

"Maybe," Solomon allowed, feeling his way. "But I would like to help you find out. It's my mystery as well as yours now. There are doctors who might be able to help you remember."

"Oh, I don't care for doctors. I don't even mind anymore that

I don't remember. I can live with it. I'm happy with who I am."

It was a gift Solomon had never acquired. He had always been discontented, always looking… Until Constance.

But his visitor was rising to his feet, and panic filled Solomon.

"I've got a ship that sails on the evening tide. Interesting to meet you, Mr. Grey."

"You won't consider staying?" Solomon blurted.

A frown flickered. "You mean it, don't you? I could rob you blind, bleed you dry."

"You wouldn't find it as easy as you seem to think."

Johnny's smile flashed, a dose of charm that was almost familiar. "No, I don't suppose I would." He hesitated. "Look, I can't do that. I can't live off a stranger pretending it's fine because he *might* be my rich brother."

Then he knew Solomon was rich. He had made inquiries of his own before coming here. For some reason, that gave Solomon hope. He pushed the card back across to the table. "Keep it. You can find me again if you want to. Or if you need my help. I would rather you didn't vanish again completely."

Those eyes were curious now. Johnny didn't feel the emotions Solomon did, but he might have felt their echo, a desire to belong.

Solomon stood because he didn't know what else to do. To his surprise, the seaman thrust out his hand, and Solomon took it. The man who might have been his brother smiled and walked away. Solomon could hear him whistling as he strode off up the street.

CONSTANCE ROSE IN good time for her "evening salon." She felt much more rested and steady, and enjoyed her light supper with the women who would grace the salon this evening. They were expecting several important guests as well as the usual "passing"

trade, and so musicians had been hired for a musical evening.

There were plenty of jokes about that among the women, laughter over how music put some gentlemen in the mood, and others grew too philosophical to wish for more than a shoulder and a sympathetic ear.

After a difficult case and a tragic outcome, the familiar banter and companionship was just what Constance needed. By morning, by the time she saw Solomon again, she would be back to normal and ready for the next case.

Although perhaps they should take the time, as they had promised, to look for a house to live in and a clergyman to marry them who would not throw up his hands with horror and eject Constance from the church.

It would be a very odd wedding, one side of the church filled with the respectable and wealthy, and the other with her eccentric mother and a rabble of old convicts and whores, reformed and otherwise. Not that most of these women were incapable of behaving like ladies for a short time at least, and they would, for her. She just wondered at the man who was prepared to tolerate it.

It came upon her suddenly that she didn't want anyone else at their wedding. Not the stuffy disapprovers or even her own friends. This was about Solomon and Constance, no one else.

She would speak to him…

With her stitches still in place, she made a light, flimsy head-dress to cover the bandage and match her gown. Then she went downstairs to play her part once more.

The recital was well attended, with a duke's heir, an earl, a government minister, and a senior bishop among the guests. Wine flowed, along with delicacies from the kitchen, and various musical pieces were rightly applauded.

The musicians took a break, and the guests mingled, chatted, and laughed, much like at any soiree—or so Constance imagined. She gave in to requests and sat down at the pianoforte to sing. She had just finished a rather naughty little song in French—

greeted with much laughter and appreciation—when Solomon strolled into the room with Dragan Tizsa and another gentleman she recognized as Lady Grizelda's youngest brother. He had been present that first night she had met Solomon… And was that not Sir Nicholas Swan?

As usual, neither her guests nor the women made any unseemly fuss. But Constance had to force her legs to move, to stand and walk across the room to greet them. Her face burned. What on earth were they doing here? In her territory? Why had Solomon brought them? She was appalled to think of Dragan playing Griz false in this way—which was laughable, perhaps, but Constance's disappointment was intense. She had grown stupidly romantic since Solomon…

Her stomach jolted. *Was* she being stupidly romantic? To imagine fidelity in Solomon? Would any man feel obliged to be faithful, whatever his vows, to a—

"Constance," Solomon said, taking her hand and kissing it and then her cheek. "I hope you don't mind our uninvited arrival. I brought some friends to see what you do here."

Constance blinked, the inevitable joke rising to her lips before she saw the deeper meaning in his eyes. Her flippant words died unspoken and she smiled brightly, offering her hand to each of the newcomers in turn.

"I confess I am somewhat surprised to see you gentlemen here," she managed. "Welcome as you are."

"They were not fully aware of the charitable nature of your establishment," Solomon said. "I am trying to persuade them to donate."

"Our coffers are always open," Constance said weakly, grasping with some relief that these particular gentlemen were not here for the favors of her girls.

"So how does this work, then?" Sir Nicholas asked her.

They stayed for barely an hour, but by the time they left, she had a considerable amount of money to lock away in the desk of her private sitting room.

"I shall have to keep this separate," she said worriedly. "I have never had a charitable fund, as such. Why did you do this, Solomon?"

"I thought it would help blur the lines. I know your perceived lack of respectability has begun to hurt you, and I think that is my fault. So I feel obliged to do something about it. It does not change the nature of the place. Your clients will not now know necessarily who is here for the girls and who for the charity and the conversation. The world might be discreetly aware of what goes on here, but they will also know it is a charity that you and everyone here is contributing to."

"There will be no favors in return for charity," Constance said firmly.

"Of course not." He took her hand. "Are you pleased? Should I have asked you first?"

"Perhaps… No. No, I think it is good. I-I've never wanted to be worthy of anyone before."

"Neither have I," Solomon said. "Will you marry me, Constance?"

"You know I will."

He rested his forehead against hers. "Johnny came to see me today. I think he is David, but he doesn't know. He doesn't know me. He remembers nothing before recovering from an illness in a Marseilles hospital ten years ago. He's gone back to sea."

There was nothing she could say to make that better. So she simply put her arms around him and held him.

"I quarreled with him," Solomon blurted. "The last time I saw him. I can't even remember why now. I just remember being angry. And David being angry too as we stomped off in different directions."

"Siblings quarrel," she whispered. "It mattered to neither of you. It has no bearing on whatever happened to him, except that it did not happen to you too."

Part of him wished it *had* happened to him too. She could feel that among the guilt as his arms tightened. He would learn to live with it again, in time, with her help.

"Will he come back?" she asked.

"I don't know."

"I think he will come back."

They embraced in silence for a long moment.

His rough cheek caressed hers. "Constance? May I stay?"

Her heart bumped. "Always," she said simply, and led him through to her bedchamber.

It began as comfort, warm and welcome and intimate. But desire had always been there between them and it flared all too quickly, taking Constance by surprise. But then, everything took her by surprise that night, from his gentleness and tender worship, to the wild passion he ignited in her. His own, he kept at bay as though she were a virgin, teaching her pleasure until she leaned to please him more and more. And by then it was too late to stop, and she never wanted to again. Ever.

This was joy.

In wonder, she lay in his arms as their breathing gradually came back to normal. She realized he was smiling, stretching out like a large, satisfied cat.

"What are you so pleased about?" she asked, although she knew perfectly well.

"Because now you will *have* to marry me," he said. And then they were both laughing because there truly was nothing they could not overcome together.

ABOUT THE AUTHOR

Mary Lancaster lives in Scotland with her husband, three mostly grown-up kids and a small, crazy dog.

Her first literary love was historical fiction, a genre which she relishes mixing up with romance and adventure in her own writing. Her most recent books are light, fun Regency romances written for Dragonblade Publishing: *The Imperial Season* series set at the Congress of Vienna; and the popular *Blackhaven Brides* series, which is set in a fashionable English spa town frequented by the great and the bad of Regency society.

Connect with Mary on-line – she loves to hear from readers:

Email Mary:
Mary@MaryLancaster.com

Website:
www.MaryLancaster.com

Newsletter sign-up:
http://eepurl.com/b4Xoif

Facebook:
facebook.com/mary.lancaster.1656

Facebook Author Page:
facebook.com/MaryLancasterNovelist

Twitter:
@MaryLancNovels

Amazon Author Page:
amazon.com/Mary-Lancaster/e/B00DJ5IACI

Bookbub:
bookbub.com/profile/mary-lancaster

www.ingramcontent.com/pod-product-compliance
Lightning Source LLC
Chambersburg PA
CBHW072109300726
48975CB00003B/765